THE ICE IN OUR VEINS

She has always known the sea would take something from her. She never expected it to take everything.

Elin of Frostwake has always lived between two worlds: bound to the land by love, but called to the sea by blood.

When pirates capture her twin brother, Elin trades her selkie pelt for his life—and loses him anyway.

Stripped of her birthright and left with nothing but grief, she joins the Silvamari navy with one purpose: to hunt down the man who destroyed her life. But vengeance, she learns, cannot fill what grief has emptied.

Aboard the warship *Maren*, she is drawn into a kingdom already breaking beneath the weight of a merciless sea god–and into the orbit of Lieutenant Edward Graves, whose quiet, steady presence threatens the walls she's built to survive.

As Elin fights, grieves, and learns what it means to keep living, she begins to understand that survival and love come with their own costs. And that some fates cannot be outrun.

The Ice in our Veins

T. René Thornhill

DRØM PRESS

First edition May 2026
Published by DRØM Press LLC

Book design by T. René Thornhill
Map by T. René Thornhill

ISBN 979-8-9956824-0-0 (paperback)
ISBN 979-8-9956824-1-7 (hardcover)

www.trenethornhill.com

"October 14, 2009
I am writing a story called Vampires Love. Guess that's all for today.
-Goodnight"

While eleven-year-old me might be disappointed to learn that I don't write about vampires anymore and haven't the slightest idea what happened to that story...she'd be thrilled to know I actually finished one. And published it.

This one's for her.

AQUERIOS
FROSTWA
STARFALL SEA
SABLE ISLES
SIDON
WAVECREST OCEA
VOLCARA

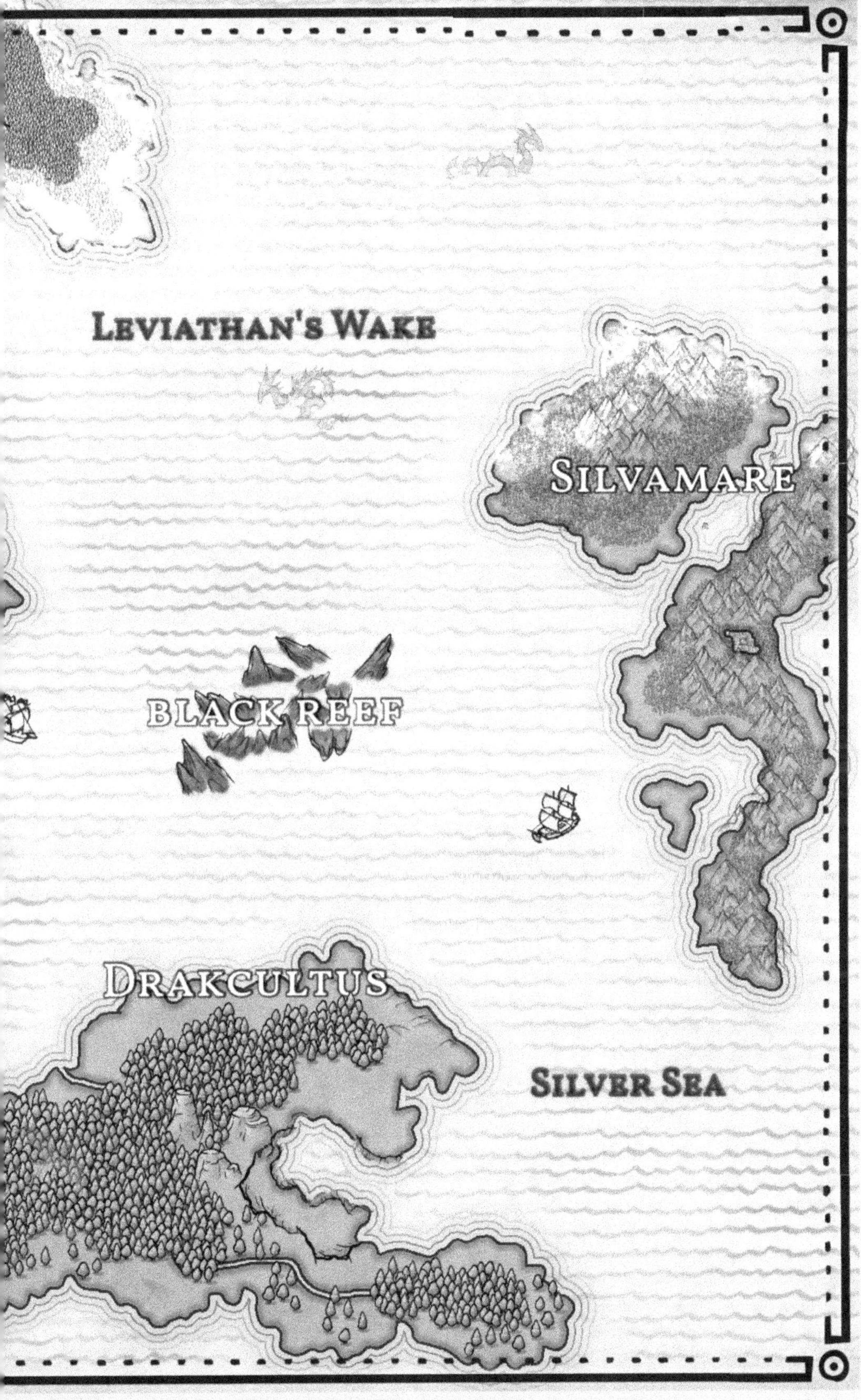

LEVIATHAN'S WAKE
SILVAMARE
BLACK REEF
DRAKCULTUS
SILVER SEA

Pronunciation Guide

CHARACTERS:

Elin   EE-lin
Anik   AH-nik
Ila   I-la
Arnaq   AHR-nahk
Kova   KOH-vah
Tven   tuh-ven
Sereia   suh-RAY-uh
Reina   RAY-nuh
Hatra   HAH-truh

PLACES:

Drakcultus   DRAH-kul-tuhs
Silvamare   SIL-vuh-mahr
Volcara   VOHL-kah-ruh

OTHER:

Amphiptere   AM-fih-teer
  -a winged serpent, with wings and no legs.
Yaranga   yah-RAHN-gah
  -tent-like home of some nomadic Northern indigenous peoples.

GODS:

Cosmir   KAWZ-meer
  -God of the sky.
Terron   Teh-ruhn
  -God of the earth and life.
sea god
  - name is stricken from record

"**Selkies**, sea-bound shapeshifters of North Aquerian origin, are known to shed their pelts and walk upon land in human form. Their legends share many commonalities with the tribal histories of Frostwake, and most end in sorrow: stolen pelts, broken vows, and the inescapable return to the sea.

These tales, passed down through generations, explore the tension between freedom and captivity, love and longing, and the untamed call of the ocean. Though often portrayed as gentle, selkies possess a dual nature: capable of mercy, yet equally of wrath.

Whether such truths are to be believed remains a matter of debate. Still, as their numbers dwindle, they remain—controversially—exempt from the sea god's annual Tide, for fear of extinction in a time when so many species have already been lost."

—Excerpt from *A Compendium of the Sea Folk of Aquerios*, housed in the Old Kingdom Library of Sidon

Privation of the Heart

FROSTWAKE - SEPTEMBER

Chapter One

The village stirred beneath a muted dawn, its quiet broken only by the whisper of snow settling on rooftops and the crunch of footsteps as Elin and Anik loaded their sleigh.

Every exchange came with a nod or brief conversation as they gathered offerings for the shaman. The villagers' emotions clung to Elin's skin like burrs in wool: gratitude, fatigue, and suspicion tangled together. She tried not to hold on to any of it, returning each greeting with a practiced smile that did not falter as she and her brother carried on through the snow-dusted cluster of homes.

The provisions were for Tven, the island's shaman and the guardian of Terron's Forest. They were a revered and enigmatic figure, sought when decisions became hard and answers elusive. Centuries after the sea god began demanding an annual sacrifice of souls, Frostwake's dependence on shamans was absolute.

Each village took turns making the journey, offering goods in exchange for their prophetic counsel. Yet, Elin was uncertain about the business of prophecy; once you knew what lay ahead, that knowledge couldn't be undone, and she preferred to meet the future as it came—one day at a time.

Nearing a yaranga set apart from the rest, she turned towards the shy-orange glow of the encroaching sun, unwilling to reminisce on the memories lingering inside. Not when *he* and his family were gone, and she was left alone with the burden of remembrance.

Elin quickened her pace, distancing herself from the empty shell, as if she could outrun the emotions it conjured, losing herself in earlier conversations with the villagers. Her sense of displacement grew, fueled by their unspoken words and expectations.

"I can't understand it," she murmured, adjusting the leather strap across the sled's load. "After all this time, they still believe I'll leave with the others."

Anik rolled his blue eyes with theatrical exasperation. "And yet, here you remain."

A smile brightened her features. She shoved him, causing the snow in his silver hair to flutter.

"No selkie resists the sea forever," he added, a wry note beneath the tease. "It simply hasn't been done."

Rather than argue that just because it hadn't been done didn't mean it couldn't, she shrugged, feigning indifference. She never joined a migration; that feat alone had taken great effort.

When the selkies returned in the autumn, Elin shifted and hunted alongside her mother and the others, dragging fish ashore for the village. The intrusive cries of the sea lessened, granting her a fragile semblance of solace.

Come spring, when the deep freeze of winter thawed and the ice sheets retreated towards Frostwake's rocky shores, the selkies once again took their leave, leaving Elin alone on the glacial isle, rooted only by the nails of her will. It was her love for her father and her brother that kept her grounded.

"Then again, I suppose if someone were going to do it, it would be you, Elin," Anik added after a long pause. Despite the playful annoyance in his tone, confidence washed over her at his words—because he meant them.

From her periphery, she observed her brother, envying his effortless stoicism. Born without a pelt of his own, she wondered if there was a part of him that envied or pitied it. It wasn't something they'd ever discussed. Despite Anik's composure, he had never been one for serious conversations; as a boy, one might say he had an aversion to them.

As they stepped into the clearing at the heart of the village, she pushed the thought from her mind. It wasn't fair to think of Anik that way—as he'd been. He was allowed to change.

Gulls fluttered, pecking through fresh snow and squawking at one another in the empty center. She loosed a breath and watched it bloom in the cold air before fading; only then did she realize why the morning was quiet.

"The chief's not here," she noted, gesturing towards the elaborate yaranga at the village's center. "Where do you think he went?"

It wasn't common for the village chief to leave unannounced, and it was even rarer for him to leave the village unprotected. The usual sparkle in Anik's pale blue eyes dulled. "The congregation's meeting with Silvamare about patrol routes."

Elin cast a nervous glance towards the grey horizon. "I heard about the raids, but for Silvamare to send an envoy..." she exhaled. "How did you learn of this?"

"You were snoring, and I couldn't sleep," he said, looking at her pointedly. They paused in front of their last stop. "So I rose early to prepare the sleigh. I saw them leaving and asked, but they were in a hurry—they'd received notice at the last minute."

Elin reached for her pelt, fingers worrying the edges. He pulled her into a tight embrace. "Hey—nothing's going to happen to you. They won't touch you."

She relaxed in his arms. Though she feared what might come if she crossed the raiders, she feared more what her brother would do to keep his promise. Whatever it was, she knew it would never be worth the cost.

He released her and turned, reaching for the final sack of supplies still sitting outside the yaranga—the quiet stirrings of the family waking filtered through its hide.

"I did learn that Silvamare sent their spare heir with the envoy," he grunted, tossing the last sack onto the sleigh. He glanced back at her, smirking. "Rumor has it he's handsome."

Had he expected her to blush? To swoon as if she were a girl from a child's fairytale? She lifted a silver brow.

"If I wouldn't leave you for the sea, what makes you think I'd leave for a prince?"

His laugh was hearty as he retorted, "So the sea's the greater temptation?"

"Of course," Elin grinned. "I'd rather lose my wits to the sea than end up in some palace, drowning in silks and politics."

Gasping, hand to his heart in mock horror, Anik said, "Not the silks!"

She slung an arm around his shoulders and pinched his cold cheek. "Sorry. You're stuck with me."

Anik pulled aside the flap of their yaranga and stepped inside. She followed, pausing at the threshold. Her gaze trailed up the smoke-stained beams arching overhead, resembling the ribs of an ancient leviathan.

Then she spotted her mother's coat hanging on its peg—embroidered with waves and stitched with seals, its blue threads faded from time. *Soon,* she told herself, her mother and the other selkies would return from their annual migration. Perhaps then her father would be in better spirits.

Deep in the embrace of shadows, their father lay curled beneath a mound of old blankets, one arm draped over the family dog. The dog raised its head, blinking once, then twice, before thumping its tail and settling back in. Their father stirred, a rough grumble escaping him as he blinked in the dimness.

"Good morning," Anik said, louder than necessary.

He grunted his reply. Blankets fell to his waist as he sat up. His blond hair clung to his forehead as he squinted at Anik, his blue eyes ringed with sleeplessness. His gaze flicked to Elin, softened—then slid to her mother's coat. When he looked back at her, his stare hardened like ice.

"Every time you walk through that door," he muttered. "I think you're your mother. You stay, and it feels like she never left." His jaw flexed. "It'd be easier if you'd just go with her."

Elin's chest tightened.

A surge of anger rolled through the room, coming from Anik. "Don't. That's not fair, and you know it."

He did. Their father's regret lingered beneath his other emotions, but it wasn't strong enough to take the words back. No matter how hard she tried to prove to him she was different, he could not accept it. Why wasn't it enough that she stayed?

Sorrow rolled off her father like a tide, cutting as grief always was, especially when it carried blame. Except her mother wasn't lost to them, only gone. It was a temporary pain, wasn't it? Her mother would return, and he'd be happy again.

Was it a choice to waste away in the absence of love when it wasn't truly gone? She hoped it wasn't, because she couldn't understand how anyone could choose to live this way—to treat their family this way.

Crouching beside her father, she wrapped her arms around the broad curve of his back and promised herself she'd never let someone love her, only to leave them in this kind of ruination.

"Do not drown yourself in mead while we are away," she whispered. "We'll be gone for only a few days. You don't have to disappear with her."

He said nothing; the only sound filling the silence was Anik rifling through his things and the wind against the exterior walls.

Rising on weary legs, she sorted through her own belongings before rolling up her bedroll. She scratched the dog behind its ears and stepped out from the confines of her home.

Outside, the air was chilly; the sunlight warm, hazy through a layer of sea mist hanging above. With it came the bustling sounds of the village as it began its daily affairs.

Elin welcomed the warmth bathing her face, trying to ignore the irritation in Anik's silence, sharp as urchin spines. Through the lacing of her lashes, she stole a glance at him as he fumbled with his gloves, jaw tight. The words he spoke next were unsurprising.

"He chose our mother, knowing what she was and that she would leave. If he weren't our father—" Anik dragged a hand over his mouth.

"He just—he shouldn't speak to you that way."

Indeed, everyone knew a selkie was of two worlds. To love one was only to be loved half as much. It was for that reason that she wasn't sure love was a choice.

The snow crunched beneath her feet as she loaded her bedroll onto the sleigh. She met his blue gaze across its load. "A selkie's first love is the sea. I can't blame him for wanting to keep his distance."

"I can, because I know your first love is us. And staying with us year after year is a choice you make because of that love." He approached her, holding a waterskin in each hand, and handed her one.

A tired, lopsided smile curved her lips as she narrowed her eyes with suspicion. "You've done something, haven't you?"

"You know me well," he grinned. "Although what it is I've done," he tilted his head, a dimple forming in his right cheek, "I will not say. Not yet, at least."

"Oh, for Terron's sake," she sighed, lowering herself onto the bench seat of the sleigh. One reindeer in front chortled as if bemused.

Anik settled in beside her, taking the reins. He clicked his tongue at the reindeer. They lurched forward, hooves crunching the snow into glittering shards.

A heaviness overtook her as it always did when burdened by what she felt from others. She wished she could shut it off—close out the world and be left with only herself. One's own emotions were more than enough to navigate, but to also feel the ones of those around her was exhausting.

Unscrewing her waterskin, she peered inside and recoiled.

"Anik!" His name was a screech from the back of her throat.

A small fish blinked up at her, sluggish in the sloshing water. She fished it out, holding it by its wiggling tail with a wrinkled nose.

"As a seal, this might have been tempting."

She looked away from the wriggling fish and reached around Anik's neck. "But like this?"

She gagged, dropping it down the back of his parka. He howled, thrashing and flailing until the fish flopped free onto the sleigh's floor.

With exaggerated disgust, he flung it away from the sleigh. "I thought you'd appreciate the snack," he said, feigning offense.

She scoffed, leaning back as the sleigh slid beyond the village's edge. Ahead, the mountains loomed, their peaks etched in white light. Snow glittered across the expansive coastal plain like a frozen sea, too beautiful and bright to look at for long. She pulled on the hood of her pelt, shielding her eyes, and settled in for the journey.

By midday, the coastline had vanished, obscured by distance and the mirage of light on the snow; the roar of waves had faded to the hush of wind over the tundra. Now, there were only rolling hills giving way to the slow rise of Terron's mountains ahead. At its foot, trees stretched wide and dark like a slumbering beast curled beneath the peaks.

They set up camp before dusk; the solemn sentinels of pine watched them. Nearby, the reindeer grazed, steam curling from their nostrils as they drank from a narrow stream fed by melting snow. Anik busied himself with the bedrolls, as she coaxed a flame to life.

Worn as a coat, her selkie pelt hung heavy over her shoulders. The slick fur shimmered in the firelight, catching hues of silver and grey as she moved. The world shrank to the oppressive heat and stinging smoke as she retreated inward, her thoughts floating away like scattered embers.

Last spring, her mother had asked her again.

"Come with me, Elin, just for a season."

She'd almost said yes. The sea had been a relentless cry in her ears, calling her name. Yet, for her father and Anik, she stayed. For the boy she grew up with, the one who made her laugh, even in the moments she thought she couldn't.

The selkies left just days before the Black Tide approached their shores.

Kova hadn't survived the spring's Tide.

He'd always been flirtatious with her, garnering attention—she'd been happy to give it, though it had never been serious. Elin could not allow herself to love. She'd been proven right when his name was drawn, and he was seized by the chief's men, dragged to the coast, and offered to the sea god like so many others every year.

On the night of the Black Tide, the rest of the village moved inland, leaving their sacrifices behind. When she'd awoken the next morning, she knew he was gone.

Adding another branch to the fire, she stared into the flickering orange heart, wondering what the sea god did with their souls; why he demanded them at all. Was it punishment? Tribute? Did he care which lives were given and which were taken by force?

It was hard to revere a god who ruled the sea when it possessed such a cruel hunger.

She thought of the old stories the elders used to tell on autumn nights around great fires, about a boy who wandered off onto thin ice and was dragged beneath by hands of water. *"Don't stray,"* they warned. *"The sea god likes the curious best."*

The fire crackled, drawing her awareness back. Embers spiraled skyward like fireflies locked in a dance.

Anik dropped beside her with a grunt, showing her two fistfuls of foraged berries. He handed her a handful before popping the rest into his mouth with a sigh.

Before eating, she whispered a quiet prayer. The surrounding air seemed to exhale, coaxing the spindly pine branches to stir.

Terron—the God of Life—lived in all things born of land, or so she had been told. The wind is his breath; the boreal forest is his heart. In autumn, tribes came bearing offerings, giving thanks for food and shelter before winter's grip returned. Some remained year-round, sharing the woods with mammoths so large they could uproot pines with a single sweep of their tusks.

Elin ate a berry, savoring its bright, juicy tang, eyes drifting towards the mountain peaks, now bleary with the pinks and purples of the fading sun.

It was believed that when traversing that high up, one could be present in Cosmir's realm—the closest anyone could get after the death of the winged beasts of the southern isles, the only way left to know his touch.

The God of the Sky—the keeper of the stars, the moon, and the sun—

was not a major god in Frostwake. Cosmir's winged serpents—amphipteres—never came here, and the sky, aside from its beauty, offered little comfort in the endless dark of winter. Still, some climbed the mountain's spine to sing into the thinning air, before winter's snows erased the trails and access to Cosmir's realm vanished beneath treacherous glacial ice.

There was nothing to fear from Terron and Cosmir; they were kind, if not apathetic. If only the sea god—a lasting terror in everyone's lives—were as perfunctory.

Pulling her selkie pelt tighter around her, she stared up at the awakening night sky. She wondered which fate would find her first: the hunters who plundered the coasts and ice shelves hungry for her soul, for her pelt, or the thunderous call of the sea, waiting for her to at last give in.

"**While** most magics are wrought of elemental nature, rarer still are those touched by the gift of foresight. The origin of such sight remains unknown; for while many magics are descended from the first bond between mortal and godly beasts, and thence passed down through bloodlines, prophecy stands apart. Those whose eyes are clouded with visions, whose ears are attuned to the call of futures yet shaped, are most often gathered within Sidon's Order of the Prophetess—a sanctuary for the oracles, founded in the wake of the Tide and spared from its summons, for the knowing is deemed more precious than gold.

In all recorded history, there is but a single account of an oracle who serves beyond the reach of the Order, dwelling in solitude in the northernmost forest of the known world."

— *The Beasts of Magic*, housed in the Old Kingdom Library of Sidon

Chapter Two

They woke before the sun to a world still painted in shades of blue under waning stars and a fading moon. Glittering ice laced the sleigh's straps as they broke camp and set off towards Terron's Forest.

The reindeer slowed as they neared the forest's edge, uneasy about what awaited within.

The trees towered above them, tall and ancient, allowing little light through the dense foliage. With needles as dark as ink and ice clinging to every limb, the trees' brittle fingers stretched in every direction. To cross beneath the canopy was to step between worlds, or so it felt.

Elin tightened her pelt around her shoulders as the air shifted, pressing down on them.

"You can sense it, can't you?" Anik murmured, his voice no more than a whisper. "It's like we are insects beneath a hovering boot."

Nodding, Elin said, "Pray we're fast enough to scurry if it ever comes down."

A breathy laugh escaped him. Neither spoke again; words felt intrusive beneath the trees' silent gaze. She recalled their carefree childhood, racing through Terron's Forest during autumn celebrations. Time had a way of making the soul more wary of the forest's presence, however divine it may be.

Just beyond the tree line, a familiar beast stirred in a clearing covered in white.

As they drew closer, Anik slowed the sleigh to a halt. With the deliberate, unhurried motion of icebergs, the beast stood, rising to its feet. Snow fell from its flanks, drifting down like ash. Towering and regal, it displayed its ivory tusks and deep-set eyes.

The mammoth observed them. No matter how many times Elin visited Terron's Forest, the beast's majesty never failed to amaze her. Its dark eyes studied them, assessing their souls. With a powerful, snow-scattering puff, the creature moved aside, letting them go by.

The path twisted between gnarled roots and ice-crusted stones until the forest gave way to another clearing. Tucked away in the thicket was an odd building, part yaranga and part cabin, built from wood, hide, and bone, weathered by time. It leaned into the land as if it had grown there. She imagined its roots stretched all the way to the heart of the island.

Anik parked the sleigh just outside the home. She followed him wordlessly to the front door. The door was built of narrow wooden slats, each carved with waves, flame, wind, and stone. At its heart, an eye had been etched into the grain.

She winced as Anik knocked, almost laughing at herself—as if the carved eye might flinch beneath his knuckles.

The door creaked open, allowing them to enter.

Inside, odd relics dangled from the rafters and sat in mismatched pairs along the walls. A tall, gleaming candleholder stood beside a short, rusted one. A fur-lined stool sat opposite a bench of bare, polished stone. A painting of constellations hung beside a charcoal sketch of a grave.

Turning in slow circles, her gaze moved from one object to the next. Each visit, she challenged herself to notice something new.

A kettle whistling from deeper inside the house made them both startle. She grinned at Anik, who smiled back, shaking his head.

A steady, deliberate tapping followed.

Tap. Tap. Crack.

The persistent noise led them onward until they stood before a shell-strung curtain.

"Vines call to blood, and blood to stone," the voice murmured. "So strange, this magic—how surrounded and yet so alone."

She froze, a sudden chill running down her spine.

"Tven?" Anik called. "It's us."

Movement stirred behind the curtain, making the shells clatter together like chattering teeth as Tven stepped through.

Dressed in white furs, Tven was almost indistinguishable from the walls around them. Even though they weren't physically imposing, their aura commanded attention, filling the entire room. Brown skin, marked by the sun and wind, showed the deep lines of their years. Their clouded eyes possessed a faraway look, and they seemed to be perpetually catching whispers unheard by others.

Their wrinkles deepened into creases when they broke into a smile. In the firelight of the hearth, the tattooed eye on their forehead appeared to come alive, its gaze shifting with the reflected flames.

"I haven't seen you in ages," Tven mused, "and yet...just yesterday."

Anik grinned.

"Did I look good when you saw me?"

A moment of frowning scrutiny passed over Tven's lips before they broke eye contact and turned, offering no reply.

"The gods are like children," they said, strolling past a cluttered shelf. "They grow up and leave home, never to be heard from again. Utterly useless."

Elin blinked in surprise. As a shaman, Tven was a mouthpiece for the divine.

"What have they done to rouse your irreverence?" she asked.

Tven's face softened as their gaze drifted, unfocused, towards the crackling fire.

"My allegiance is to the one who takes sorrow...and reveals what's yet to be seen."

A remarkable clarity settled in their eyes as they turned to look back at her.

"Thank you for the supplies. The forest gives, but not in dried fish and soap. There is only so much an old soul can do themselves." Their lips twitched, almost smiling. "And I despise getting dirty."

Anik chuckled.

She offered a polite nod, her eyes scanning the tidy room. Every surface was well-organized, despite their many possessions.

"What are your plans from here?" Tven asked, as if they didn't already know.

"Hunting, mostly," Anik shrugged. "We'll head south to the coast. Should be back home in a few days."

Perceiving something unseen, Tven cocked their head. Bracing on the table, they leaned forward, then pulled back. "The sea carries both prince and pirate this week...though which bleeds first, I cannot say."

Elin's body tensed, and Anik's smile vanished. "We've heard," he said. "You probably know that there have been increased raids in recent months."

Tven nodded, then turned and walked towards the door, heading for the sleigh loaded with supplies. She and Anik swiftly handled the load with their selkie strength as Tven reorganized the items on the small table by the kitchen, arranging them all in orderly lines. When everything had been placed, they stepped back.

Tven pulled Anik into a firm embrace. Anik paused, taken aback by the shaman's unexpected affection. He pulled back, offering a curt nod, then proceeded to the door.

"Be well," Elin said, following Anik out.

In a flash, Tven's hand seized her wrist, the unshakeable clamp of their fingers stopping her retreat. A startled gasp escaped her as she jerked back from the unexpected touch, though their hold on her did not release.

"Remember this," they whispered, their voice echoing not just in her ears, but deep in her mind. "Some burdens are not yours to carry."

Her lips parted, but no sound escaped.

Tven released her without further explanation.

She swallowed, her throat dry, and offered a single, hesitant nod, trying to process the outburst. "It's...always good to see you."

Tven didn't blink, but they raised their voice just enough for Anik to hear.

"It was...is...and will be...a great honor to know you both. Thank you for the supplies."

Elin released a deep sigh as she emerged, her hands sweeping down her legs to dispel the last icy remnants of Tven's touch. She stood beside Anik, feeling the rough texture of the woven blankets as she helped to rearrange their items in the sleigh, making sure it stayed balanced.

"What do you think that was about?" he asked.

"I don't know, they are as mad as they are wise. Much of the time, their advice isn't understood until it's too late or simply not at all."

She couldn't hide the tremor in her voice. Bewildered by her own reaction, feeling as if Tven's words were the tremor before something worse.

"Who's the irreverent one now?" Anik teased.

She opened her mouth to insist it wasn't irreverence, only frustration that everything involving divinity must be so vague, but a huffing sound interrupted them.

The mammoth had found them. It stood just beyond the path, watching them, as steam curled from its trunk. Its eyes met hers, and then Anik's. It took a slow step forward, then another. Her heart lurched in her chest, her heartbeat a loud pounding in her ears. She could feel Anik's rising panic like a fire crackling to life.

Anik reached for her arm as it hovered above them to protect her, but she shrugged him off as the mammoth lowered its majestic head until its trunk brushed her shoulder, and she and Anik were between its tusks. Its breath was warm against her skin.

Unable to explain how she knew what the mammoth wanted, she placed her palm between its eyes, and matted hair scraped against her skin as she stroked the spot.

A rush of unfamiliar sensations flooded her, leaving her hollow and brimming all at once. Even Tven's mammoths were creatures of duality—as gentle as they were violent. It was unusual for them to come so close to people.

The mammoth rumbled in its chest and then slipped quietly into the trees.

Anik exhaled, wide eyes staring into her own. "You're either blessed or doomed."

She surveyed the mammoth's return to the snowy field beside Tven's home; unease curled in her gut. She thought of making a quip—that she was clearly blessed since they weren't skewered on its tusks—but instead asked, "Is there a difference?"

They climbed into the sleigh, the only sound being the creak of wood beneath them. The reindeer didn't wait for Anik's command this time as they lurched ahead. Even they'd had enough of the oppressive weight of Terron's Forest and were eager to escape out into the open tundra.

"In recent years, the isles of Aquerios have struggled to produce enough children to replace the depleting population and to meet the annual sacrifices to the Tide. Our Governess of Health and Population is working tirelessly to uncover the causes and remedy the matter, with some success.

Unfortunately, not all isles welcome our assistance. Drakcultus has outright refused. King Talon declared that his kingdom—his island, as he stressed—is the seat of the gods and will not be allowed to fall.

And yet, over the last five centuries, was that not also what Volcara and the Sable Isles believed? Before they failed to meet their tithes, and the sea rose to consume them all? I can only pray his heir proves less of a fool than he."

— Correspondence from Yada, Governor of Foreign Relations, Sidon

Chapter Three

Tven's words, like the bite of cold air in her lungs, refused to leave her, even as the trees thinned and the potent scent of pine gave way to brine; the unease wouldn't settle.

Anik hummed a half-formed tune, lost in thought, his thumbs tapping against the leather reins. He looked ahead unperturbed, as if the forest's peculiarities didn't affect him.

"Elin, I can feel your thoughts from here," he said, not looking at her.

Her fingers tightened around her pelt. "Does anything they say actually have meaning? They're always so cryptic. It's exasperating."

A snort of amusement escaped Anik. "Of course it does. Doesn't mean I'm about to lose sleep over it." He shrugged. "Tven's meant to be enigmatic. It's what they do."

"If what they say is divine, we shouldn't ignore it," she said.

"No," he agreed. "But we don't have to worry over every rhyme they mutter as truth."

As they reached the top of the ridge, the weathered village came into view below.

The village was little more than scattered huts on the rocky coast, with nets hung on driftwood posts and thin smoke rising from narrow chimneys. Only a generation ago, this village would have been loud with the laughter of children and the chatter of bustling life. Now, only the gulls drifting overhead, shrieking their songs into the blue sky, accompanied their approach.

Two figures stood by the water's edge, dark shapes against the muted backdrop of the misty, grey sea. Elin recognized them at once by their pelts. The sleigh glided closer. She hopped off, boots biting into the snowy ground with a series of loud crunches as she rushed to meet them.

"Arnaq! Ila!"

Their faces lit up as they turned, their eyes finding her.

"Look what the sea dragged in," Arnaq called.

Ila threw both hands in the air.

Snow sprayed beneath Elin's boots as she barreled into them, arms flung wide, laughter spilling from her. Nearby birds broke into flight. Ila's selkie hood slipped back as they collided. Arnaq grunted as the three of them embraced in a tangle of limbs and silver braids. The months between them ceased to exist.

"You're back early." Elin hadn't expected to see them for at least another month. "Is everything all right?" The words came quickly. "My mother—"

"She's fine," Arnaq said.

Elin started to speak again, but Ila's grin flashed as she interrupted. "We're getting an early jump on the search for mates."

The selkies' eyes flickered towards Anik as he emerged from the spot where he'd tethered the sleigh.

Arnaq gave him a playful wink before turning her attention back to Elin. "I can't believe no one has claimed him yet."

A wide smile stretched across Anik's face, his blue eyes sparkling with mischief as he closed in.

"Claimed me for what?"

Ila brought a hand to her mouth. Neither answered.

"They're looking for mates," Elin explained.

A blush crept up Ila's neck, but Arnaq's grin only widened.

Anik leaned towards Arnaq. "I am a person of interest, then?"

Arnaq moved nearer, her finger tapping her lips. With a theatrical hum, she inspected him, a slow, deliberate assessment. "It's tempting."

"You two must find your own bed," Elin grimaced. "I will not have my sleeping space defiled."

Ila laughed. "You could do worse, Arnaq. He has a strong physique and a decent face."

"Decent?" Anik let out a scandalized gasp, his eyes wide with disbelief.

Arnaq gave his shoulder a reassuring pat. "You're charmingly rugged."

Ila's smile wavered as she glanced between them. "Truthfully...it's been harder," she admitted. "I mean, you know. Fewer selkies are falling pregnant."

"Even fewer are birthing pups with pelts," Arnaq added, voice dropping.

The words hung in the air, a tangible presence between them.

Elin didn't need to look at Anik to feel it. Something sharp flickered through her—gone before she could name it.

Anik inherited all the attributes of a selkie, though born without a pelt, he could never shift. They never spoke of it. And while the call of the sea was not as loud for Anik, there were times when it was hard for him to ignore it. They used to huddle together beneath the stars when they were younger, on nights when they both felt its call. They had sworn they would eventually leave. The two of them would board a vessel and explore the world.

They'd never gone. They were needed here; that was the excuse, at least, but she couldn't be certain if family or fear kept them there.

Ila must have noticed his shift, too, because she said, "Don't mind me. My spirits sink when I'm on land."

Anik offered a tight-lipped smile.

"Come," said Arnaq. "We should find a place to stay."

They left the shoreline behind, strolling through the quiet, solemn village.

Her stomach clenched with unease as they walked past the vacant homes.

"Why did you choose to come to this village?" she asked. "There aren't many options here. Next year, other villages will be forced to offer up more sacrifices to prevent consolidation."

Ila's fur prickled; the fine hairs on her pelt stood on end. "We're not here just for ourselves. We're here to help them, not live off them."

What Elin meant was, why choose a village with so few potential mates? She started to form the phrase, but Ila interrupted.

"Unlike the stories, our comings and goings aren't so selfish. We survive by being useful; you know that," Ila said, voice sharpening.

"That's not what I was getting at."

Ila's shoulders slumped; she ran a hand over her face and then gave her head a shake. "Sorry, that was unfair. We're just...on edge."

"What happened?" Anik asked, resting his arm across Arnaq's shoulders as they walked.

"The hunting's been relentless," Ila said. "We spent half the summer running from the *Lady*."

Elin inhaled sharply. "The *Lady*?"

Arnaq nodded. "Hatra commands her now, and she's worse than anyone who's come before."

"She and her first mate, Ivan," Ila added. "They're hunting us for their enjoyment. Not just for the pelts anymore. They collect them as trophies and end up killing us as soon as we hand them over."

"They're spreading lies about us, trying to convince people we charm sailors to their deaths," Arnaq added. "Her first mate believes we're a divine mistake that must be set right. Any selkie he gets hold of, he kills or pelts. We call him the Butcher."

Elin's grip tightened on her pelt.

"His preaching is an excuse to justify the attacks. They're angry we're spared from the Tide. Not that they're any different. They've run away from their islands to avoid sacrificing themselves," Ila said, her voice a blade. "If we're such a divine disgrace, why keep our pelts after stealing them? They just want our strength and the healing that comes with possessing it."

If Ivan thought they were a mistake, what would that mean for them if others believed him, too? How far could Silvamare's protection go? The pirates weren't the only ones who felt bitterness towards them for their freedom from the Tide's demands.

They wove through the heart of the village, pausing at a rack of dried fish, where an elder sat, his gnarled fingers tying a net.

"We'd like to buy some for the road and a place to stay for the night," Elin said, lifting her satchel.

The elder's kind, clouded eyes lifted to meet her own. "Keep your coin;

I don't need it. Take any open hut. If you intend to hunt during your stay, return with anything you can spare. That will settle the matter."

While her village could use the food, they were better off than here. She intended to share some of her catch with the struggling people anyway.

Anik answered for her, "Of course, we're happy to trade. Anything else the village needs?"

With a groan, the elder sat back onto a crate. "If you come across any clams or good wood for bow frames, we're short."

"It's as good as done," Anik said, gathering only what they needed.

As they left, the four walked the well-trodden stone paths that meandered between the leaning huts, towards the small central gathering place.

As they settled onto a bench just a few feet from the open fire, a comforting heat settled against Elin's exposed face.

Years of harsh winters had left their mark on the fire pit stones, with deep cracks and a charcoal-blackened surface. A hushed conversation between two younger women ebbed in and out of hearing.

"You're lucky you were here," one whispered. "I was away..."

"The prince was with them," the other replied. "They made use of the empty huts..."

"I heard he's charming."

"He was...asked questions about our needs... performed a fire show for us. I've seen nothing like it..."

Elin shuffled a little nearer, trying to picture the spectacle of heat and light.

"He told one of our stories," the woman continued, "the selkie man who lost his pelt and then drowned himself in the sea."

The second woman's voice dropped. "I'm surprised he knew it."

That story was as familiar to Elin as it was to every selkie child. His wife destroyed the selkie man's only escape to the ocean, leaving him stranded after he was tricked into staying. The man's plan was to wait for his son's coming of age, then he'd seize his pelt and flee towards the ocean.

He failed. The story ended with the father drowning, and the son returning from the waves alone. The story was meant to impress upon selkie pups that the sea's call remains eternal. Be discerning in your trust; always remain vigilant. The constant whisper of the waves will forever pull at the soul, with or without your pelt.

The prince's telling of that story meant he knew more than most about their culture; maybe he was more than a ceremonial figure, giving weight to his kingdom's promises.

When darkness descended, the village square came alive with the flickering dance of firelight. Across the snow, shadows stretched long and thin. Elin's ears picked up the distinct sounds of laughter behind her: Ila's ringing cackle, Arnaq's sultry purr, and Anik's quiet chuckle.

Behind her, Arnaq trailed her fingers down Anik's arm, moving over his lap—

"Okay," Elin said, pushing to her feet. "I refuse to witness this." Flashing them a saccharine smile, she added, "Don't let the sea spirits catch you with your trousers down," and slipped away.

Stripped of its comforts, she stumbled into the hut she'd secured earlier. It was blessedly quiet. Darkness swallowed her as she slipped inside, finding her chosen spot in the corner, her bedroll, and a cozy mound of extra furs awaiting her. Burrowing deeper into the bedding, she inhaled the scent of pine and whiskey from whoever had rested there before. It stirred something that felt like memory, though she had none to claim— an ache for places she'd never been, a home she didn't yet know.

Once, this had been a family home, full of laughter and love. Now it was an abandoned shell, unused not for any defect, but for the simple absence of anyone to claim it. So many were these days. Love, if it didn't vanish with the Tide, still had a way of slipping through the cracks, carried off by grief or by time. She couldn't tell which frightened her more.

The darkness had held her gaze for many hours until a flickering amber light and a faint sound of movement at the door announced Anik's arrival. The lantern's glow illuminated his wide, goofy grin and the rosy flush on his cheeks.

"You have a very self-satisfied look about you," she mumbled, a knowing smile on her lips.

With a sigh that filled the room, he threw himself onto the bed facing hers.

"Should we expect a pup this spring?" she asked.

"Only if we're lucky," he said, still grinning like a fool.

A soft laugh escaped her. "I didn't know you were already thinking about children."

"I wasn't, not until Kova was taken," he said. "It made me really think about how fragile it all is, you know?"

The idea of being an aunt warmed her. The prospect of motherhood filled her heart with even greater love, but her eyes were drawn to the pelt beside her, its sheen in the dim light offering promises that felt more like threats.

"Yeah," she whispered.

Her skin tingled with a premonition that her deepest longing would eventually prevail. That one day, the sea's pull would become louder than the sound of her name. The thought of abandoning a child or a partner, however brief the separation, was something she couldn't bear.

How many years of her life, and those of Anik and her father, had her mother missed?

She didn't want her life to end up as a cautionary tale whispered around a crackling campfire. It would have been easier if she'd been born like Anik, but she hadn't. Wishing did no one any favors; she shouldn't count on an unseen force to save her.

Would her heart have been so divided between her terrestrial existence and the allure of the sea if her family hadn't been a factor? This hesitation didn't seem to plague the other selkies as it did her.

Anik's contented sigh filled the air as he tucked his hands behind his head, his mind miles away from her own. Her grip tightened on the blankets, gaze fixed on the thatched ceiling above, her heart caught between the warmth of what could be and the chill of what might be inevitable.

"**Twins,** in the annals of Aquerian history, have ever been regarded as both blessing and bane, no matter the isle of their birth. Though rare, such births are a boon to the preservation of life in the wake of the sea god's Tide, which each year claims its due. Yet the fortune is seldom unshadowed, for amongst twins it is nearly always so that one enters the world marked for favor, and the other for misfortune. This belief, rooted in legend and reinforced by generations of recorded lineage, speaks to the delicate balance between abundance and loss. Whether this division of fate is a divine decree or mere superstition remains contested amongst scholars. Still, the pattern endures, etched in the memory of every islander who has seen one twin flourish whilst the other faltered."

—*Outcomes of Twin-souls*, housed in the Old Kingdom Library of Sidon

Chapter four

As morning broke, Elin and Anik traversed the rough coastline, where the towering cliffs diminished into short, stout shapes, revealing the sea's jagged inlets.

"I'm going inland," he declared, shifting the weight of his quiver on his shoulder. "I might find some foxes. Who knows, maybe something bigger. Their fur should trade well. Don't forget, we owe that old man some of our catch."

His gaze flickered from the sky to her face. "I'll be back before dusk."

She nodded, her focus turning to the smooth, obsidian water. A hint of a smile played on her lips, and her brown eyes shone with mischief as she teased. "Perhaps I'll pick something for your waterskin."

"Don't you dare!" he groaned, the sound pained, then a wide grin flashed across his face as he pivoted to face the trees.

"Love you."

"Love you," she called after him.

His footsteps faded. She watched him disappear into the dense foliage before setting the baskets down next to a sturdy block of ice and undressed.

Layer by layer, she peeled away wool and leather, folding her clothes into a tidy pile. Far on the horizon, ships drifted like ghosts, difficult to make out through the sun's glare. The wind, fierce for the season, stung her exposed skin with its chill. She welcomed it, the thrill of the impending shift a low thrumming in her very core.

She dove headfirst into the Starfall Sea, the salty spray hitting her face.

Water surged around her like silk, cool and languid. The pelt adhered to her. The change was instant and breathless, transforming her physique into something more agile and robust, ideal for rapid travel through the ocean's depths.

She plunged deep, slicing through the cold sea. The memory of the world above grew distant as it vanished.

There were no voices here, no responsibilities or fragile hopes trapped in human flesh—just the current and blissful silence.

Welcoming her second nature, she danced through the kelp beds, skimmed under floating ice shelves, and dove between silver schools of fish to watch them scatter. With a fluid motion, she rolled and twisted, surrendering herself to the ocean.

The persistent ache in her chest faded, replaced by a profound joy, like the warm embrace of a long-lost friend. Here, she shed the roles of daughter, sister, and villager, no longer a woman suspended between the sea and the shore.

It was easy to forget herself here.

Her world narrowed to instinct.

She had to wrestle for the memories of Anik's crooked smile and her father's tired eyes, the villagers who waited for their next meal, pretending not to hope that life would get easier.

Only then did she slow, remembering that the sea needed nothing from her, but others did. With one last twist, she turned towards the deeper darkness, her hunt commencing.

She hunted with rhythm, gliding through the currents with practiced ease. Each time she snagged a fish, she surfaced enough to throw it into the waiting baskets on shore.

Then she dove again and again.

She found herself in a trance, mesmerized by the steady flow of catch, surface, toss, dive.

Sometimes, she let herself drift, the gentle tide guiding her through swaying seaweed forests and beneath vast, shimmering ice shelves.

Once, a pod of narwhals passed, and she felt their strange, echoing calls vibrate deep within her chest. She swam with them for a time, letting their song fill her.

It was by sheer will that responsibility always called her back.

As the hours moved groggily and without notice, the sea shifted. The current, once a gentle guide, now fought against her, its invisible grip pulling her further into the depths.

She struggled against the sea's protest as she swam towards the surface; the effort daunting and its insistence terrifying.

Her muscles ached in protest as she broke the water's surface and heaved herself onto the shelf. As the wind shifted, the sounds of voices, carrying shouts, reached her. She froze halfway on, her pelt clinging damp against her back as she peeked around the ice pile.

Out from the cover of the trees, distinct shapes started to appear. From the edge of the woods, a cluster of men fanned out; one tripped when something yanked him. His gloved fists clenched a rope that was as taut as a bowstring, disappearing into the dense treeline.

She stilled. Her eyes narrowed in concentration, her gaze focused on the hazy surroundings. The rope was tugged again, and Anik stumbled into view.

With a crash, he fell down, his descent a rapid slide along the ground separating the forest from the massive ice shelf. He was jerked back onto his feet. Blood matted the silver at his temple and ran down the side of his face, a bright trail of red.

His boots carved twin furrows through the snow as his heels dug in resistance. With a sharp twist, he drove his shoulder into the attacker behind him, hard enough to knock the pudgy man off his feet.

With a curse, the man slammed his fist into her brother's jaw.

She let out a gasp, her hand pressing against her lips as Anik fell to his knees.

Her pulse hammered against her eardrums, a frantic rhythm.

Two more men emerged from the trees. Anik had put up a fight. An arrow stuck out of one man's shoulder, and another protruded from his leg. With a noticeable limp, he rested his weight against his tall, lean companion.

She sank deeper into the cool water, her attention fixed on the group.

From the corner of her eye, a shadow rippled on the ocean's surface. She thought with a willful desperation that it was only a whale—massive and breached, but her will couldn't make it so. Her stomach dropped as her gaze swept across the horizon to where the shadow lingered.

Sails like torn wings whipped from its masts. The vessel bobbed in the tide, indistinguishable from a predator ready to strike; the carved remains of a leviathan clung to its prow.

The ship bore Silvamare's flag—or what was left of it.

Sage green canvas hung burnt and tattered, strung upside down in a mockery of distress.

Her breath clouded before her, crystallizing and sparkling in the sun's glow. The sun had dipped low, spilling gold across the sea and snow like a beacon.

She followed it, blinking. Her eyes struggled to catch up with what her mind already knew—what her heart wished to deny—until they again landed on Anik.

He was shoved onto the ice, close enough that she saw the strained expression he tried to mask as his knees struck the frozen ground.

The tall, slender man now circled him, his one eye a startling ice blue while the other was a milky white, marred by injury. A blackened cutlass twirled and spun in his hand.

She'd heard tales of Ivan, the *Lady's* first-mate, infamous as the Butcher of the Black Reef, and they were all grim.

"Let's try this again," he drawled, as if discussing a mundane matter. "I saw the two of you out here before your parting."

Anik said nothing. He was thrust forward by the portly man with the aquiline nose. He threw up his tied forearms to stop his fall.

Ivan tilted his head, lifting a chunk of Anik's hair with his blade. "Silver locks like this are hard to miss."

Blood slid from her brother's brow and dripped onto the snow.

"Where is she?" the Butcher asked, dropping the blade.

Somehow, Ivan had seen them before they separated. She thought of the ships on the horizon, considering the possibility that they'd been hunting. She searched the area for anything that could be used to free herself and Anik. There was nothing.

The raider, with his sharp, hooked nose, slammed Anik's face against the frozen ground before he and Ivan hauled him back to his knees. Blood trickled from his nostrils.

Her fingernails clawed into the shelf, the relentless sea pulling at her with its might, threatening to drag her beneath the waves. It could not have her; it could not save her. She would not leave him.

"You don't have to make this difficult," Ivan murmured. "Call her."

Anik spat blood onto Ivan's face.

Ivan raised a hand to wipe it away.

Anik's gaze shifted, sweeping the shelf beyond. When he met hers, stillness descended. The wind came to a halt. His blue eyes widened a fraction as he gave an almost imperceptible shake of his head. It was the smallest movement, but Ivan saw it anyway. In a flash, he was behind Anik, a black blade pressed against his throat.

Her breath caught as she scrambled onto the ice.

"Elin, go—" Anik was cut off as the blade pressed deeper.

It didn't matter what the sea, the wind, or what Anik wanted, not when his life was at stake. Ivan stood with such perfect stillness that she wondered if he were carved from stone. The blade drew blood. A thread of red slid down the column of his throat.

"Stop!" she cried, lifting her arms in surrender. "Don't."

A smile snaked across Ivan's face.

"Well," he breathed, looking her up and down, "there you are."

Hooked nose stepped forward, arm outstretched. "Hand it over."

The words crumpled something in her soul. Her hands gripped the hem of her pelt.

"We're doing you a favor," Ivan said. "No one should be of two worlds."

She stilled.

"You're a thing that does not belong. A mistake," Ivan tilted his head. "You know it, don't you?"

Anik's silver hair glinted like the blade threatening his life. His eyes, a wild blue, wide with panic, held hers. "*Run,*" they said. "*Run.*"

The plea was as clear as any prayer. He had to know she wouldn't; that she'd sooner bleed out on the ice than leave him. She had no weapons, no plan—only her instinct and strength. Even that would fail her if Ivan's steel struck first.

They didn't have a chance, but she'd go down fighting.

Please. Help me.

Her prayer went out to Terron, to Cosmir, and to the cruel keeper of the sea, seeking any who would hear.

"I am not a patient man, Elin," Ivan warned, narrowing his eyes at her.

Shouts rang out in the distance, beyond the treeline. Elin tore her gaze away for only a moment. The Butcher of the Black Reef snarled at the sound of approaching sleighs.

"Now," he yanked on Anik. "Or I'll slit his throat and toss him to the gulls."

Her brother's blood was already staining the snow, and she loved him more than the sea, more than herself. Without question, her hands moved, peeling the pelt away and feeling its weight leave her as she tossed it across the ice.

Hooked nose lunged for it, clutching it to his chest like stolen gold, then raised it high like a banner of conquest.

Elin remained motionless, exposed and fractured.

The sleighs were getting closer. The pounding of feet on ice drew nearer.

From behind, two explosions ripped through the air. The ice shelf trembled, a sharp crack echoing before it tore apart. Jagged fissures spread beneath her. She stumbled sideways, crouching low to steady herself. Her back stung against the spray of snow and jagged pieces of ice.

Still, she could not look away from Ivan's smiling face. He hadn't so much as flinched.

"See?" Ivan asked, looking down at Anik. "You were never meant to have both. There should never be two of anything."

Ivan turned his saccharine smile on her.

"Eat your heart out, selkie bitch."

And then he slit Anik's throat.

Chapter five

The sound was a wet whisper of steel on flesh, but her world cracked open around it. Anik's body crumpled forward, his strength slipping from him like a thread pulled from a seam.

Ivan shoved him aside, as if his life was of no consequence, then turned and ran for the awaiting rowboat. Her pelt flapped in the pirate's grip as he ran, a stolen banner snapping behind him.

Elin screamed as she scrambled across the ice, reaching for her brother. "No, no, no, no, no."

Her knees hit the ground next to him, hands pressing to the wound at his neck, trying to contain the pulsing blood.

"Anik, hold on," she cried, trembling fingers slick with red. "Help is coming. Just—please."

Fighting broke out around her—the remaining raiders clashing with the warriors spilling from the treeline—but she kept her attention on her brother. His eyes searched for hers, wide and shining with tears.

"Don't leave me, please," she breathed.

He nodded, bound hands reaching for her cheek. The cold tips of his fingers brushed away her hair. Sorrow thickened in her throat, stealing air.

Another explosion shook the shelf; shards of ice tore around them. She leaned over him, shielding him from the blast.

His aura was fading.

"Hold on," she whispered over Anik.

His mouth opened once, then stilled, his light extinguishing like a dead star in the night sky. She clung to him, drawing him into her arms.

A scream tore from her. She choked on it, consumed by a spreading numbness. She couldn't feel anything but the blood soaking into her hands and the vast, echoing absence of where her brother had been.

A hand grabbed her shoulder. With a snarl, she threw them off, curling around Anik's body.

"Give her space," someone commanded, before draping a coat across her shoulders. The sensation was so light that she barely perceived it.

Without releasing Anik, she looked up at the surrounding chaos.

Out at sea, the pirates were rowing fast towards the escaping ship, her black sails spread like the wings of a vulture.

They wouldn't retreat unscathed. From the shore, a crimson arc blazed across the sky. It hit hooked nose mid-stroke. With a terrified screech, he flailed his arms and legs, then fell with a splash into the dark, cold water.

Another arch of fire followed, blazing with intensity. Her tear-filled eyes were fixed, unwavering, on the source of the flame.

With hands clenched at his sides, a young man stood at the ice's edge, flames flickering along his knuckles.

The prince of Silvamare.

He launched another stream of fire towards the fleeing boat—but the *Lady* had already caught wind. Her sails billowed in a violent gust, filling faster than any natural wind could carry. Within seconds, she vanished into the open sea.

Elin didn't move as she cradled her brother's body—as if she might pour life back into him with touch alone. The coat slipped from her shoulders, crumpling in the snow.

The Frostwake warriors gathered around, their bodies a shield against the biting cold, yet an icy shiver ran down her spine, intensifying the hollow cavern deep in her chest.

She wished it had been her instead.

"Elin," someone whispered. "We need to move him."

She tightened her hold, looking up at the warrior who'd spoken. He was from her village; they must be near the congregation.

"It's time," he said. "We have to—"

"No," her voice came out hoarse.

A hand hovered near her shoulder. Someone else reached for Anik's tied hands, cutting the rope away. She held him tighter.

"We'll be careful with him."

Her fingers dug into the fabric at his back. If she loosened her grip, even for a breath, he would slip farther from her. Already, he was different, too heavy and too still.

"I promise," the warrior said.

Her hands trembled. She pressed her forehead to Anik's, breathing in, trying to make herself let go. With the sense of peeling away from a sheer rock face, she let go.

The warriors moved quickly, as though speed might soften the cruelty of it. They lifted him from her arms.

Her hands fell into her lap as she followed their movements. They laid Anik's body on the back of a sleigh, untying his hands. Someone found his discarded bow and laid it across his chest.

She got to her feet and followed; the sleigh bumping and swaying as it went.

What was time, really, when it bent and contracted on a whim? Each person seemed to move through it differently—some, like Tven, teetered between its three states. Which she was in now, she couldn't say; she only knew it wasn't the past. Because that is where her brother was now, and she could not be there with him any longer.

The crunch of her boots on the frozen ground echoed in her mind. Indistinct voices murmured, carried off on the wind. The sticky sap of Anik's blood adhered to her skin, flaking in the creases of her palms.

Ahead, a new village loomed, full of strangers.

They came because they had witnessed her brother's attack in the woods. The royal envoy was on a hunt, just as Anik had been, but they were too late.

A woman she'd never met touched her face; her rough fingers scraped Elin's cheek.

"Poor girl," they whispered. "We heard..."

Another voice from nearby. "We're so sorry…"

A hand on her shoulder.

Arms wrapped around her.

Too many hands touched her.

Too much of their sadness and grief poured inside her, mixing and churning with her own.

She couldn't breathe.

When their feelings too closely resembled her own, she couldn't push it away.

It all pressed in like a final wave before drowning.

Grief.

Pity.

Anger.

Questions. Whispers.

She was choking on it.

She was too raw. A soul flayed open and stinging. Her thoughts had nowhere to settle.

Space. She was starving for space.

"Elin—"

She bolted.

The coat fell from her. Her feet pounded over snow and rock. She ran until the wind screamed and the sea rose to meet her.

She didn't stop. She dove in.

Cold water swallowed her, but there was no shift.

No slick fur sliding over her skin or the soft ache in her bones as her body morphed.

Just her mortal flesh.

Ice seeped deep into her veins, burning through her muscles and her heart.

She sank deeper, chasing silence and stillness—anything that didn't have a voice, a heartbeat, or a feeling.

There was no solace or safety.

Even here was defiled—a reminder of what had been and would never be again.

Only when her lungs began to burn did she scream. A voiceless sound that only the water heard. It cleaved out of her, vanishing into the deep, swallowed whole by the sea that once called to her, but there was no song now.

It was not until her body rebelled, when the need for air roared louder than grief, that she surfaced, gasping and cold.

Alone, and no longer whole.

"**What's** a skinned selkie but a beast, struck low, bleeding out on the ice? You've not taken the breath from its lungs, but the fire from its soul. And tell me, what's a body worth, if it walks and breathes yet carries no soul at all?"

— *Musings from a Fisherman, A Collection*, donated to the Royal Library of Silvamare as a gift

Chapter Six

Water surged around her ankles and streamed down her body as she reached the shore, her silver hair clinging to her face. Her lips had turned a startling shade of blue. They'd never done that before.

Ila and Arnaq waited nearby. In silence, they drew near, their faces masks of composure, yet a hairline fracture in their control allowed glimmers of their inner turmoil to escape. Their unspoken pain surfaced, a current that flowed into her own sorrow. It left the taste of ash on her tongue.

Elin exhaled a long, slow breath. Ila held up the coat she had dropped, its familiar scent filling the air as she offered it. A shiver ran down Elin's spine as she pulled it on, the weight a small comfort against the gnawing emptiness. It was thick and soft, so soft she could almost imagine it was her pelt.

She watched over his body that night, unable to sleep.

Ila and Arnaq returned to help with funeral preparations. It seemed they had journeyed to this village not long after she and Anik had set out that morning.

When someone died in Frostwake, the bereaved would create pine wreaths and arrange wood for the funeral fire. The sounds of work carried from outside as some worked on the raft, preparing to send Anik and the fallen warriors on their final journey to the sea.

The fire's heat kissed her face as she washed the blood from her brother's skin with trembling fingers. She untangled the knots from his silver hair, careful not to snag it. When she was done, she snipped off a small lock and tucked it away in her coat pocket.

A villager brought him a tunic, the rich blue fabric trimmed with plush fur and intricately stitched with threads as stark as bone. She dressed him, taking her time—clinging to every second she could steal.

There hadn't been enough.

When she reached his throat, her hands froze at the wound.

Arnaq moved forward, her hand supporting his neck as she wrapped a soft blue scarf around it, the same shade as his eyes.

He appeared serene, as though he were asleep and on the verge of waking.

Elin sat beside him for a long while, tracing the lines of his palm with the pad of her finger.

He used to fidget; his fingers were always moving when nervous or deep in thought. He enjoyed holding the sleigh reins and the honest work of a day's labor.

All of that had disappeared.

There was an old belief that twins were two sides of one coin, one marked for favor, the other for misfortune. She never believed it; she and Anik had always been extensions of each other, balancing for the better. Their souls were intertwined in a way that no others could understand; losing him did not feel like the gods looked on her in favor.

She once held the conviction that a soul resided in everything. That the trees had hearts, the rivers memory. That bones possessed stories and their pelts, pieces of themselves.

She had given up her pelt.

Anik had been another piece of her.

And now? Now she was unsure what remained.

A stranger had stolen all that light.

There was no rhyme or reason to the injustice. A single blade, a passing whim, and the stark black sails of a ship that sailed on and on. How is it possible for a heart to exist in someone capable of such malice?

Were some things born hollow?

Ivan?

The sea god?

Did they feel anything? Or did they just take and take and take?

Her vision blurred, and she slipped her fingers from Anik's.

She only registered her tears when Arnaq crouched down and enveloped her in a wordless hug.

Elin didn't resist; she leaned into it, letting herself be held, if only for a moment.

Ila and Arnaq guided her outside; the wind blew, its whispers carrying through the yaranga walls, lifting the scent of pine from the fur coat on her shoulders.

The sea churned beneath a sky of iron and ash, and mist dragged itself low across the ground. She tracked the mist's path, scanning the crowded village, until she landed on two men engaged in conversation near the path's edge.

One stood straight, a hand pressed to his chest, fingers worrying the fabric above his collar. The other, dressed in insufficient layers, rested against a post with an air of relaxed weariness, his arms folded. Elin recognized the first man from the ice shelf. He'd been the one to cast his fire at the raider's ship.

As she approached, their eyes followed her, a silent curiosity in their gaze.

"I can't express how sorry I am," the prince said, his voice heavy with remorse, "for your brother and what they took from you."

She offered a brief, rigid nod, her heart heavy with a weariness that made her want to escape the well-meaning words of sympathy. Another scream threatened to bubble up. Was it irony that she wished to crawl out of her own skin?

"Forgive me for my lack of manners," the prince said, bowing. "I am Silas Blackwater, and this is my lieutenant, Edward Graves."

He gestured to his lieutenant.

The grey morning light highlighted the deep brown of his skin. Tall and broad-shouldered, Edward stood a head taller than Silas.

Elin's fingers curled tighter around the coat's collar, recognizing the name. She glanced at the stitching on the sleeve cuff, which showed the rank of Lieutenant Edward Graves.

"This is yours?" she asked, the words scratching her throat.

"It was," he shrugged.

Her pulse beat in her ears as she studied the coat's dark fur. "Do you want it back?"

"No," Edward said, shaking his head.

In a woolen tunic and trousers, he had to be cold. "Why not?" she asked.

"Because it's yours now," was his only explanation.

Her eyes stung. "Thank you—for the coat. For giving me space...with him."

She swallowed against the burning in her throat.

Edward shifted, his arms tightening across his chest.

"Don't thank me," he said.

A few tears fell anyway, leaving damp trails on her wind-chapped cheeks. She swiped them away before turning to the prince.

"Will you go after them?" she asked.

Arnaq squeezed her hand.

"The *Lady*?" Silas's jaw clenched. "We leave first thing tomorrow. I'd like to do so sooner, but there are still things we need to finish here."

She gazed out at the rhythmic crash and pull of the waves. "You must put a stop to this."

"We will," Edward said. "If—when we can catch them, we'll try to get your pelt back, too."

She didn't expect the offer; the thought that her pelt might not be lost forever—that she could reclaim a piece of herself—

"That is very kind. Thank you."

Silas gave a small smile. "We will stop them. You have my word."

With a desperate grip, she clung to his reassurance, the only solid thing in a world that felt on the verge of collapsing around her. She had to believe him.

"**Studies** long conducted in Sidon have shown that the loss of a twin is akin to the severing of one's own limb. Learned physicians contend that twins, in essence, partake of a single soul, conceived, nurtured, and delivered into the world as one. It is not unreasonable, therefore, to reckon them a singular entity. The death of one often gives rise to an unyielding melancholia, and in graver cases, to a madness from which there is little return."

— *The Twin Archetype,* from *A Compendium of Sibling Dynamics in a Post-Tide World*

Chapter Seven

The sky bloomed in violet and gold, like an evanescent bruise, as she helped lay Anik in a boat lined with wool, placing his hands over his chest. Someone mended his bow; it now rested beside him. A wreath of pine from Terron's forest crowned his head. He looked how she imagined a king might—maybe he'd been one in another life.

It was easy to imagine he was only dreaming—perhaps of a life with Arnaq, where come spring, she'd tease him as he fumbled with the complexities of diapering.

Her mind drifted to impossible futures. She wanted him to wake with one of his crooked smiles and call her over to tell her some half-formed joke or recount a strange dream.

She wanted to deny it—pretend this was all some cruel trick—but she couldn't. Not when his body lay still and cold, about to be returned to the gods.

A few men from the village pulled Anik's boat towards the sea. She turned a band in her pocket, twisting it around her fingers. *Wait*—she'd almost forgotten.

She stepped forward as they prepared to push the boat into the tide.

"Stop," she said.

The men stilled.

She waded into the water, the cold lapping at her legs. The boat bumped against her, grazing her shins as she halted its release. From her coat pocket, she pulled a thin band she'd been weaving since the morning—a band of her hair braided with his.

She tied it around Anik's wrist, her fingers trembling.

"I have one too," she whispered, lifting her arm to show the matching band wrapped tight around her own. "So we'll be together always."

She leaned down and kissed his brow.

"I love you," she whispered before gripping the boat's side and pushing him out to sea.

The boat drifted, adrift in the tide, rising and falling with each wave. Walking backward towards the shore, she never took her eyes off him, terrified that if she looked away, his memory would slip through her fingers.

The warrior from her village stepped forward, dipping an oiled arrow in flame. He pulled back the bowstring and then released it. The arrow sliced the air, arcing across the sky like a falling star, landing on the kindling at Anik's feet.

Flame caught in a flash, licking upward and spreading. The boat burned as brightly as an amber sun on the dark sea, growing smaller with each passing breath.

She stood there long after the last flicker of light had vanished.

She thought about the gods and their roles: Terron, who shaped the land and gave it life; Cosmir, who painted the sky and carved stars into the heavens; and the sea god, who demanded sacrifices and took without asking.

But tonight, she didn't know who to pray to. Who would listen? Who would care?

Immersed in the soft lapping of waves, she stayed on the shore, thinking of the selkies. Soon they would return, their pelts glinting in the surf, laughter carrying over the rocks. They'd swim, hunt, and roam the waters like they always had.

She'd be left behind, her choice stolen with her pelt. The sea would no longer call to her in the same way, stranded on land, not by fear or indecision, but by theft and cruelty.

If she hadn't fought it—if she'd gone with her mother—would Anik still be alive?

Was this punishment?

She didn't know how to return home without her brother.

Her father would blame her, hate her even.

And her mother...she couldn't think about her mother.

The crunch of footsteps came from behind, and her muscles tightened in anticipation of the approach. Unable to bear the touch of another's emotions, she tried and failed to bring a wall of her emotions up and around her. She inhaled shakily and turned to face the incomer.

She blinked in surprise as she stared up at Edward Graves, then recalled whose coat she'd been wearing. Clutching the fur closer to her chest, she asked, "Have you changed your mind?"

He cocked his head, furrowing his thick black brows. Realization seemed to dawn on him as his gaze shifted to the white of her knuckles. He relaxed his brow and shook his head. "About the coat?" he asked, appearing to suppress a shiver. "No. I wanted to check on you."

Elin's heart froze. "That's kind, but I don't want company."

"Are you sure?" he asked, taking a step closer.

Looking back out over the sea's horizon, she said, "Yes." It came out more curtly than she had meant.

Edward said nothing, but she'd yet to hear his retreating footsteps.

"I keep thinking there's more we could have done," he said. "I don't understand how she did it."

She? Elin turned once more to face the lieutenant. "Did what?"

Eyes locked on the horizon, Edward's jaw ticked as he said. "How she stole our ship. Our best sailors were on the *Leviathan*. They shouldn't have been able to take it." He raised his hand, gesturing his frustration. His grief and confusion swirled around her, churning her stomach. "It just doesn't...doesn't make sense," he said.

Elin raised a brow. Anger sizzling across her skin. He was talking about Hatra, the pirate queen. Narrowing her eyes, she snapped, "None of this makes sense." Wishing to be alone, she added, "If you're looking for answers, you won't find them here."

She looked away once more, closing her eyes against the night and squeezing them against the sting of tears.

"You're right," he said. "I'm sorry."

Her shoulders softened at the sound of his retreating footsteps, but then he paused. "I wish you well, Elin."

Her throat tightened at the sound of her name, and all she could think as she inhaled his scent embedded deep into the coat was that she wanted him gone.

Sitting on the rocky shore, she stared at the horizon until night gave way.

Faint streaks of pink and lavender teased the edges of the sky.

A new day was coming, and she wasn't ready to meet it.

The sun didn't pay attention; it rose whether it reigned over joy or a world on fire.

What did Cosmir care of man's suffering, when he was a god, untouchable and unmoved. He painted the sky in soft colors, touching the water and casting a warmth she couldn't feel. Life dared to keep going, and that, more than anything, made her want to scream—if she had any voice left to do so.

She stood slowly; her legs stiff from lack of use.

The fire that had consumed Anik's boat still blazed behind her eyes. She reached for the band of braided hair wrapping her wrist. It was damp, with small granules of salt crusted in the overlapped areas. She rubbed her thumb against it.

Anik wouldn't want her to stay here. To sit in the aftermath and rot away, buried by a place that had always torn her in two.

A voice echoed in her mind, "Stop feeling sorry for yourself," it said.

"Stop being sad. Stop doing nothing. Make them pay."

The voice was her own. She turned from the sea; the sun warming her back as it rose and began to walk.

Anik's death wasn't her fault.

She understood that—deep down, buried beneath the grief and the guilt, under the howling what-ifs that plagued her every time she closed her eyes.

However, the scenarios continued to play on a loop.

What if she'd learned to fight?

She could have approached, feigned surrender, waited for the right moment, and slit their throats the way they did her brother's.

Was there a version of the story where they both walked away?

Or was she always meant to lose him?

The questions didn't help; they only cut her further, picking at her bones like carrion birds.

The past was fixed, unmoving, and unforgiving. Anik was gone, and she was still here, but she could do something.

She could learn to fight, get her pelt back, and make Ivan suffer for what he'd done.

If Ivan wanted her to eat her heart out, then she'd return the sentiment.

She pressed on from the beach, a fierce promise burning in her chest and coursing through her veins.

The raiders would bleed at her hands. She would hunt them to the edge of the map if she had to. No other selkie should endure what she had. No one should be hunted, stolen from, or broken for someone else's profit, pleasure, or corrupted sense of right and wrong.

Elin turned her attention to the docks, intent on finding the prince.

The world blurred past in smears of morning light as she hurried to the dock, where the gangway of Silvamare's ship remained open. She moved with quick, fluid steps. If it were not for the solid reality of her body, she might be mistaken for the wind. Unlike the wind, she'd made only a single step onto the platform connecting the ship to the dock when she was stopped.

Two sailors blocked her, blades drawn. She flinched, stepping back, wood groaning beneath her feet.

"Please," she said. "I need to speak to the prince or the lieutenant."

One sailor let out a dismissive snort. "A person of your standing doesn't initiate these kinds of discussions." He twirled his sword, the sunlight flashing off its edge. "State your business, and perhaps we'll pass along the message."

Her hand moved to her side, reaching for her pelt—only to find silver strands of her hair instead. That hollow ache pressed inside her, but she shoved it down and squared her shoulders.

"I will pass on my own message, thank you."

The officer shrugged. A black curl slipped across his brow. "Then I must inform you that your request is denied. Now, take your leave."

"Excuse me—"

"We're preparing to sail," he said. "Hatra has captured one of our vessels. We mean to take it back."

She opened her mouth to argue, but then paused, her eyes fixing on Edward standing on the ship's deck. He tossed his head back in a fit of laughter, a sound that felt foreign to her ears.

"Edward!" she called.

Turning, his eyes met hers. His smile disappeared after he quietly spoke to the others. Then he approached her, followed by two men. She recognized the prince, but beside him stood an older gentleman, a man unknown to her.

"I told her—" the sailor began.

"Thank you," Edward cut in. "I'll take it from here."

They stepped aside.

Elin didn't wait for pleasantries. "I want to come with you," she blurted.

Edward's eyebrow shot up, gaze shifting to the older man whose face was deeply lined and worn, softened by a neat beard threaded with silver. The man watched her with clear, intelligent eyes, assessing her.

The silence was broken by the thud of ropes against the masts and the piercing screech of gulls overhead.

Edward cleared his throat. "This is a warship, Elin," he began. "We do not carry passengers."

Heat rose to her cheeks, but she couldn't back down. "I am aware, but I could be of use. Please," she hated the break in her voice, the vulnerability of that word.

The men studied her: Edward with concern, Silas with curiosity, and the other—

"What skills do you bring?" the older man asked. "This won't be a ceremonial voyage. We don't have room for liabilities."

"I'm strong," she stated with a swift, almost breathless certainty. "Much stronger than I look."

Edward crossed his arms, leaning against the ship's railing. "Out there, strength alone can't save you. You have to know how to fight."

"I want to learn," she said. "It can't be any more dangerous out there than here."

The older man angled his head, a thoughtful expression on his face. "What can you offer that my crew doesn't already have?"

She met the captain's steely gaze. "I can sense storms before they near."

All three men straightened. The captain narrowed his eyes. "Even without your pelt?"

Her lungs ached as if a question had physically struck them.

She inhaled; the frigid ocean air stung her nose. "Yes, even without it. I can still sense the pressure in my bones."

Silas's mouth opened, then closed again. Edward rubbed at the stubble lining his jaw.

"Welcome to my crew," the captain said.

A sharp gasp escaped her; her eyes widened in surprise. She feared she'd have to resort to begging, but the captain offered little resistance. He turned to Edward. "Train her starting tomorrow."

Her knees nearly gave out with the rush of relief. "Thank you," she whispered.

Then, louder—steadier. "I mean it. Thank you, because I'm going to find Ivan, and one way or another, I'll feed the Butcher his own heart."

A low whistle escaped Silas's lips.

Edward regarded her with quiet curiosity, something unreadable flickering in his eyes.

The captain, who introduced himself as Howie, extended a hand. "Let's ensure you live long enough to see it done."

She shook his hand as she climbed aboard, looking back only to wish she had the time to say goodbye.

PART II

The felicitous Nature of Revenge

THE HIGH SEAS SEPTEMBER-FEBRUARY

"**few** things drive a dead soul like revenge. It's the only fire that can catch in the cold ashes of despair and stir a ghost to walk again. But vengeance is only a bandage covering the wound without curing it. The hurt that birthed it remains a sickness deep in the bone."

— *Musings from a Fisherman, from A Collection,* gifted to the Royal Library of Silvamare

Chapter Eight

Weeks passed, slipping by like dreams—each intangible and indistinct, remembered only in fragments of light and movement.

Elin had grown used to the ship's movements, the rise and fall of its deck, the stomping of boots at dawn, and the smell of the sea. The sleeping quarters were crowded, and hammocks creaked with every swell. It was a sound she wasn't sure she could sleep without—the only thing quieting her darker thoughts.

Under naval discipline and the prosaic tasks that defined their days, there was a strong sense of camaraderie amongst the crew. It was impossible to overlook. When sailors squabbled over cards, irritation prickled along her skin, but beneath it persisted something steadier, a warmth that settled low in her chest. When they spoke to one another or clasped shoulders in passing, their love was unmistakable.

She found herself surrounded by something like a family.

It reminded her of her own. Guilt gnawed at her like a pest lodged in her marrow. She tried and failed not to think of her father, and his sad eyes, the same soft blue as Anik's. Or her mother, likely returned from her migration to an empty home, only to learn her daughter was gone, and her son was never coming back.

Driven by her need for revenge, she hadn't said goodbye. She left without writing a single letter. To her father and her friends, it must have seemed she'd let the sea sweep her away. There were many things she regretted, but her choice to leave was not one of them.

She couldn't return to her village, not until she could tell them that Anik's death wasn't wasted—not until her own hands were stained red with the blood of the Butcher.

Edward's instructions filled her days. He trained her in the workings of the ship, explaining the purposes of ropes and sails, and the roles of each crew member. He was patient with her and firm in his teachings; there was no room for error, but his dry wit made the monotony of some tasks more bearable. Especially as he taught her the importance of sanding the deck.

He dumped a bucket of seawater over the planks; the scent of brine filled her nose as Edward handed her a rough stone. It fit perfectly into her palm.

Elin stared at the stone, then at the wet planks. "So, I just scrub the planks with this?"

Reaching for another stone, Edward crouched low, dragging the stone back and forth across the wood. "It's tiresome and inconvenient, but it is important to remove the grime and crusted salt from the deck. It also keeps water from leaking into the ship."

As she lowered herself to her knees, she followed Edward's instructions, grinding the stone back and forth over the planks. It made a grinding sound as it scrubbed away at the grime, sloshing the water back and forth. Already she knew that after some time her palms would chafe and her muscles would ache. Good. It gave her something else to focus on.

"I've never seen someone actually scrub the deck too hard," Edward said, placing his hand over hers. "You're going to sand away the plank."

She winced at the worn spot in the wood. "I'm sorry," she said. A flush reached her cheeks. Already she had failed.

With his calloused hand still on hers, he guided the stone across the plank, showing her just how much pressure to apply. A thought struck her then.

"Why are you the one teaching me this?" she asked. "As the lieutenant, you must have more important matters to attend to."

Edward pulled his hand back, creating a space between them. "I took responsibility for you."

"To train me how to fight, yes. Not for this." She lifted the stone so that it sat between them.

Shrugging, he said, "I guess I've become invested in your well-being."

She scrunched her face. "That's a terrible investment."

He brought a hand to the side of his face, smiling at her. Her eyes widened at the sight of his bright smile, and she glanced away. "Let me decide that for myself," he said.

She shook her head, returning to the task at hand. That was until Edward's hand returned to her line of sight that she brought her gaze back to his. He gently lifted the braided hair around her wrist, observing it.

"You might want to take that off while doing this. You might ruin your bracelet."

Pulling her hand to her chest, she said, "It's fine."

His eyes narrowed on the band. "What is it? It looks like your hair."

The heat of anger welled up in her chest. Under his scrutinizing gaze, she feared he'd insist she remove it.

"It is. I braided it with Anik's. I won't—can't—take it off."

Edward's eyes softened, and he nodded. "I'm glad you have something of his to keep close."

Relief was a cold wind through her. Her shoulders fell as she looked at him. A silence that felt like minutes passed between them as they stared at one another. Edward sucked in a breath and placed his palms on his thighs before rising to his feet. "Well," he said. "I think you've got this figured out. I should attend to those other matters you were so worried about."

He winked at her, turning around, and Elin could only watch as he walked away, wishing he might have stayed a little longer. Loneliness crept back in like shadows cast in the evening, and she returned to scrubbing the planks and observing the surrounding crew.

What surprised her was how often Silas lent a hand. He wasn't above scrubbing the deck or taking on extra work when a sailor fell ill or suffered an injury. Even Howie got his hands dirty when he could have assigned the tasks to someone of a lower rank; she imagined no one would think anything of it. But it seemed Silvamare's command took a different approach to authority.

One afternoon, as the sun dipped low and the sails flashed gold in the light, she found herself beside Silas. Together, they coiled rope in the shade of the mainmast.

"You work more than I expected a royal to," she admitted, glancing at the coil in his hands.

He looked up with a crooked smile; the wind tousled his dark hair. "Did you think I spent my days parading about the deck like some fabled prince? What do they teach you in Frostwake?"

She squinted at him. "An unfair assumption, it seems."

He chuckled, leaning against the mast. "I serve as my father and brother's voice," he said after a moment. "In matters of state—negotiation, governance, the sorts of things that don't require them directly. My brother, Prince Linden, doesn't travel well."

"It sounds like you carry the burden of a crown without wearing one."

His gaze met hers, his eyes flickering as if she'd pressed an old wound. She almost apologized, but he gave a shrug.

"As long as the kingdom's cared for, and the people I love are safe, I can bear it."

There was no bitterness in his voice.

Conversation with the prince came as easily as speaking with a friend. Though the idea of forming a friendship seemed unlikely to her. He was accustomed to conversing with people from all walks of life. Of course, he knew how to make her feel comfortable, too.

Despite being surrounded by the crew, the weeks had been lonely. Anik's absence was an ever-present rupture in her world. So she'd cling to the illusion of comfort.

Chapter Nine

Elin scrubbed the deck on her knees. The sandstone block scraped against her palms, salt and grit biting into her raw skin after days of nothing more. Back and forth, she scoured the wood, shoulders aching. She had been promised training in combat—learning to fight with both her hands and a blade. All she'd done since boarding the *Maren* was scrubbing decks and menial chores.

Was she expected to drown the Butcher in a bucket? Or run him through with a broom handle?

Sweat dripped from the tip of her nose. She swiped it away and sat back on her heels as Edward walked past to check on her progress.

"How's it coming along?"

The sweltering sun beat down on her.

"When are you going to train me?" she snapped. "I'm not here to be your free labor."

He raised a single eyebrow, unfazed by her outburst. "This is part of knowing how to survive out here."

She folded her arms, narrowing her eyes at him.

"It's just as important to know when not to use a blade as it is to know when to use one." He stepped beside her. "I understand you want revenge, but right now, it's more important that you understand the ship, and that your head is clear when you learn to fight."

She opened her mouth to argue. He held up a hand.

"I'll train you, but not while your grief is still running the show."

Leaning against a crate, he crossed his muscular arms. "Elin, you don't have to be fine. What you need is a clear head. Pain can cloud your judgment."

His words made her squirm. She dropped her gaze, ashamed of the tears threatening to fall. "It hardly seems fair that you can judge my state of mind," she argued. "You don't even know me."

He let the silence stretch, waiting until her tears had receded before speaking again. "When Silas and I were younger, he'd sneak out of the palace. He'd find me helping my father in his workshop."

Unsure where the conversation was heading, she asked, "What's his occupation?"

"Carpenter. His business helps supply Silvamare's ships. He dabbles in smaller projects too, making wooden toys for children. I enjoyed it, but it was his work, not mine. I wanted to pave my own way, so when Silas joined the navy, I figured, why not?"

Without a word, she nodded, her mind wandering, as it often did when conversations turned to families. Not that she didn't care; she just couldn't get past her own ache. Every memory, every story she might've shared, circled back to Anik or the selkies. It hurt too much to share those parts of herself.

"Why are you telling me this?" she asked.

He shrugged. "You said we don't know each other. I am trying to amend that."

She looked away, attempting to smother her smile. It would be easier not to like him.

He said nothing more, and for that, she was grateful.

By dinnertime, Edward had convinced a few sailors to teach her their favorite card games. She sat cross-legged on the deck with them, watching as coins and scraps of paper changed hands. The rules were fast and confusing, the slang another language, but they laughed when she lost and cheered when she bluffed her way into a win.

"You're cheating," Milo—the sailor who had barred her in Frostwake—pointed a calloused finger at her.

"I am not," she replied, though she wasn't sure if that was true.

"Careful," another drawled. "Sluagh'll come for you if you are."

A few of the men snorted.

Perry, the Drakcultian wind-wielder, stiffened beside her. "Please don't say that."

"Oh, gods," Milo scoffed. "It's only a story."

"It is not wise to speak its name at sea," Perry muttered, eyes flicking towards the dark water beyond. "Not unless you wish to draw its notice."

She glanced between them. "Sluagh?"

"A creature of sorrow," Milo said with a grin. "Feeds on grief. Floats about unseen until it finds someone miserable enough to suit it."

"Or until you mock it," Perry whispered.

Elin tilted her head, drawing on old stories from home. "Like a water spirit?"

Milo shrugged. "Call it what you want, but if you're going to cheat, don't make it so obvious."

Laughter rippled through the circle as the game resumed, coins clinking against wood.

A faint chill traced the length of her spine as she reached for her next card. She told herself it was only the wind.

For the first time in weeks, she didn't feel like a ghost of herself.

Edward lingered nearby, watching. The corner of his mouth tugged upward. When the laughter faded and the crew wandered off for their night shifts, he handed her a plate stacked with bread and smoked fish.

She blinked at it in confusion. "I'm not—"

"You are," he said. "You skipped breakfast again. You'll start fainting if you keep it up."

She hadn't meant to skip meals; eating had simply become another task she couldn't bring herself to care about. As she stared at the plate, it became difficult to ignore the way her gut growled at her.

"I can't train you if you're at risk of fainting with a blade in your hand," Edward added. "Fuel the body, fuel the mind."

Concern radiated off him in steady waves, warm and uneasy. She took the plate, realizing too late that she trusted him to know what she needed—even when she didn't. She picked at the plate; the first few bites turned her stomach, but she forced herself to keep going.

When she finished, she handed the empty plate back, giving the most sincere smile she could manage. "Thank you."

His gaze moved over her, a deep line forming between his brows.

"What is it?" she asked.

"Nothing," he said. "You have a beautiful smile."

She rolled her eyes. "Then why do you look like it pained you?"

"It didn't." His voice quieted. "It's just...the first time I've seen it."

She looked away and thanked the night's cover for concealing the blush rising up her cheeks. Then she stood, brushing imaginary crumbs from her borrowed trousers. Part of her wanted to lean into it, but the louder part screamed, "*Run! This isn't safe.*"

"Goodnight," she muttered.

"Goodnight, Elin," he said as she walked past.

As she reached the door to the hammocks, she tried not to think about the way his emotions had shifted, softening into awe before crashing back into concern. He shouldn't worry so much about her, but gods help her, a small part of her was glad he did.

"**Though** a selkie's strength is lauded in seafaring myth, reliable accounts of their performance in battle are scarce. When pressed, they fight with startling ferocity, but their passions run deep and unchecked—an untempered blade, swift to strike yet prone to snap."

— Naval Records of the Old Kingdom of Sidon

Chapter Ten

Edward at last made good on his word. He woke her in the early hours of the morning, before the bell marked the shift change, and dragged her from the dark warmth below deck into the open air.

Above, the sky was a canvas of silvered clouds and fading stars. A thin mist clung low over the sea, turning the horizon into a blurred seam. The *Maren* cut through the calm swells of Leviathan's Wake, water sloshing against the ship's hull. Behind them, their companion ships sailed, one on each side.

The rigging creaked overhead.

Only two sailors lingered near the bow, speaking in low voices as they kept their watch. They paid her and Edward little mind.

He shrugged off his coat and rolled his shoulders. Pale morning light traced his frame as he stretched. She followed suit, watching the muscles along his back tighten and shift beneath his shirt.

Heat rushed to her cheeks as he lowered his arms, looking at her with a hint of amusement.

"We're starting with our hands," he said.

Elin tilted her head, a flicker of challenge lighting her expression. "You will regret that."

A corner of his mouth twitched. "Maybe."

He closed the distance without warning. On instinct, her palm shot towards his throat; he deflected it.

She pivoted.

The ship dipped with the swell of Leviathan's Wake. She embraced the motion, pressing the advantage too soon.

Edward gave ground just enough to invite it. He caught her wrist mid-strike and turned with the movement.

The sky flashed where the deck had been. Her back struck the planks with a breath-stealing thud.

Before she could twist free, his knees pinned her hips, and his forearm braced across her collarbone, immovable as the mast behind him.

She was at his mercy. Her pulse hammered against her ribs.

"Breathe," he whispered.

The word barely reached her.

For a fractured instant, the deck was no longer wood but ice, and she was helpless again, reaching for someone already slipping away.

She shoved him hard.

He pulled away, removing his forearm.

"Elin."

His voice was steady, a rope leading her back to herself.

The ship snapped into focus around her: the scent of tar and salt, the constant creak of rigging.

"It's one thing to have strength," he said, meeting her eyes. "It's another to know how and when to use it."

Heat climbed her neck, prickling her skin.

"I nearly had you," she muttered.

"You didn't."

He eased his weight away and stood, offering his hand.

For a moment, pride kept her on the deck.

Then she took it, rising to her feet once more.

"Ready to go again?" he asked.

She raised her chin. "Yes."

Instead of attacking directly, he guided her, showing her how to position herself, where to shift her weight, and how to scan for her opponent's next move.

This time, when he came for her, she evaded him.

She started watching his hips, noting the way his weight shifted.

When he stepped in, she saw the turn in his hips a fraction earlier than before. She moved with it, but was still too slow. Catching her around the waist, he used her momentum to spin her away. She stumbled but didn't fall.

"That's better," he said, already repositioning.

The mist along the horizon was thinning, pale yellow threading through the silver sky. It struck the handsome planes of his face, lining it with gold.

Forcing her gaze away, she shifted her attention to his hips, catching his movements faster than before.

She sidestepped; the moment his back was turned to her, she kicked out. He pivoted towards it, catching her leg before she could land the blow.

It wasn't until the morning bell chimed, marking the daily shift change, that they separated.

Training had become the best part of her day.

Edward drilled her on disarming, footwork, and stances that adjusted for the shifting deck. He didn't go easy on her.

Every day, she improved, learning quickly. Her selkie blood made her faster and more agile than most of the crew, and she had endurance most of them couldn't match—except for Edward.

They trained early, before the ship fully woke, or later, when only the night crew stirred. She learned how to anticipate movement, read tension in someone's shoulders, and know when a blade was coming before it was swung.

He was quiet when she needed quiet, firm when she hesitated. There were moments when her guard dropped that she'd realize he was watching her, his gaze extending beyond mere observation. It was growing difficult to ignore the warmth of his attention. The feeling was sweet on her tongue, but heavy on her heart.

A loud, splintering crack snapped through the air as her wooden blade cracked against Edward's with enough force to send a jolt up her arm.

Her breath came fast, but she wasn't tired. For the first time since she'd set foot on this ship, her heart soared, every part of her thrumming with exhilaration.

She felt the old urge to rush him and resisted.

Ducking his next swing, she drove forward, leveraging the sway of the deck to propel herself into him. Edward stumbled back, surprised by the strength behind her lunge. She struck again towards his left shoulder, then his side, each blow sharp and controlled.

"Good," he said, deflecting the last hit. "You're using the ship to your advantage."

"It's not the only thing I can use to my advantage," she said, lips turning into a half-smile.

He raised a brow. "Is that so?" he asked, gaze falling to her mouth.

She smiled fully, feinting high before swiping her leg behind his knees. He dropped like a sack of grain. Before he could recover, she was on him, the dull edge of her practice blade pressed against his neck.

Her heart stumbled, and she quickly withdrew.

Elin's ears perked up at Edward's laughter, a joyous sound that steadied her.

"Well done."

"It was too easy," she said between breaths, "You let me do that."

"I didn't," he replied, still smiling. "You're stronger than you look."

Gesturing to her hair and the markings along her temples, she said, "Of course I am."

"Fair enough," he conceded.

She extended a hand. He took it, and she pulled him to his feet with little effort.

Edward had gone easy on her in those early days, but now he was pushing harder, fighting dirtier, keeping her always guessing, always watching.

"Complacency kills," he told her.

They sat close, sweat beading on their skin from exertion. On the horizon, the sky smoldered with streaks of amber, smothered by the deepening indigo of night. The last light clung to the waves in fractured ribbons.

It was much warmer now that they were away from Frostwake. She hadn't known a heat like this. It left her wondering how much she had yet to experience—how much more there was to see and learn of the world.

"What does Silvamare look like?" she asked, surprising herself with the question.

Edward tilted his head back, thinking.

"Green," he said finally. "There are forests that cover the island from the beaches to the cliffs. A strait cuts through the middle, letting the sea through."

Elin closed her eyes, trying to imagine it. "It sounds beautiful."

"It is," he said. "I've sailed to all the surviving islands, and nowhere compares to home."

A soft ache brushed against her. "You miss it," she said.

"I do. Especially the food," he groaned. "My mom's bread, river trout, fried apples..."

She laughed. "You had me at bread."

He grinned, then fell silent.

Elin glanced at him, waiting.

"We left not long after the last Tide; we've been at sea for many months."

She couldn't explain her curiosity, but the words tumbled out before she could stop them.

"Have you lost someone to the Tide?"

His eyes squinted, reflecting the glow of the lanterns. "Yeah, a few."

Her heart clenched, a sympathetic pain mirroring his own.

"Four Tides ago, I lost a good friend," he said. "She was the smartest person I'd ever known and kinder than anyone deserved."

"I'm sorry," she said. "What was her name?"

His shoulders rose and fell, yet the gesture couldn't conceal the sadness that lingered. "Cassidy."

She hesitated before leaning her head onto his shoulder, a silent offering of comfort. He loosed a shaky breath, "I thought I'd never get past it. I don't claim to be over it now, but I can say the grief gets quieter. It's taught me not to waste time."

She nodded, hoping that the same might someday be true for her.

"And you?" he asked, resting his chin on the crown of her head.

She pursed her lips, considering how much of herself she wanted to share. If Edward could share his loss, it was only fair she offer something of herself in return.

"Most of my friends are selkies...but I had a human friend," she said. "Kova," her voice strained on his name. "He was called on this year for the Tide, ripped right out of my arms."

It burned behind her eyes, and she blinked it away.

"You've lost a lot this year," he said.

"Yeah." The word escaped as a breathy scoff.

His gaze lingered on her, as if there was something he wanted to say—but chose not to.

She didn't pull away as their heads leaned together in the quiet stillness. A warmth washed over her; their shared sorrow softening something sharp inside her.

"In all my years plying the waters of Leviathan's Wake, I have never seen the ancient beasts. They vanished with the drakes—perhaps the merfolk with them—long ago. Yet my grandfather swore he once heard their song. His ship broke apart in a storm, and the mer came for him, leading him by their voices back to land. The beasts and the mer were the gods' most cherished children.

It chills me now to think on it. If the gods would let one of their own devour their children, what hope has the man on land? Perhaps we are here only to feed the endless hunger of the King of the Seas."

— *Musings from a Fisherman, from A Collection*, gifted to the Royal Library of Silvamare

Chapter Eleven

Elin's laughter rang out as she sprinted past the berry thicket, drawing a groan from Kova. Pine needles squished beneath her bare feet as she ran light and fast through Terron's Forest. A flutter in her chest made her feel as if her heart had grown wings and was eager to carry her away.

Anik was close behind her, closing the gap with long strides, his teasing taunts breathless, making her giddy with anticipation.

"Can't catch me!" she shouted, rounding the giant trunk of a pine.

"I always catch you," Anik called, grinning lopsidedly.

It was autumn, and the village had pitched its shelters just inside Terron's forest, preparing for their yearly celebration of thanks for their good fortunes.

Smoke curled from fires, and selkies cloaked in their pelts moved about the camp, helping to set up the remaining shelters. Her mother stood near their shelter, a string of shells woven through her silver hair, laughing as her father whispered something in her ear—he looked younger, happier, his blue eyes bright with mischief.

Her mother caught her eye.

"Come on, pups," she called, waving a hand. "It's nearly time to eat!"

Ignoring the call, Elin bolted, a shriek escaping her lips as Kova lunged again, almost sending her tumbling. Anik grabbed her wrist, tugging her just out of Kova's reach. They spun together before collapsing onto the dry grass.

"Hey! I almost had her!" Kova yelled.

They only laughed as their father approached with feigned menace in his step.

"You two better listen to your mother," he warned, scooping Elin into his arms.

Squealing, she kicked her legs as he spun her.

"Settle down, love," he said through his own laughter.

Then he stopped spinning, and the world's warmth washed away. Her father's arms turned to ash, sifting between her fingers as she fell.

The ground was no longer grass but ice, slick and unforgiving in its biting cold. Its expanse was endless, stretching from one horizon to another.

Overhead, the sky turned black, and the surrounding air thinned. The forest was gone.

Anik, Kova, and her mother stood at a distance on the cracking surface. She tried to reach them, but the ice fractured beneath her mother and Kova.

Their eyes locked for a fleeting moment before the ice splintered and they were plunged into the darkness below.

Elin screamed their names, but no sound came.

Only Anik remained—no longer a boy, but a man. She looked down at her hands, her fingers gouging into the ice. They were no longer the hands of a child but of a woman. She looked back at her brother. Across from her, he stood, his sterling hair identical to hers, his blue eyes too vibrant, too cheerful for this desolate reality that now only lived in her mind.

She tried to run to him, but her feet would not move. He opened his mouth to speak. A trail of red marred his neck, and blood pooled onto the ice below.

The world lurched, swallowing everything whole—and when she fell into its dark embrace, it was with relief.

She spilt from her hammock with a startled gasp; the ship tipped with a great swell. The air filled with the muffled thuds of bodies tumbling onto the floor, accompanied by groggy curses and the ship's complaining creaks as it settled.

Elin blinked into the darkness. Sweat clung to her neck as she burrowed back into her hammock, folding herself into a ball. The persistent trembling of her body kept her from sleeping. She lay there until the first light appeared in the sky.

As the first hints of dawn filtered through the porthole above, she pushed herself upright and peered outside. The world beyond the glass was cast in soft grey; the sea was still.

It reminded her of the selkies. The silvery light shimmering off the sea's surface made her think of Anik's hair, and how it glinted like the silver strands threaded through her own.

When the sun broke through the clouds, golden and warm, she felt his bright and easy smile. Veins of blue split the clouds, as piercing as his eyes.

The world pressed close, in stifling waves, the air too heavy to breathe. She hurried to the washbasin; stiff fingers gripped its sides. Unable to see her reflection in the sloshing water, she lifted her gaze to the mirror.

She didn't recognize the person in it. Leaning forward, she inspected the shimmering spots showing beneath her collar and freckling the sides of her face until they faded near her temples. Her brown eyes stared back with the same emptiness she felt now.

Her skin had darkened under the ocean's sun, and the long silver strands shimmered brighter than before in the glass.

She'd become a stranger to herself.

Splashing her face with water, she scrubbed at it as if she could wash away the memories of that day on the ice.

She had no pelt to tuck around her shoulders. Edward's coat had only offered a temporary reprieve, and no longer smelt of pine and whiskey, only of her. There was no promise from the sea to hush the grief that tangled within her chest.

Her long hair clung to her damp skin—silver ropes that restricted her breathing. Ropes that would drag her under.

She shoved her hair back, her reflection mocking her.

And bolted.

Cold boards slapped beneath her as she ran down the narrow hall. Entering the galley, her hands shook as she opened and closed drawers, searching for something—anything—to ease the weight dragging her under.

She slid open a drawer, finding what she'd been looking for.

The sharp knife slid through her hair with a crisp sound, like a blade cutting through straw; strands fell to the floor in pale ribbons. She gripped the ends too tightly, sawing them off in uneven chunks.

Her breaths grew ragged and quick in the quiet.

Morning light spilt through the porthole in thin gold beams, illuminating the hair scattered at her feet.

Laughter carried from the hall, two voices, carefree and too loud for the hour.

Elin froze.

Edward and Silas entered, mid-conversation, grinning—until they saw her. The laughter died, like a note cut short.

The sight of them made her avert her eyes, overcome by a flush of shame.

"Silas, give us a minute," Edward said.

Silas hesitated before stepping out without a word.

Edward approached slowly.

"Elin," he coaxed, "let me help."

She couldn't move, couldn't speak. She'd become a statue, wishing the floor would open up beneath her and swallow her as it had her mother and Kova.

"Please," he whispered.

She tightened her grip on the knife. "I don't want anyone holding a blade near my neck." Her voice was a brittle whisper.

"I understand," he said. "I would never hurt you, Elin. I swear it."

When she met his gaze, she didn't see pity, just concern.

"I have sisters," he added. "I used to help them with their hair when they were too little to do it right."

Her fingers shook as she handed him the knife.

He stepped in front of her, trying his best to keep the blade in her line of sight. His hands were gentle as he murmured instructions, "Tilt your chin...good...hold still..." but mostly, he said nothing.

The silence deepened as he worked to even out the edge of her hair. It fell like snow, carrying a weight Elin hadn't realized until now.

She watched it collect on the floor, piling at her feet.

Tears slipped down her cheeks, quiet and unannounced. He wiped them away. She hadn't known hands like his could be so gentle.

When he finished, she sank to the floor and didn't move. The knife clinked as he set it aside.

He sat beside her without a word and wrapped an arm around her shoulders.

"Is this okay?" he asked.

She nodded, leaning into him without thinking. He stiffened for a moment before relaxing, running his fingers up and down her arm as he held her.

They stayed that way for a while, silver strewn across the floor like fallen threads from a life that wasn't hers anymore. She didn't know how to carry her grief, only that she had to keep moving, keep fighting, until it no longer drowned her.

"**Elemental** magic originates from the first bonding of man and beast. These first wielders, The Firstbound, rid the world of its earliest curses and monsters. Though the beasts are gone and the blood of the Firstbound diluted by time, their magic still thrums through the blood of many, growing weaker with each generation."

—*The Beasts of Magic*, housed in the Old Kingdom Library of Sidon

Chapter Twelve

Since finding her in the galley, Edward kept her busy. She was half-convinced he was making up tasks just to keep her distracted. She rose before the sun and worked until well after sunset. Each night, she had only the energy to drag herself to bed and fall into a sleep so deep that not even her dreams could find her.

Tonight, Edward placed her on mid-watch with Milo and Perry—whose relationship was one of equal parts admiration and disdain.

The night breeze whipped through her shoulder-length hair, tossing the uneven ends in every direction. She held it away from her face, watching as Perry worked to shift the winds in their favor. In the pale light of the moon, Perry's brows drew tight. A sheen of sweat matted his blonde hair to his forehead.

Through the whistling wind, Perry called out an order.

Elin approached the mast, calling out to Milo, who clung to the rigging, managing the sails. She did not know what the orders meant, but as Milo adjusted the sails and the wind blew taut behind them, she watched, impressed by his skill.

Returning to Perry's side, she said, "I haven't felt wind magic before. It's remarkable."

Perry looked up to where Milo was descending the rigging. "Tell him that."

She followed his gaze, watching as Milo yanked another line tight.

He shouted down to Perry, "You wouldn't be so impressed if you knew he doubled our travel time to Frostwake. Took us two months to get there. It should have been one."

Her muscles locked. Milo and Perry continued to take shots at one another. Their voices dulled, as if she'd slipped beneath the waves.

The image of the *Leviathan's* sawed-off figurehead flared behind her eyes. Silvamare had been late to Frostwake. Regular patrols against the pirates would have already taken effect along their coastline if they'd gotten there earlier. Anik's death—the theft of her pelt—might have been avoided.

Her stomach churned as the ship heeled.

"I wasn't trained on the sea—" Perry stopped speaking; his control over the wind faltered. Air lashed across the deck, and she planted her feet to stop herself from swaying.

Perry called another order. She almost missed it.

Clouds blocked the moon, plunging them into darkness.

"Why were you sent to Silvamare if you were not ready?" she asked Perry, anger edging into her voice.

Milo shouted from his position above. "Because his king sends Silvamare his weakest."

"That's not true," Perry said.

"Why would your king do that if Silvamare and Drakcultus are allies?" she asked.

It was Milo who answered for him. "Our alliance is out of necessity, not loyalty."

"We were allies before the Reckoning—" Perry began.

Milo climbed further down the rigging. "Silvamare was never allied with Drakcultus. But history likes to forget that the Araceli were Silvamare's oldest allies."

She shifted her stance. Even on this ship, there were fractures in trust and uncertainty.

"The Araceli still rule beside the Gaiano," Perry said between clenched teeth. The air pulled away from Elin, thinning as Perry worked it around the ship.

Moonlight flooded the deck as the clouds parted. The sheen of sweat on Perry's forehead now beaded and ran down, dripping from his brow and his nose.

"I don't trust Drakcultus," Milo dropped onto the deck with a rope in hand. He stepped closer. "Not when your princess is prophesied to destroy kingdoms."

Elin knew of the princess's prophecy, but she never gave it much thought. She had never cared about the politics of other islands. She fiddled with the band of silver hair around her wrist.

"If you fall, it won't be by the princess," Perry said. "Her prophecy is exaggerated. If anything, you should be more fearful of me. I sleep right above you."

A counter-gust blew, causing Milo to stumble. Smug satisfaction flickered across Perry's face.

Narrowing his eyes, Milo said, "And don't forget that I sleep right below."

For all their posturing, Elin could feel their threats were only half-hearted. The world was growing larger, more dangerous with each passing day. She had far more than the sea to fear when the politics of one island were enough to shatter lives across the whole of Aquerios—enough to upend hers. And she didn't yet know what she would do about it.

"The passions of the heart do not always bend to the mind's reason, just as the passions of the mind care little for the heart's unrest."

— *Musings from a Fisherman*, from *A Collection*, gifted to the Royal Library of Silvamare

Chapter Thirteen

They were sailing deep into the Wavecrest Ocean, where the skies shifted on a whim and the salt air stung their skin. The crew worked harder to steady the sails against unpredictable gales, and the constant motion of the sea became as regular as breathing. What had once felt foreign had rooted itself into the fabric of Elin's daily life—and so had Edward.

They trained constantly. Tentative sessions of footwork and balance developed into fluid exchanges of blows and counters. She now had a dangerous edge, a result of Edward's instruction. Cutting her hair had not freed her from grief, but it had eased its hold. Once again, she could breathe around it.

A new confidence blossomed within her, one she'd never had before. She no longer reached for a coat or her pelt, as if she might sink into it and disappear.

Edward seemed to notice the shift, too.

He watched her more often now, whether in passing, curled up reading in a corner, or when she laughed at Milo's ridiculous card-playing antics. His gaze always held something soft and steady, as though he were learning her by heart.

To her dismay, she missed him when he wasn't around. To become used to his presence was a risk she couldn't afford—not when she feared a loss like that again.

Still, she inched closer when they were absorbed in conversation, felt her heart swell when he smiled at her.

Most evenings, she'd find herself with Edward and Silas, the slap of cards and the gentle clinking of cups accompanying their shared stories or comfortable silences. The prince always surprised her. He carried a hundred myths and tales in his mind, which he spun with dancing flames—a natural storyteller. There was a fire in him that didn't match his quiet demeanor—fury at injustice, a deep need to see the world change.

One night, after another raucous round of cards—which she would have won if Silas hadn't cheated so obviously—they lingered at the table while the rest of the crew filtered away.

Silas stood, stretching his arms with a yawn. "Goodnight, you two," he said, heading for the deck.

"You're sleeping...out there?" she asked.

He paused, glancing over his shoulder. "Sometimes," was his only explanation before disappearing behind the door.

With a raised brow, she looked at Edward, her silent question hanging in the air.

He shrugged. "It's not for me to say."

His tone was final; he wouldn't betray his friend's privacy. She respected that about him—his unwavering loyalty.

Alone, the silence between them turned awkward. Elin started to fill it, but Edward spoke first. He smiled, and she tried again. "I should go too."

They both rose to their feet, their shoulders bumping. They stepped back, murmuring soft apologies, but neither moved. The space between them thinned until it felt like even breathing might shatter it.

Her pulse stuttered. She thought of the time she went cliff diving with Ila and Arnaq. How they stood at the edge, the sea crashing against the rock face.

She could feel Edward's unsettled warmth brushing against her thoughts, stirring beneath her skin. His hands twitched at his sides, as though he didn't know what to do with them. The air between them thickened, charged with something restless and aching. It made her dizzy.

For a moment, she couldn't tell where his emotions ended, and hers began. The sensation hummed through her chest, pulling her forward—like standing at the edge of the cliff before the jump.

They stared at each other, neither speaking. The ship groaned underfoot, the only sound between them as she stepped closer, the fear of the plunge building beneath her skin. He leaned in, stopping just short, letting her choose.

The pull towards him had crept up on her—harder to resist than she liked, but resisting what felt natural was nothing new. If she jumped, there would be no taking it back. This would be more than a passing kiss. Her breath caught.

She pulled back, unable to choose the fall.

"Did you know," her voice was barely louder than the creak of the wood, "some selkies are empaths?"

His lashes fluttered, blinking away his surprise. "I didn't," he said hoarsely.

With her chin tilted upwards, her eyes met his. "Please," the word was shaky, "try to control your feelings when I'm around. They confuse me."

He took a small step back, and she felt the sudden tightening of his emotions; the warmth between them recoiled. She hated this part of herself. When someone felt the same thing she did, their emotions tangled together until she couldn't tell whose heart was beating in her chest.

His hand twitched at his side, as if he wanted to reach for her. His throat worked around a reply. "I didn't know. I'm sorry."

If only she could swallow her words, reverse the flow of time, and undo the hurt she'd caused, but she was in no condition to love or be loved. She didn't wait for him to say more; she turned and walked away.

Thoughts buzzed in her skull like bees, so she climbed the narrow stairs and slipped onto the upper deck.

The night air embraced her—a soft breeze brushed her face as she took in the stars glittering above in the velvet black sky.

Silas was sprawled out on the deck near the railing, arms folded behind his head, eyes turned upward. He looked peaceful, almost as if he belonged to the stars themselves.

Elin had forgotten he was out here. She hovered for a moment, unsure whether she should interrupt.

"Needed some air?" he asked without looking at her.

"Yeah," she said.

He patted the space beside him. "Join me."

She hesitated, then sat beside him, drawing her knees to her chest.

"My mother used to tell me the stars were where the gods carry our souls," she said after a while. "When someone dies, we look for them in the sky. I never believed it; they all looked the same every time I looked up. I didn't bother when Anik...when he died."

Silas turned his head towards her, quiet and listening.

"There's a peak in Frostwake," she added. "A sacred one, with steep slopes. The wind is treacherous, but some still climb it each year to pray to Cosmir, whether for mild winters or for their loved ones."

"I'd likely try if I lived there," he admitted. "It's far too cold."

She grinned. "That it is."

Tilting her head back, she traced the constellations. "The stars are beautiful tonight."

"They are," he said. "Though it's the moon I love to watch most."

She turned her head, resting her chin on her knee. He was still staring upward, something wistful in his expression.

"Why is that?" she asked.

His lips curved into a small smile. "It reminds me of someone—someone I miss."

His feelings were a blooming warmth, gentle beneath his words. A tender ache of longing, soft and steady like the moonlight itself.

The feelings didn't tangle with hers. They didn't pull at her chest or send her pulse skittering. It didn't blur the edges of her thoughts or make her question whose feelings were whose.

In this quiet moment beside Silas, when she could so clearly feel the shape of his heart, without clouding her own, the truth was an undeniable thing. Edward's emotions didn't confuse her; they matched her own. And that frightened her more than anything else.

It was impossible to pretend she wasn't drawn to him—nor that he felt the same.

She stayed beside Silas, letting the silence stretch between them undisturbed. He didn't say anything else, just stared at the moon like it held every answer he ever wanted.

Elin was no longer looking at the stars, too aware of her own heartbeat. Everything inside her buzzed, a hum beneath her skin.

When she stood, he looked up at her. "Going to bed?"

"Yeah," she said, brushing off her trousers. "Sleep well, Your Highness."

He gave her a lazy salute. "You too, Elin."

She walked away with her pulse unsteady, wishing she could slip into the sea and quell her thoughts. Because the tugging in her chest was her greatest fear come true, and if she wasn't careful, she was going to drown Edward Graves.

Chapter fourteen

She did not want Edward Graves. He could not want her.

Staring blankly up at the hammock swaying above her, and wrapped in Edward's fur coat, Elin fidgeted with the band around her wrist. It wasn't only that she feared hurting him. Edward was just as much a danger to her as she was to him. They had been strangers only months ago. How could she trust her broken heart with someone she scarcely knew? What did it matter that he was gentle and kind?

As she brought her bracelet to her face, she analyzed the overlapping strands. "*What do you think, Anik?*" she asked before dropping her arm, knowing what he'd say. She didn't want to hear it.

Edward was there for her when her world fell apart. It was gratitude that she felt. Or so she told herself. Proximity was the enemy, the threat against her heart. What she needed was distance, and she knew how to get it.

Quietly, she slipped from her hammock, clutching Edward's coat in her hands. She tiptoed through the narrow corridor of the ship in search of Howie's quarters. The hour was late, but she had to do this now— before she could change her mind. Squeezing her eyes shut, she knocked three times on his door.

For several moments, there was only the sound of the ship and the distant sound of the night crew working above. Then there was the sound of footsteps. Elin stepped back from the door as it swung open.

Howie stood wide-eyed, looking up and down the corridor. Then he took in Elin. "What is it?" he asked. "Has something happened?"

Worry swirled around him, and she felt guilty for waking him. "No, nothing is wrong. I'm sorry, it's just—" She chewed on her lip, looking down at the fur coat.

"Do you want to come in?" Howie asked.

Elin nodded, and Howie stepped aside, letting her inside his quarters.

It was dimly lit by a small candle beside his bed. There was a small sitting area around the fireplace and a large table scattered with papers and instruments she didn't recognize. "I am sorry for waking you," she said.

Howie waved her off and gestured for her to take a seat by the mantle. Sinking into the leather, she let out a deep sigh.

The fire in the fireplace flickered to life as Howie lit it. He groaned as he rose to his feet and brushed off his hands. "I'm sure what you woke me for is important."

Elin buried her face in her hands. Suddenly, she missed her friends and her mother with an ache sharp enough to hollow her out. She'd give anything to talk to them now. "Howie," she said, suddenly tired. "I want to work the night shift."

Howie sat across from her, leaning forward on his elbows. "Switching to the night shift means you won't be able to train with Edward."

Looking up from her hands, she met Howie's steely gaze. His eyes narrowed. "Did something happen between you two?"

She shook her head. "I just need some space."

"I see," Howie leaned back. "There is no shortage of men who'd love to move to the day crew, so that should not be an issue. As for training..." he ran his fingers through his beard. "I can see if Silas'll step in. How's that?"

Elin's shoulders sagged. "That will do. Thank you."

Rising from her seat, she brought the coat close to her chest. "Will you do one more thing for me?" she asked.

"I suppose that depends on what it is," he said.

She extended the coat, and Howie reached for it. "Can you return this to Edward for me? I don't need it anymore."

"If you're sure," he said.

"I am."

"Should I be worried about you, Elin?" Howie asked.

The corners of her eyes crinkled, careful to give him the truest smile she could manage. "No, you should not. Sorry again for waking you, Howie. Goodnight."

"Goodnight," he said, walking her to the door.

He closed it behind her. Rather than go back to the crew cabin, Elin ascended the stairs, returning to the deck.

Nearly a week had passed since she switched to the night shift, and in that time she hadn't once seen Edward. How he felt about her sudden absence she could not say; it was better not to know. Besides, there were things about the night she hadn't had the chance to fully appreciate before.

The sky glittered above, a thousand shards of light watching over them. The stars were different here than at home, and between tasks she was meticulous in identifying new constellations. Some she even named. If she looked hard enough, she could make out a mammoth in the south, so she named it after Tven. Another to the east appeared to be a warrior drawing a bow; that one was Anik. Others she gave simpler, less meaningful names to, like fish and hut. It was silly, but it passed the time.

Tonight she and Silas took training easy, moving through sets of drills. He'd been careful to avoid mention of Edward, and she wondered if he knew anything of what transpired between them. If he did, he hid it well. Though she supposed that came naturally with his role. Royalty had all manner of things to hide. It was just one part of the many games they played—one she never wanted to understand. And yet, when she looked at Silas, all she saw was one big contradiction.

She kicked out, and Silas dodged. He lunged, and she blocked.

Silas looked like a sailor, dressed in the same naval uniform as his men. He kept watch and maintained the ship just as well as he led it. He was secretive yet open. Refined yet relaxed. It led Elin to question if he was a prince playing as a sailor or a sailor playing as a prince.

She parried away from Silas, called for a break, and reached for her water skin. Gulping it down, she wiped away the water that spilt from her lips.

"You know," she said between breaths. "I still don't understand why you joined the navy. You put yourself in danger when you could remain safe in your palace."

A laugh escaped him as he shook his head. "You sound like my parents." He looked around the ship until he found a spot away from listening ear, then gestured with his head for her to follow.

"Every year I have to watch my people live in fear of being sacrificed to the sea god," he said, sitting on the steps to the quarterdeck. "Against the Black Tide—against the god—I am useless to them."

"Still," she said, sitting beside him. "There are ways to be helpful to your people that don't involve a sword and months at sea."

His expression turned contemplative. "It's not enough. The pirates threaten to destabilize the balance the islands have worked so hard to achieve. People like Hatra and Ivan think they can run away from the responsibility of the Tide and steal and murder at their leisure without consequence. If we allow them to go on unchecked, more might join them."

"Do you think so?" she asked.

"People do all kinds of things when they're scared," Silas said.

She couldn't argue with that. And she also understood why there were people who fled their homes for the sea. People like Hatra and Ivan, who didn't want to wait for fate to feed them to a monster whose hunger was never sated. What she could not understand was what they became afterwards. In trying to outrun a monster, they'd become one themselves.

"It's been centuries since the last island fell," she said. "Surely you don't believe a few pirates will bring the rest down."

"Elin, Frostwake's population is plummeting. Your shorelines need patrols from other islands because they're under attack. You yourself have been a victim of piracy. It wouldn't take much for another island to fall. After that, it will only be a matter of time before the rest of the world falls with it."

Straightening, Elin turned to face Silas fully. "Aquerios has survived the fall of islands before."

He gave her a pointed look. "And it's been dying ever since."

Out on the horizon, the black water of the sea trembled. She didn't like to think about it. The Black Tide was a constant cloud over their heads, a whisper in the back of their minds, a reminder that every soul was living on borrowed time. If only she could shift into something else, something that would take her far from the sea. "It's too bad we can't shift into something like a bird. We could fly away. Do you think birds have such thoughts of the gods and doom?"

"No, I do not," he said.

She turned back to him, smiling. "You don't think?"

Silas raised his brows in bemusement. "Sometimes I wish I could not."

"Perhaps thinking wouldn't be so tiresome if we didn't also have to feel," Elin mused.

"That is what makes us human. Though it is important not to let our feelings rule our thoughts."

"Easier said than done," Elin replied.

"True," Silas rose from the steps. "We should get back to work."

Elin thought about her conversation with Silas long after they'd returned to work. Now that her watch was over, she remained troubled by it.

Feeling was what made them human, but it also made them flawed. Her brows drew tight as she thought of her father. She didn't know that she missed him, but worry rooted itself in her stomach. How did he take the news of Anik's death? Was Mama there to grieve with him? Ila and Arnaq said her mother was fine when she last saw them, but anything could have happened in such a short time.

Entering the crew's cabin, she approached the shared writing desk shoved in the back. Sunlight streamed through the portholes with the rising of the sun. Elin pulled out a sheet of parchment and sat down, tapping her nail against the wood. She stared blankly at the sheet, unsure of what to say, only that she should say something. After several minutes, no words came, and she put the parchment away.

Later, she told herself as she dropped into her hammock. The canvas groaned beneath her. Someone dropped the curtains over the porthole, plunging the space into near darkness. In the dark, her eyes fluttered shut, and her limbs weighed heavily. She had the sensation of sinking as the world quieted to only her breathing. Her skin grew hot as she thought of the night she nearly kissed Edward.

Again, she felt the dizzying spell pulling her under. Her heart raced as she imagined the brush of his lips against hers, the way his chest would feel beneath her palms. Her breath quickened; the cabin's air suddenly felt too stale. She'd gone days thinking of Edward as little as possible; even so, in the quiet, he found his way back into her thoughts. The distance was not helping; it only made everything worse. She wanted space, and she got it. He let her have it without protest, and now she wanted him more.

Somehow he'd become the lone raft in a dangerous sea, and yet his safety felt like the real threat. She could swim to the raft, but that did not mean it was safe. It did not mean that the raft would not break apart or that her weight would not cause it to sink beneath the waves. Damn Edward Graves.

Elin dragged herself from her hammock to the wash bin, feeling the cold water slip across her cheeks before falling back in. The smallest ache worked its way through her bones, making the markings at her temples tingle with the suspense of a shift. It was gone as soon as the water returned to the bowl.

She closed her eyes, thinking of the blissful silence of the sea. Remembering the last time she sifted and let herself go in its embrace.

If only she could dive in now—silence her mind. Just for a moment. A moment to breathe. To pause time. To think—or not to think.

The need for fresh air overrode her fear of running into Edward. She made her way to the deck, the morning air whipping through her hair as she approached the ship's side. She stared out at the ships trailing behind and then leaned over the railing for a better view of the glittering water below. A part of her wanted the ship to lurch and send her toppling over, but she couldn't surrender herself. Not yet. She made herself and Anik a promise she was determined to keep. Still, she reached her hand out as if the sea might reach back.

Heat washed over her cheek, and she followed the sensation until she met the gaze of Edward from across the deck. His body was tense, as though he were prepared to dive in after her should she fall. She tore her gaze away and returned inside the ship with her heart in her throat, but this time Edward followed.

"Elin, wait," he said.

She almost didn't, but it sounded like a plea. With a deep inhale, she turned to face him.

"I'm sorry," he said. "I don't know what I was thinking. I was wrong to confuse you. It wasn't my intention." He spoke quickly as if worried she wouldn't give him the time to finish what he wanted to say.

"I appreciate what you have done for me," she said. "But I can't be around you right now. I already have friends. I don't need more."

"But you have none on this ship," Edward said.

Elin scowled, knowing that wasn't entirely true. Maybe Howie and Silas were not her friends, but she knew they looked out for her just as Edward had. But Edward could not be her friend. Friends did not think about each other the way she thought about him.

"I think that's for the best," she said. "My presence is temporary."

Edward's face softened as he took her in. "Everything is temporary, Elin."

"Then you should move on from me in no time," she replied, turning on her heel. She let out a shaky breath and walked into the awaiting darkness of the crew's cabin with her heart lodged in her throat.

"**The** Black Tide came on the day of Reckoning. From the depths, the sea god himself rose and demanded penance in blood. Those who refused were shown the cost of defiance in the ruin of their island and its people. For nearly five-hundred years, Frostwake has yielded its souls in the pale dawn of spring. Sidon weeks later. Silvamare bleeds at summer's first breath, and Drakcultus at its dying light. Each year, the Tide claims more, and with each offering, the world withers a little further."

—*The Birth of a New World: An Aquerios Compendium*, Old Kingdom of Sidon Library

Chapter fifteen

Silas

The black smudges on the map marred Volcara and the Sable Isles like a wound left to rot. Aquerios paid for time with souls.

The pirates were only a minor threat to Aquerios's stability, but it took very little to bring a kingdom to its knees.

Silas stood in the middle of Howie's quarters, staring down at the map rolled out across the table. He rubbed his neck, listening to Edward and Howie debate their approach to the Black Reef.

"We don't know that Hatra is actually seeking refuge in there," Edward said. "We will risk our ships and our men."

"It's better than aimlessly sailing all four seas," Howie deflected. "I sent a bird to the King. He'll learn soon what's become of the *Leviathan* and its men. Patrols from Silvamare to Sidon'll be searching for her soon enough. If she's not in the Black Reef, then it's one spot we can rule out. If she is there, we'll need a plan of attack."

Silas narrowed his eyes on the map. The Black Reef was situated between Silvamare and Drakcultus, and because of its difficult terrain, sailing near or within the Black Reef was often treacherous. Only the most skilled sailors could navigate it—and even then, their ships rarely came out unscathed.

"We may need to sacrifice one of our ships," he said, pointing to the eastern and western passages. "If we leave one side open, Hatra will likely escape."

"What about the men?" Edward asked.

"It will be crowded, but we'll converge on the *Maren*."

Howie scratched at his beard as he stared down at the map. "And use Perry to direct the empty ships to one passage while we enter on the other side. Smart thinking, Silas."

"It could work, but only if Perry is strong enough. He has grown, but is still unpredictable," Edward said.

"It's true," Silas said. "Perry has only just begun to prove himself."

"Ah, have a little faith. Perry'll be fine—" Howie started to say before a knock sounded on the door.

"Come in," Howie called.

The door creaked open, and Elin stepped in. Her large eyes widened at the sight of all three of them. "I'm sorry for interrupting; I didn't realize you were in a meeting."

Howie waved her off. "How can I help you?"

"I've finished my tasks for the day and am looking for more."

Silas raised a brow. He hadn't seen Elin sit in days—not since he and Edward found her in the galley with her hair strewn all over the floor.

"You could try relaxing," Howie suggested.

Elin's face fell. "I like to stay busy."

Her gaze moved around the room, pausing on Edward and then the table.

"Is that a map?" she asked. "I haven't seen a full one before. May I?"

Howie gestured towards the map. "Of course."

Silas watched her closely as she crossed the room. Her eyes narrowed, skimming across the worn parchment as she trailed her finger from island to island, pausing when she reached the blacked-out islands to the west.

"Are these meant to be Volcara and the Sable Isles?" she asked, brows furrowed.

"Yes," Silas said.

She stared a moment longer, lips pressed into a thin line.

"They're blacked out."

Edward nodded, pointing to the way the trade routes skirted around the islands. "They are no-sail zones."

Elin's brows furrowed. "Why?"

"You can't go there anymore," Silas explained. A shiver like the cold edge of a blade skated down his spine.

"I've always wondered why no one returns to the islands," she said. "We could reestablish the population in these places, couldn't we?"

Howie walked away from the table. Silas watched as the captain riffled through a pile of books.

Edward cleared his throat, returning his attention to the map.

"No," Edward said. "Ships that sail too far into Volcara's waters never come back, and no ship that we know of can sail into the Sable Isles. The sea pushes the ships away."

Elin's fingers glided over the population numbers labeled near each island. Not long ago, he and Howie added risk assessments for which islands were most susceptible to fall. As she neared Frostwake, Edward leaned past her, guiding her attention away from her island.

"Here is Silvamare," Edward said, turning to look at her. He was close enough that their noses nearly touched. For a moment, neither of them moved.

Her eyes were wide as she stared at Edward, unmoving. Silas tilted his head, watching as the selkie spots at her temple shimmered.

Edward pulled back quickly.

Elin blinked several times before taking a step back. "I've always wanted to travel," she blurted. "I never thought I'd actually do it. I knew the sea was big, but I didn't realize how small we all are until now."

She stole another glance at Edward before returning her attention to Howie. The captain was smiling at her.

"Thank you," she said. "Sorry again for interrupting your meeting."

Howie walked across the room with a book in hand. "You can look at it anytime. Here, take this," he held the book out for her. "Working the mind is just as important as working the body. It's a compendium about the different islands."

She took the book, examining its front before flipping through the pages. "Thank you," she said, smiling up at Howie. It almost met her eyes.

"Now go relax, Elin," Howie said. "That's an order...from your captain."

Elin nodded, giving her best salute before turning on her heel. The door creaked shut behind her.

Elin left silence in her wake. The three of them stood, staring blankly at the map. Silas couldn't look away from the black paint marring the lost islands, then at Frostwake. He knew why Edward had diverted Elin's attention. Though he wasn't sure hiding her island's struggles from her was the right thing to do.

"Does Elin know how close Frostwake came to needing support this Tide?" Silas asked.

"She hasn't mentioned it," Edward said. "I imagine she's aware of her own island's struggles."

Silas chewed his lip; Frostwake's borders burned in his vision. Volcara and the Sable Isles failed to meet the sea god's quota. The Tide took everything—thousands gone in a single night.

It was never a matter of *if* it would happen again, only when.

"It wouldn't take much," Silas said. "A plague. A bad winter. Famine. If they can't stabilize their population, it won't be long before it falls— even if we gave extra souls, we couldn't go on forever." Eventually, there would be nothing left to give.

"This isn't something we need to talk about with Elin right now. She's dealing with enough." Edward said.

Silas knew that. They all knew that. That day on the ice was one he would never forget. "The world will not stop for her to heal."

"I know that," Edward said. "That doesn't mean we have to worry her about something that may or may not happen. Knowing isn't going to save her island. Some things don't make you stronger, Silas. They just break."

Howie began to speak, but Silas cut him off, narrowing his eyes. "Your feelings towards Elin are clouding your judgment."

"That's not it at all. Maybe you just don't understand because you've never had to lose anything."

Heat flared beneath Silas's skin. "How long will you hold Cassidy over me?"

Edward shook his head incredulously. "I'm not."

Silas narrowed his eyes. "How long will I have to repent for saving your life? If the roles were reversed, you would have done the same."

Shaking his head, Edward looked up from the map. "No, Silas. If it had been Sereia in danger...I would have laid down my life to help you."

Silence seeped across the room, weighing heavily upon them. If he hadn't stopped Edward from rescuing Cassidy the day her name had been drawn for the Tide, Edward would be dead. He'd always told himself he could live with Edward's resentment, but he'd never asked himself if Edward wanted to live without Cassidy.

Silas glanced towards the door, jaw tightening.

Edward was getting close to Elin. Silas had seen what love drove him to do—and what it cost when it was taken from him.

Silas thought of Sereia.

He hadn't understood it then.

He did now.

If Edward chose to risk himself for Elin...he wouldn't stop him.

"Well," Howie said. "I think that's enough for the day. I'm going to think on our plan of attack. You boys go do something more productive than wagging your tongues."

"A fight is not won by speed, nor strength, but by the ability to see the moment that matters and seize it. Those who strike from the heart strike wide. Those who strike from the mind strike true."

— Journal of Silas Blackwater, Second in Line to the Silvamare Crown

Chapter Sixteen

The clang of steel sounded across the deck, sharp as the crying gulls along the coastlines of the Aquerios. Elin shifted her footing, bracing against the roll of the ship. She'd demanded to learn, to be given the opportunity to practice, and despite her aching muscles, she reveled in the chance to spar with the Silvamari crew.

It pushed her beyond what she'd learned from Edward and Silas—and gave the sailors a chance to test themselves against a selkie's strength. They didn't know how many of Hatra's crew carried stolen pelts. The *Lady* had captured the *Leviathan*, the sister ship to the *Maren*. To underestimate Hatra and her crew would be a deadly mistake. Every match was meant to harden them all for the battle waiting ahead.

She sidestepped a strike, her blade singing as it parried Milo's. The crew had taken turns against her all morning, but Milo fought with a dogged intensity that made her teeth clench. He circled her like a shark, sword steady, sweat curling through the hair plastered to his brow.

"You've got fight in you, northern girl," Milo said between breaths, driving her back with a heavy blow. Boots pounded the planks while the crew cheered them on. "But that doesn't mean you belong here."

Elin gritted her teeth; she wasn't looking for belonging, nor did she care what Milo thought of her.

"Your captain invited me aboard. We share a common enemy."

"You're a liability," he swung his blade low; she caught it just in time. The blade's vibration ran up her arm. "You couldn't protect your brother from Ivan; how can we trust you to have our backs?"

The words lanced through her, like salt ground into an open wound. The world fractured. Images came creeping in like a swell—her brother and the cutlass glinting in the fading sun, the blood pooling onto the ice as he fell.

Her vision smeared as emptiness gave way to white-hot rage.

She swung out, grip faltering as Milo twisted. The blade ripped out of her hand. Then she was flat on the deck with his boot against her chest.

The crew's shouts blurred as pressure built in her ears.

Noise warped—stretching thin and watery, as if carried through the ocean depths. A heaviness settled low in her ribs; it was not entirely her own.

Milo's expression softened as he pulled back, offering his hand. "Don't take it personally. I was ordered to get under your skin," he whispered. "Truth is, I respect you as much as anyone else here."

Ignoring him, she rose without help. Anger sent her muscles trembling. "Who told you to do that?"

Milo hesitated, lips thinning. "Can't say."

Her gaze flicked to Edward at the far side of the deck, steel rasping as he sharpened his blade. She stalked towards him, but another voice halted her advance.

"It wasn't him."

Silas stood at the edge of the sparring circle, his calm, grey eyes locked onto hers.

"Why?" Her voice was hollow to her own ears.

"You needed to learn." He closed the distance between them. "When the blades come out, you are not Elin; you are not a sister or a daughter or even a friend. You are an instrument of battle. If you let your heart steer you, you'll falter. The cost of faltering in an actual fight isn't a bruise on these planks. It's death."

Her throat ached. "You think I should just carve my heart out and leave it behind?"

"I think you need to learn when to sheathe it," Silas said, lowering his voice. He rested a steadying hand on her shoulder. "So you can protect the ones who are fighting beside you. And so you can live after you get what you came for."

The tears in her eyes only fed her anger; embarrassment welled up in her. Silas's regret hung heavy in the air.

She shoved it away.

He was telling her to stop using the one thing that had kept her from answering the sea's call, the one thing that fueled her fight. What would she become if she sheathed her heart? She'd be empty.

Was that such a bad thing? An empty creature can't feel pain, can't suffer loss. Empty creatures can't drown themselves in sorrow.

The sea was screaming, shouting her name—though she was the only one who could hear it. It had quieted the day she lost her pelt. Now it was a force.

Elin.

Elin.

She was a nail and the sea a hammer.

Elin.

Each cry of her name drove her deeper. When she thought the deck's boards might give out from under her, the growing pressure lifted like a dispersed cloud.

Heat rolled in its place. She hadn't noticed Edward's approach, nor the beginnings of his argument with Silas. The anger in his voice pulled her out of her trance.

"She wasn't ready for that," Edward said. "You should have consulted me and Howie before planning something so dangerous."

"What's dangerous is having an unstable partner in battle. Have you forgotten that I am the Crown at Sea? I have more authority than you or the Captain," Silas countered.

She turned to Edward, "I don't need you to come to my defense."

He didn't seem to hear her. His eyes were narrowed on Silas, and a pang of guilt ran through her for causing their discord.

"Believe me, Your Highness, I haven't forgotten. Nor have I forgotten that you, too, have been an unstable partner in battle. Or have you forgotten that until recently you were struggling with your own contr—"

"That's enough!" Howie commanded, striding across the deck. "Look around you." He gestured to the crew on the ship, watching their leadership fight amongst themselves.

A shrinking feeling came from both men—shame.

It did not remain contained between them. It spread, slow and suffocating, until even the sailors at the rail and in the rigging shifted, casting nervous glances towards the dark water.

"Sparring is over. Return to your duties," Howie ordered. They quickly broke apart, following the command.

"Edward, I should have told you of my plan," Silas said. "Elin, I am sorry for the pain it caused you, but it's also imperative that you aren't so easily driven by your emotions. People like Hatra and Ivan will use them against you. Don't let them."

"I understand," she said, though the words felt thin. "And you—" she turned to Edward, lowering her voice. "—need to stop stepping in like that."

His brow creased. "Like what?"

"Like I need protecting."

"You were—"

"I was handling it."

He held her gaze. "You weren't."

Closing her eyes, she inhaled deeply. Pine and whiskey warmed her senses.

"Then let me fail," she said. "Stop making my problems your own; they're mine to carry."

His brown eyes softened, but she felt his frustration growing beneath the surface. "You don't have to carry them alone."

She didn't want this—didn't want him looking at her like that. For years, she carried the fear that she'd abandon someone to the sea's call. She'd done it anyway, hadn't she? Even though her father resented her and her mother's absence was frequent, she'd still left them without a word.

A skinless selkie could not find safety in the sea, no matter what it promised. If it was calling to her once more, she didn't want the burden of leaving anyone else who might care behind.

"Edward—I can't. I can't give you what you want."

His jaw tightened. "You haven't even asked what I want."

Edward opened his mouth to say something more, then stopped, his attention gripped by the sudden silence of the ocean.

Elin followed it, eyes widening. The sea was preternaturally still, as if something was pressing upon it, flattening out its crested peaks.

"What is—"

Water shot upward in a towering dark veil, swallowing the sunlight.

An explosion of sorrow tore through the ship—sharp as a scream inside her skull.

The world went black.

"The Sluagh, a sorrow-born entity of unknown origin, is shaped not from souls, but from the remnants of emotion left behind after great loss—fear, longing, despair made manifest. Its rise is traced to the earliest Tides, when grief first mingled with saltwater and the sea learned to carry what the living could not.

Though often described as a single creature, scholars argue the Sluagh is more a resonance than a being: a wandering echo that feeds upon the fractures of the mind. It slips into the thoughts of sailors and shore-dwellers alike, growing heavy on their pain, drawing them towards the deep before drifting on in search of its next unwitting host.

Accounts agree on only one certainty: escape comes not through force, but through the acceptance of one's own sorrow. Yet even this offers no mercy to the Sluagh itself. No ritual has succeeded in easing the entity's torment or ending its quiet plague upon the seas."

—Excerpt from *A Compendium of Oceanic Dangers*, housed in the Old Kingdom Library of Sidon

Chapter Seventeen

Not all monsters wait for the cover of darkness. While it is true that many take shelter in the shadows, some of the most fearsome hide in plain sight. They strike when you least expect it, when you're least guarded.

Elin knew that temptation came at any time of day, that it would be easy to slip from herself, to become a vessel for something else. So when the sea pulled, she pushed.

Somewhere on the ship, screams and weeping filled the air, but she could not see it—she was trapped in her own mind. She tried to follow the sounds back to the deck, to where reality waited.

Cold sea spray struck the back of her neck as something splashed into the water.

It would not claim her.

She would not—she would—she—

A great blackness consumed her as sorrow swelled in her chest. It clouded her sight, stuffed her nose, and filled her lungs.

She was nothing more than fear and pain, suffocating in it. If she could wash it away, scrub enough of herself raw, she might get clean. It might all end.

"Elin, my little seal," a voice sang in the darkness. "Elin, where have you gone?"

"Mother?" It was like talking underwater.

"Why did you leave? Why did you leave us?" Her mother was crying. Elin could feel the chill of sorrow webbing like morning frost across her skin.

Elin searched the dark. "I—I didn't—"

"You did," her mother cried. "You couldn't face what you'd done, so you ran."

"No, you don't understand."

"If you'd just listened, Elin!" Her voice had become shrill. "If you hadn't fought the sea—if you had obeyed—Anik would still be here."

"Please," Elin choked on her silent tears. "Please, it wasn't my fault."

Rivers of salt fell from her cheeks, turning into a puddle of ice at her feet.

It spread before her like a shelf.

She knew what awaited her. It didn't stop her from lifting her gaze. Anik lay sprawled, bleeding out on the ice.

"You did this!" their mother bellowed.

"Mama," Elin's voice was little more than a whisper.

"Ivan would never have bothered Anik if you hadn't been there. Your brother would be alive. He didn't need you, Elin. No one needed you to stay; no one cared! You should have come with me." Her mother's words cut like ice on raw skin.

Any fight that remained in her dissipated. She'd run dry.

"Little Elin lost her way,"

Shivers racked her delicate frame. She took a step back, then another, shaking her head as if she could rattle the voice out of her mind, but it only grew louder.

"Come, take a dive in my deep waves,
And home is what you'll find."

Crouching to the ground, she covered her ears with her hands. Rocking on her heels, she hummed to herself, trying to drown it out.

It was going to take her. She didn't have her pelt, and the sea was coming for her.

"Sink or swim,
Either way,

I'll drown you in my love."

Another cry escaped her lips. "No—no, please. Please," she pleaded.

"There is no escape from the call below,

I'll pull you from up above."

She didn't know when she'd done it. Only when salt filled her nose, and the sharp sting of water hit her back, did she realize she'd risen from the deck and fallen into the ocean below.

Edward had grown accustomed to accepting what was out of his hands, or so he liked to tell himself.

The muggy, stifling air flattened the ocean's surface.

The deck dissolved as a phantom hand wedged itself between his ribs.

He was in the courtyard.

Cassidy's name rang in his ears as the priest read it from a slip of parchment.

"No," he heard himself say, before tearing through the crowd.

He had no plan. Only the certainty that his friend, the woman he loved, had been condemned. Two guards flanked his sides, closing in before he could reach her.

He swung out, landing a blow. The second never did; something cracked against the back of his skull, and he lost consciousness.

The courtyard dissolved.

He was kneeling in Silas's chambers, palms braced against cool stone.

"I beg you," he heard himself say again.

Silas refused.

Edward rose anyway; if he could not have Silas's support, he'd break in. He would reach Cassidy, or die trying.

Silas returned with a glass.

"If you are going to attempt to save her, will you have one last drink with me, then?" Silas asked.

He took the glass.

The liquid burned on its way down.

The room blurred, and the sounds of the outside world faded into a dull roar.

Silas's betrayal hurt more than the sedation.

Again, darkness fell over him.

The Sluagh did not linger long in the distant past.

It pressed harder, finding fresher memories.

Blood on the ice.

Elin screaming.

He'd reached her too late; he was always too late.

The Sluagh moved on from memory, preying on futures yet to pass.

Elin lost to the sea, slipping beneath the black water.

Her eyes distant and unseeing.

With each iteration of these losses, he was hollowed out further.

Do something.

Move.

Fight.

He tried. The images did not shatter. They increased, separating and connecting, splintering into a rapid succession of scenes that seared themselves into his consciousness.

This isn't real. I am not here.

He clung to the refrain as the Sluagh forced him to accept each loss, each failure as it came to pass, lest he become consumed by them.

The courtyard returned. Cassidy's name. The blow to his skull. The drink. The fall.

This isn't real.

He failed to save Cassidy and Anik. He cannot save Elin.

The Sluagh pressed harder, waiting for him to resist—to deny it, to unravel.

He let the truth stand.

Cassidy was gone.

Anik was dead.

Elin's fate was not his to command.

He could not change what had been, nor could he control what would come. He could only choose what he did next, and that would have to be enough.

With that, the hazy black that once consumed his senses fell away. Sunlight warmed his skin, and the ship came back into view.

Sailors were scattered across the deck, some lost in a daze, while another scratched at his face, desperate to snap out of it.

He scanned the deck for Elin.

A flash of silver caught his eye. Elin was backing up towards the ship's rail.

She was crying.

If she fell over, he'd lose her, either to the sea or to the Sluagh. Even if Elin had to save herself, she didn't have to be alone.

"Elin!" he shouted across the deck, but she could not hear him.

The salty breeze swirled through Silas's hair as he tilted his head back, feeling the sun's warmth kiss his skin. He felt the soft, fine sand beneath his palms, so different from the rocky shores of his home.

He'd made it to Drakcultus on time for the spring convergence.

With a furtive look from under his lowered lids, he observed the figure beside him. Her fair skin shimmered as she basked in the warm sunlight.

His heart skipped; this was it.

In anticipation of his departure from Frostwake, he had vowed to himself that this would be the moment he'd finally lay bare his feelings. But the words died on his lips as a small frown creased Sereia's mouth. Her eyes fluttered open, immediately finding his.

A raw, accusatory pain filled her gaze. "Why don't you love me, Silas?"

She leaned closer; a curtain of black hair fell over her shoulders. He opened his mouth to confess, but the truth remained locked within, unspoken.

His voice was silenced by something unseen, and the lengthening quiet intensified Sereia's suffering.

"Is it because of the prophecy?" she whispered. "Because you fear what I'll become?"

The salty kiss of the sea vanished, giving way to the stagnant air of a room sealed for ages. As heat flared under Silas's skin, terror surged through him as he remained speechless.

A sad smile touched Sereia's lips, but it soon shifted into an agonized grimace.

"You have no interest in me." Her laugh was brittle. "You're as afraid of me as the others."

Leaning closer, she rested her chin on his shoulder. "It's okay."

"*No, it's not,*" he wanted to say.

Flames surged from his arms and spread, engulfing the island. But it wasn't Drakcultus that was on fire.

Silvamare went up in flames, and he watched it all from a distance, like a bird of prey.

Hungry flames laid waste to the mountain forests.

His family's screams echoed within the stone palace walls as they were cooked alive.

The slow gong of the island's bell towers rang in his ears. He spun around, his gaze wide with alarm. Sereia stood several paces away, her face a mask of silent agony as her skin blistered and peeled, the acrid smell of burning flesh filling the air.

Amidst the chaos, one thought refused to be real.

He could never hurt Sereia like that.

Even if he lost hold of his flame, she would be untouched.

Despite not having the power of fire, Sereia was incapable of being harmed by it. This was a dream. A trap.

Where had he been before this?

The memory eluded his grasp, slipping away like water. A voice, as familiar as his own, broke through the mist.

Edward.

They were on the ship, and they had been arguing. The sea had quieted, exploding into the sky.

At that moment, he understood they had sailed into the Sluagh.

The world returned in a flash of light. The dizzying shift left him disoriented as he struggled to regain his composure.

There was shouting. Sailors who had freed themselves were attempting to rouse others; while some were slumped over the railings trapped in their own minds, battling the Sluagh's influence.

Edward was sprinting towards the ship's railing.

"Edward!" Silas yelled.

His head snapped in his direction.

"Elin went over!" It was his only explanation before he threw himself over the side of the ship.

Silas swayed across the deck, passing sailors in various states of repose, some on their knees and others sprawled out.

Perry stood amongst them, frozen in a rigid trance, his eyes vacant and his chest rising and falling with rapid breaths. He knew they couldn't afford to lose their master of the winds.

"Perry," Silas said, his voice rough as he gripped his shoulders and shook him. "Perry, look at me."

He stood frozen, his eyes as vacant and unseeing as polished stones.

Silas's stomach lurched. With a more vigorous shake, he tried again, but it was futile.

"Damn it," he muttered.

Jaw clenched, a silent prayer escaped him, a plea that his next attempt would be successful.

He placed his hands on Perry's arms.

"Forgive me," he whispered.

The conjured flame singed his skin.

Perry let out a gasp and stumbled backward, choking out a cry.

Silas steadied him.

"Your Highness—what? What is happening?"

"A Sluagh," he said. "I need your help to wake the others."

Perry's gaze became sharp. His teeth chattered as he asked, "What do I do?"

"Try to wake as many as you can. Try without magic first," Silas said. "If that doesn't work, try shock. Cut their air, slice their skin, anything to jar them out of it."

Perry swallowed hard, then nodded.

They split without another word. Perry dropped to his knees beside Milo and slapped his cheek, then again with more force.

Silas didn't linger to watch. He moved past the two sailors who were curled up on the planks, attempting to wake them as gently as possible. He continued his search across the deck, his eyes scanning for his captain.

Howie knelt, as if preparing to withstand an invisible tempest. His jaw was clenched tight, his hands trembling, every muscle taut with visible resistance.

"Howie," Silas breathed, dropping beside him. "Come back. None of it's real."

Howie couldn't hear him; his mind was somewhere else entirely. The distant look in his captain's eyes as he pushed himself upright was a clear sign he was fighting a losing battle. Silas tried to restrain him, but despite Howie's age, he was strong.

Silas burned him, just as he had done to Perry, but he remained undisturbed in his trance. The Sluagh dragged Howie into the abyss of his deepest wound, threatening to engulf him.

Silas called out to the men as the captain moved closer to the edge of the ship. "He's going to jump!"

More crew members came to lend a hand. Howie fiercely resisted; his powerful blows sent some of them over the railing and into the dark water.

Howie leaned over the wooden rails, his voice hoarse from shouting for his lost daughter.

"I'm coming," he said, right before he climbed over.

Silas scrambled, catching him by the leg. The force almost sent him toppling overboard, but then sturdy arms encircled him as the crew hurried to haul their captain back to safety.

Frigid water swallowed her whole.

For a moment, she could not work out which way was up and which was down. The world turned weightless and crushing all at once.

A presence—vast and endless—gnawed at the edges of her fractured soul. It fed without teeth, without hunger as she knew it. It absorbed her fear, her anguish. Her guilt.

Loneliness rang in her ears like a scream.

The boundaries of her body dissolved until she did not know her hands from the sea, her heart from the surrounding dark. Her name fell out of reach. The world was a colorless void, a wide expanse of nothing at all.

And within that nothing, she felt it more clearly.

It was hollow. The water spirit did not consume because it relished suffering.

Never having known the sensation of warmth, it was consumed by an endless numbing—it was grief with nowhere to rest.

For one terrible moment, she understood how easy it would be to loosen what little held her together. To stop resisting and become as shapeless as the sorrow pressing against her.

No more sharp edges or guilt. No more love.

No more love.

That was the difference.

Even now, in the dark, there were tethers connecting her to others. They stitched her together, anchoring her to something beyond the void.

Each silver-spun thread that formed these tethers was memories and emotions, desperate and solemn, that had come from someone before. They did not belong to her, nor to it.

Memories came trickling in one after another.

Anik's laughter echoed, a sound of pure delight, as his head tilted back and a spark of mischief danced in his eyes.

The memory did not bring her peace.

It hurt.

Loving him hurt more than watching him die. His living brilliance was so overwhelming that it cleaved her soul apart, a wound deeper than any blade could inflict.

The darkness pressed in, eager to dull it. She could let it go; it would be easier, but the threads did not dim; they glowed brighter.

Kova's stubborn loyalty.

Her mother's hand, warm and familiar, resting in hers.

Arnaq and Ila's antics.

Edward's steady presence at her side.

Love was not always soft. It burned, carving space inside her wide enough to hold the grief without hollowing her out.

The surrounding sorrow trembled. It did not know how to exist where warmth endured.

Elin understood then.

The water spirit was not wicked. It was untethered.

She was not.

Her grief was hers—sharp and arduous, the cost of love.

The water spirit could not have her pain, because it was hers to bear.

The threads brightened, radiating a steady heat. Its vast darkness recoiled, withdrawing like a tide pulling away from the shore.

But as it retreated, something brushed the silver threads anchoring her, a cold, ancient filament intertwining with hers.

It clung to her in recognition of what she offered—warmth in the cold.

The world around her heated and flared; light burned her eyes like the sun reflecting off a sheet of ice. She shut them against it.

They were still closed when something grabbed hold of her.

Heart thrashing, limbs scratching wildly, Elin opened her eyes as she fought off her attacker. Then stopped.

Before her, Edward was suspended in the water, his legs working to keep him afloat. He'd come for her.

He must have witnessed her fall into the water. She had tried to keep her heart guarded against him. But how was she meant to do that when he dove into dark waters for her?

When he looked at her as if he couldn't live without her?

It was a dangerous thing—to matter that much to someone.

He motioned, checking if he could take her hand again.

She nodded.

Hands clasped, they pulled each other upwards. They broke the water's surface, gasping in the fresh air. Daylight shone once more, sparkling along the ocean's crested peaks.

"Why did you do that?" she scolded. "You could have been hurt."

Edward wiped water from his eyes. "Would I really just surrender you to the Sluagh?"

"You have people who care about you—a family. Promise me you won't take such a reckless risk for me ever again."

She would not be the reason Edward Graves left this world. She would not be his ruin.

"I can't promise that."

Elin started to protest, but Perry called down from the ship.

"Are you two alright?"

"Yes," Edward said without looking at the Drakcultian.

Their faces were only inches apart, his grip still tight on her. His eyes darted over her, searching for any sign that she'd been harmed.

She hadn't, but he had. Her nails left marks on him from their struggle.

His right cheek bled from a shallow cut. Without a thought, she reached out, wiping away the blood.

Realizing her mistake, she met his steady gaze. His eyes closed and the rhythm of his breathing stilled.

She pulled back, and he released her.

With a creak of rope, Perry let the rowboat down from the ship, and Elin, Edward, and a handful of stragglers climbed aboard.

As another rowboat splashed into the water, more sailors searched the surrounding sea for their lost shipmates.

With the help of ropes and pulleys, her boat was lifted and drawn towards the deck. Edward deboarded, then reached down to help her out. Her limbs were leaden, making resistance difficult, yet a part of her welcomed the excuse to feel his skin against hers.

On the deck, the sailors' faces were expressionless, their eyes distant. Some worked without thinking, their minds still reeling from the mental and spiritual battle they had just endured, while others gazed up at the sky or absently towards the sea.

Elin was uncertain when the shift had come—only that the sea no longer pressed inward with the same crushing weight.

The darkness had fractured, unsettled, and withdrawn into deeper waters. Something of it lingered—a faint chill beneath her skin, a widened space within her chest where grief rested heavier than before.

She had not destroyed the Sluagh, but endured it.

She had met its cold with warmth—and chose to carry her grief rather than surrender.

It had loosened its hold.

For now.

Chapter Eighteen

Howie's cabin was warm with lamplight, and beneath the gentle haze of cigar smoke, it still smelt of varnished wood. Charts sat stacked on his desk, their edges curled with use.

Howie sat at the small table near the window, shoulders slumped, his hands wrapped around a mug he hadn't touched.

Elin stood near the door with Edward at her side. Lingering by the hearth, Silas crossed his arms over his chest, the firelight reflected in his eyes.

"The Sluagh feeds on grief," he said. "It drags what we bury to the surface and forces us to look at it."

Elin nodded. Her hands trembled, though she hadn't noticed until Edward's fingers brushed against hers, warming her chilled skin.

"I almost lost myself," she said, crossing to the chair near the hearth and lowering herself into it; a damp chill lingered on her skin despite the fire. "It kept pressing at my pain until it felt easier to become nothing than to keep carrying it."

Howie's brow furrowed. "Then how did you escape it?"

She stared into the flames. "I stopped fighting the truth. My life will never be what it was. Anik is gone, but not my capacity for love." She pressed her lips together. "That grief is mine. It belongs to love, and I would rather carry it than let something else hollow me out."

She leaned her head against the back of the chair, looking at the slatted ceiling. "It was only when I understood that, that I could feel it," she said quietly. "Not just my sorrow, but everyone's." Twisting the braided hair around her wrist, she added, "It was empty. Untethered."

"How did that free you?" Howie asked.

"I gave it something to hold on to," she said. "I gave it the feeling of love."

Edward's voice was low when he spoke. "That is why it left?"

"Yes," she nodded. "I don't think it knew what to do with it, and I scared it away."

"Then it can be defeated," Howie said.

"No," Elin said. "I think it's only something we can endure."

Silas drummed his fingers on the hearth, still staring into the flames. "I lost control," he said. "In my vision, I lost control of myself and burned Silvamare until it was nothing more than ash. And Sereia—Sereia was there and I—"

Fear and pain pricked at her like urchin spines. She breathed through it, pulling her own emotions out and around her, dulling the ache.

"I hurt her," Silas finished. "Which is how I knew it wasn't real. She can't burn." He looked down at his hands. "But the fear was very real," Silas said. "The grief, too."

"And you?" Howie asked Edward.

Edward's gaze flicked to Elin, then back to Howie. "It forced me to acknowledge that some things are out of my control."

He didn't elaborate further. He didn't need to. Whatever the Sluagh had dragged from him, he'd tucked those emotions back in with practiced ease.

Howie's released breath sounded like a crack. "Do you know why this ship is called the *Maren*?" he asked her.

"I do not."

"My daughter's name was Maren."

Edward moved to sit in the other chair before the fire.

"I met her mother in Sidon," Howie continued. "I was young and on a diplomatic posting." His mouth curved into a sad half-smile, as he nodded at Elin. "She was a selkie. We both knew what it was—temporary. I returned home. She carried on with her herd."

Elin's chest tightened, familiar with the story. They were always with different people, but they all shared the same ending.

"A few years later," Howie said, "a little girl knocked on my door. She had my eyes. Her mother's silver hair." His voice wavered. "Her mother sent her to me because she was mine."

Elin rose, moving to sit in the chair beside Howie. She took his hand in hers.

"She was born without a pelt," he continued. "Her mother couldn't take her on the migrations. She tried to stay on land, tried to fight the call." He shook his head. "She did so for five years, but I guess it became too difficult."

Elin nodded. "So she sent Maren to you."

"I thought I could protect her. Thought—hoped—that I could be enough for her."

"What happened?" she asked, her voice barely above a whisper.

"She missed her mother," Howie said. "Every day she talked about finding her—about the sea and how she could hear it calling to her." He looked up at Elin, pale blue eyes sharp with understanding.

"Why didn't her mother return to Silvamare?" Elin asked. "It's part of the migration route."

Howie's brow furrowed. "I don't know. Something must have happened."

Or someone, Elin thought gravely.

"Maren was eight," he said. "One night, after the Tide, she didn't come down for breakfast. Her door was open, her bed empty." His voice dropped. "She must've pretended to take her draft. I never heard her leave."

Elin closed her eyes, fighting the tears.

"I carry them both," Howie said. "Every day, I wonder what I could have done differently."

Fire crackled in the hearth, and Howie took a long sip from his mug. It smelt of whiskey.

She didn't know how to ease Howie's pain. She had no comforts, only truths.

"Even skinless selkies hear the sea," she said. "It's softer, fainter—but it's there." She met Howie's gaze. "And for children, especially without their mothers...it's hard to ignore."

She remembered the many late nights when she chose to remain in Frostwake, and how Anik would often sleep curled up next to her in their yaranga. Sometimes they would hold each other, anchoring one another to the land.

"I'm sorry," she said.

Edward hadn't taken his eyes off her the entire time she spoke. The heat of his gaze was almost impossible to ignore.

Howie squeezed her hand; his own eyes shone bright with unshed tears.

"Thank you," he said, "for reminding me that grief carried is not grief that wins."

She offered him a watery smile.

"You should all get some rest," he said.

Silas inclined his head. "I'll check on the watch."

He didn't wait for a reply. Firelight followed him as he crossed the room and slipped out, the door latching behind him.

Edward rose next, lingering a moment, eyes flicking between Howie and Elin.

"Make sure you rest too, old man," he said.

Howie nodded, scoffing under his breath. Though Elin didn't miss the smile pulling at his lips.

Edward stood at the threshold, a moment of uncertainty clouding his features. Before she even saw it, Elin felt the shift, the unspoken question he was asking. When she stood, her legs felt heavy, as if the sea still weighed her down.

"I'll walk with you," she said.

Relief eased across Edward's features.

The corridor beyond Howie's cabin was cast in soft light by lanterns swaying with the ship's motion. Their footsteps echoed against the planks; the sounds of the ship settled around them—the creaking of timbers, murmured voices, the distant slap of waves against the hull.

Elin drew her arms around herself, a chill crawling beneath her skin now that the fire's warmth was gone. Edward shrugged off his coat, draping it over her shoulders.

"Thank you," she said.

"Anytime."

They walked on, past the crew's quarters. Past the ladder leading down to the lower decks.

Elin wasn't sure where Edward was leading her until they stopped outside another, smaller cabin. It was Edward's quarters.

He opened it, offering her room to step inside. She did.

She hadn't a moment to take in the room before Edward began to speak.

"I wanted to apologize for earlier. I know you don't need me to come to your defense. You don't need me to rescue you. But Elin, you don't have to cope alone."

This afternoon was a distant memory.

"Why, Edward? Why do you care so much?"

"Honestly?"

"Yes—always."

He looked away, dragging a hand through his hair before crossing the room and sitting on the edge of the bed.

"The day I saw you and your brother on the ice, surrounded by Hatra's men—" he shook his head. "I knew it was going to be bad. I knew you were both going to die."

"You tried to stop it."

"I did, but I knew—or thought I knew—that I couldn't save you, either of you. And when they killed him—" He looked away from her. "But you survived."

"Edward—" Elin said, taking a step closer.

He looked back at her. "When you looked at me, your eyes were empty. All I could think was that this couldn't be for nothing. That I would take Hatra down myself."

"You surprised me when you came to the ship looking for me. I saw revenge had lit a fire in you. I realized the revenge I was seeking wasn't mine to take; it was yours. So I made a new promise to help you."

Elin's brow furrowed. "So, you care because you want to see me get revenge?"

"No, Elin. No." Edward rose from the bed.

Her heart leapt at his approach. She tried to ignore the instinct to close the distance between them—but when her mind told her to step back, she didn't.

The feeling lingered between them, begging to be acknowledged.

"Elin..." Edward said, lowering his gaze to hers. "When I look at you, I see someone who keeps fighting when anyone else would have stayed down. I come to your defense because I—"

He hesitated, then cupped her face with his hands, eyes pleading with hers. "I care about you."

She had known.

That was the thing he couldn't fully understand—that she had known. And it was not something she could unfeel, or unknow, or pretend away. His care had been constant for months, and she'd felt his growing affection just as she'd felt her own. But knowing the truth through her gift and hearing him choose to say it were not the same thing.

He could have kept it contained. He had kept it contained for weeks, with a discipline she felt the edges of each time he stepped back when she needed space, each time he swallowed what she sensed building in him. He could have gone on, keeping it to himself, and she could have gone on pretending she didn't feel it, and they both would have been spared this.

Her body trembled. This man had come into her life at her worst moment, and he had not shied away from the ugliness of her pain or her grief. What he offered was honest, and it was breaking her in ways she had not known she could be broken.

She thought, without meaning to, of her father.

He loved her mother to his undoing. In her absence, he stopped living. Elin could not make him happy by staying. And then she left. Scared that her presence would only be a greater burden—a threat of instability after losing Anik. How could she give herself to Edward, knowing she might not be able to stay? He'd already lost Cassidy. What would her absence do to him?

Still, he knew this about her. He knew her nature, and he wasn't afraid.

"Edward, I—"

"You don't need to say anything. I already know that you know how I feel, remember?" He smiled at her. "That's not why I'm sharing this with you. I am telling you this so that you understand. You're not alone. Not unless you want to be."

Hot tears ran down Elin's cheeks. "I don't."

Edward pulled her into a hug, and she let him hold her.

That was a mistake. Months of feeling arrived in a single breath, his and hers indistinguishable for a moment. She pressed her ear to his chest, listening to his racing heart. Edward always knew what to say—what to do.

The last person who loved her deeply, who knew her better than she knew herself, was dead. Anik's death nearly killed her too. She did not know how to give herself to Edward, not fully. Not in the way he deserved. If she let Edward become an integral part of herself and she lost him, she feared it would destroy what remained of her.

Burying her nose in his chest, she breathed him in and then pulled away.

He released her without hesitation, and that act alone made it even harder to step away. "Are you okay?" he asked.

No—she nodded anyway. It was easier than telling him the truth, and she was not sure she could have found the words for it. The kindness of it—of him handing her his heart without asking for hers in return—was unbearable.

"Goodnight, Elin."

"Goodnight," she whispered.

He turned, opening the door for her.

She stepped past him into the corridor; the door closed softly behind her.

It was not the sea roaring in her ears as she forced herself to keep walking. She could not turn around; she would not look back.

Silas was right. She had to keep her heart tucked away, even if it broke her to do it. If she didn't, Edward would be the one to pay for it.

"The Black Reef—a jagged crown of basalt and tuff rising from the Wavecrest between Silvamare and Drakcultus, born of an ancient volcanic ridge and still breathing sulfurous steam. The surrounding waters are treacherous, riddled with hidden ridges and shrouded in mist from vents far below. Though claimed by both kingdoms, its uninhabitable nature has left it effectively lawless, a perfect refuge for pirate crews who vanish into its labyrinth of stone before any navy can give chase."

— *Geological Features of Aquerios*, a common text

Chapter Nineteen

Elin stood at the bow, her shoulder-length hair whipping in the morning wind, her senses buzzing with unease.

Soon they would reach the Black Reef and—if the gods were on her side—she'd come face to face with Ivan. She might get her pelt back, and the sea would once more sing to her. How would it feel to once again carry the weight of it on her shoulders, to slip into its silken skin and shift around the water's embrace?

Her stomach turned at the thought. She rested her forehead on the ship's rail, taking slow breaths.

The Wavecrest appeared calm, but beneath the surface, something was stirring. Her bones throbbed under a growing pressure. The markings at her temples tingled as she lifted her head, scanning the horizon. From the south, an unseen tempest was awakening.

It wasn't surprising. While it was still early in the storm season, the Wavecrest had always been a volatile thing.

Turning on her heel, she descended the stairs in search of Howie.

He stood near the helm on the quarterdeck, deep in conversation with the ship's surgeon. Samson, she believed, was his name. When they noticed her approach, he gave a slight nod.

"There's a storm coming," she said, skipping pleasantries.

Howie gave her his full attention. "How bad?"

"It's not terrible, but bad enough to warrant a detour. It'll hit by evening and pass before dawn."

He narrowed his eyes at the horizon, as if trying to see what she sensed. "We're not far from the Black Reef."

A knot of anxiety tightened in her stomach. "How long?"

"With the detour," his head swayed in contemplation, "a day and a half, give or take."

Her fingers tried to curl around a hem that wasn't there.

This was why she joined the Silvamari—to find Ivan. Would the *Leviathan* be there as they suspected?

Her thoughts spun with too many maybes and too little certainty. With or without her, this was the navy's mission: to capture the pirates on the open seas; it wasn't as if her motives for revenge put these people on a path to danger they hadn't already volunteered for.

So why did she feel as if she'd committed an unforgivable crime? What was this wariness nipping at her?

The wind carried a dampness to it, hinting at the coming rain. She twisted the band on her wrist.

Howie studied her, perhaps sensing the shift in her mood. "You feeling ready?"

"As ready as I can be," she said.

Howie's gaze drifted from her to the crew, settling on each individual. A skittering sensation ran down her spine.

"You're nervous," she said.

He looked sideways at her. "That easy to read, am I?"

"No," she tilted her head. "I can sense those kinds of things."

Howie sighed, scratching his beard. "I'm always antsy before a confrontation. It doesn't matter how many times I've done it. My gut twists and my palms itch." He rubbed his palm against his elbow. "It's not fear for myself, but for them. This crew, they're the only family I have."

Elin's throat tightened. "You're an excellent captain, Howie. They know you'd never steer them into something blindly. They love you as much as you love them."

His mouth twitched into a smile. "Well, now you're just butterin' me up."

"I mean it," she said, resting a hand on his arm. "Thank you for letting me join you. For the opportunity to seek justice for my brother and for myself."

He huffed low and reached out, tousling her hair with a rough hand, as if she were a child. "You're a part of this crew now. Which means you're my family too."

Her heart squeezed. The word family hit a bruise, but it warmed her too, like sunlight on cold skin.

"Don't get yourself killed over revenge, Elin," he added with grave seriousness. "Your brother...he'd want you to live."

She squinted at the horizon, watching the distant clouds grow darker, as if Cosmir was painting the sky with a brush. Something clicked into place. Resolve. Not just to fight, but to live.

"I'll try my best, Howie," she said, lifting her chin. "But I will do this for my brother. He'd do it for me."

Howie's expression softened. "I've got faith in you, kid." He gave her shoulder one last firm squeeze before straightening with a groan. "Now, let's get this ship storm-ready."

The next few hours passed in a flurry. Sail lines were secured, gear stowed, and barrels and crates tied down. Howie barked orders with calm urgency, and the crew moved with efficiency. Elin worked alongside them, the tension of the coming storm a steady thrum beneath her skin.

When the wind began to howl, and the first fat drops of rain pelted the deck, she retreated below, shaking water from her hair as she climbed into her hammock. The ship rocked gently, and her fingers curled around the canvas edges as it swayed.

She allowed her mind to drift away from thoughts of revenge and survival.

The near future unveiled itself with vivid clarity. She'd kill Ivan, get her pelt back, and the Silvamari would capture Hatra. These weren't hopes and dreams to her—they'd become inevitabilities she clung to, like a life raft in a storm.

Beyond that was like looking through foggy glass.

Would she return home? Would her parents forgive her, knowing she'd avenged her brother? Could she stay in Frostwake, fighting the sea's pull each spring while the others left—she didn't have to fight the call any longer. Her father preferred that she leave. Without Anik, why wouldn't she go with the others?

Her thoughts drifted, unbidden, to Edward. She pushed the thoughts away—but they came back anyway.

Things between them had shifted. When he wasn't physically near her, he still found his way into her thoughts.

Her mind was a battlefield, torn between what she craved and what terrified her.

If she chose not to return home, she could travel. She'd keep her promise to Anik—the one they'd made when they were still children—to see the world. To chase stars and coastlines, and stories. The idea flickered brighter than the others, though it still wasn't right.

There was one undeniable consistency inside all the futures she could conjure: Edward. That was the problem—wanting him in a life she couldn't promise to stay in.

"I've always had this coiling of unease before a battle, a serpent of dread settling low in my gut. Ever since my first clash with pirates, it's been there. This time, however, something's changed. This chase has become personal. If I fail to stop Hatra again, I don't know what I'll do. Before I left Frostwake, I'd written a last letter, just in case. I left it for Sereia.

I hope to make it to the spring convergence. Then I'll find the courage to tell her what I feel, as Edward did with Elin—even if she doesn't return it."

—Journal of Prince Silas Blackwater, Second in Line to the Crown of Silvamare

Chapter Twenty

By morning, the storm was gone, as Elin predicted, leaving a clear sky and still seas. Rising out of the ocean, jagged black spires pierced the horizon.

The Black Reef.

As the ship drew closer, the air changed. A sulfuric smell drifted across the water, sharp enough to sting her nose. Wisps of steam curled between the rocks, hissing where unseen vents breathed heat into the cold sea.

The water churned around the spires, currents twisting between narrow passages known to wreck or trap a ship if a captain misjudged his course.

Howie handed her his spyglass. With its cool metal in her hands, she lifted it to her eye. Only a mast rose above the stone. The *Leviathan.*

A sharp thrill coursed through her as her gaze fell upon it.

It seemed a god might be on their side after all.

Howie clapped a hand on her shoulder. "That's why we hold on to our faith, kid," he said with a wink. "Because it always sides with the good."

She didn't know if she believed that; the gods had been quiet for a long time. Whether it was divine will or dumb luck, the *Leviathan* was exactly where they'd expected.

The crew gathered on the deck as Howie studied the reef through his spyglass. Standing amongst them, she shifted her weight from one foot to the other. Milo nudged her with his elbow. "Stop that," he said. "You're making me nervous."

She smiled apologetically before returning her attention to Howie, Silas, and Edward, who stood on the steps of the quarterdeck with the sun at their backs.

Edward stood to Howie's right, his face betraying nothing of what he felt. "Listen up," he called. "We have formed a plan for approaching Hatra."

"There are only two viable entry points inside the Black Reef. We will combine our ships and send the companion vessels through the pass as decoys." He pointed towards the larger eastern channel. "Perry will direct the ships through there. Once they have a direct line of sight on the *Leviathan*, Prince Silas will set off the cannons."

"If the ships are empty, how will the cannons be lit?" Milo asked.

"Before we combine our ships, the cannons'll be prepared. We'll leave a trail of powder along the deck. Silas will ignite the powder from here. The hope," Howie added, "is that Hatra will order return fire using what's left of her reserves before we enter the western passage."

Edward's eyes found hers. "With the vessels blocking the eastern channel, and us in the west, Hatra will be trapped inside the Black Reef."

A murmur of approval swept through the crew.

"Hatra thought she could come after our men, attack our ships, and sail off unscathed. We will not let the insult stand," Silas said. "Do not forget that they are cowards and have no loyalties but to themselves. We fight for our people. For those who cannot protect themselves."

The crew cheered with fists raised.

"Salt in our blood," a cry came from behind her.

"Fire in our hearts!" Silas shouted.

A wave of excitement washed over her, and when the crew's unified shout rose, she added her own voice to the chorus.

"From the sea, we rise!"

One by one, sailors from the other two ships crossed onto the *Maren*. The decks groaned under the added weight.

Perry lifted his hands towards the sky, moving his fingers as if coaxing the air to do his bidding. Snippets of his hopeful prayer reached her through the clamor of the deck, that he would find success in his task and prove himself.

The sails of the other ships snapped full a moment later, the directed gust driving them towards the eastern channel.

The *Maren* buzzed with motion as the crew prepared for battle. She squeezed through the crowded deck in search of Edward.

He found her near the mainmast. Edward said nothing as he took her hand and led her below deck. She followed without question, eyes lingering on the breadth of his shoulders. He reminded her of the towering trees in Terron's Forest—formidable and unshakeable. Though she knew no one was invincible.

The dread of the crew moved through her like the weather. She had been feeling it all morning, humming beneath the regular movement of the ship.

Inside his quarters, Edward rummaged through a trunk and pulled out a folded Silvamari uniform, sage green and threaded with crimson. A breastplate was sewn into the inside of the top.

"You need to be easily identifiable," he said, handing it to her.

She pointed to her head. "Does the hair not already give me away?"

His face was a perfectly placed mask. "Not if it's soaked in blood."

There was nothing humorous in his tone.

Her skin went cold, as if all the heat had been pulled from it. She took the uniform from him.

He turned back towards the trunk and reached inside. He retrieved a short sword, its double-edged blade gleaming.

"A friend gave this to me," he said. "I don't use it anymore."

"I already have a sword."

"That sword has a dull edge for training. It won't do you any good."

She stared at the metal in his hands, remembering the knife she'd used to cut her hair—when she was drowning in her grief. But now she'd wield a blade as a promise of death—a promise that no one else would suffer at the hands of Ivan and Hatra.

Edward's voice interrupted her thoughts.

"I won't stop you from doing what you need to do," he said. "I'll help you get your pelt back. I meant what I promised."

She looked up at him.

"And I'm sorry," he added. "For overwhelming you. I never want to make you feel like you have to feel anything back. That's not what I—"

"You don't," she said.

"I know you're grieving," Edward said. "And that even if you felt the same, the timing's all wrong."

Her hands trembled. She stared at the uniform clutched to her chest, willing her fingers to still.

"Edward—" she began.

"Elin," he said. "It's okay. We can talk after."

She wanted to tell him what was in her heart—that she wanted him on her darkest days and her brightest.

Love didn't wait for the right time; it arrived in the quiet moments, in storms, and in the way he steadied her.

She said nothing because she didn't know how to say all of that, not yet. Maybe after the battle, things would be clearer. Perhaps then the path forward would make sense. She set the blade and the uniform on the small table next to her.

If she couldn't give him her words, she could give him something else. She stepped closer, her hands catching the front of his uniform before she could think better of it.

Her name was a breath on his lips as she kissed him.

It took Edward a moment to move; then his arms wrapped around her back. He drew her closer, deepening the kiss. His breath was hot against her skin as she pressed closer.

Her heart was in a free-fall.

He held her tight as if she might slip from his fingers, as if he understood everything she failed to say.

She felt it all. That was the nature of her gift and the cruelty of this moment—she simply couldn't stay in it. She felt the warmth of his hands at her back, and beneath that the feeling behind the touch: relief. The particular relief of someone who had been holding something back for a long time and finally been set free. His breathing changed, desire pushing against restraint.

His hands moved to her hair, tangling in the silver strands as he backed them against the wall. Her heart was running away from her. They were taking this too far. Moving too fast. As if they didn't have enough time. Because they didn't.

Bit by bit, reality crept in. What would happen when she got her pelt back? When the sea called for her with a ferocity she could no longer ignore? What if she couldn't stay?

What if she left him?

It wouldn't be fair to let that fear live in him as it did her father, to make him wonder when the tide would carry her away.

Dread sluiced through her veins, cooling her blood. They were preparing for battle. People would die today. And she had kissed him. She had kissed him, and now they had something to lose.

The last time someone she loved was faced with danger, he hadn't survived. She hadn't thought it consciously, but her body understood.

She gently pushed him away. The moment her eyes met Edward's, the weight of it hit her—how much she needed him and how much it would hurt to stay away. She'd taken the plunge and dragged him with her.

She wanted him. But wanting him and being ready for what it meant were not the same thing.

For a moment, neither of them spoke.

She could feel the questions he wasn't asking. What now, Elin? Where do we go from here? He was waiting for her, the way he always waited, which was the thing she loved most about him and the thing she could least afford. He drew in a long breath, no doubt already knowing where her mind had gone.

She looked at him with tears in her eyes. "I should—I shouldn't have done that. I..."

"Why not, Elin?" he asked, stepping closer. "You act like loving someone is a mistake."

"No, but it would be a mistake to love me."

"That's not true," he said.

But it was. Her heart thudded painfully in her chest.

"Edward...I was born for leaving. When I get my pelt back, I—I don't know if I'll stay. I don't want to leave anyone behind. I won't do that to someone."

"You don't get to decide what I can survive."

"What *you* can survive?" she asked, stepping toward the door.

He stiffened.

"I won't risk being the ruin of someone I love," she said.

Edward looked away.

"I'm sorry," Elin whispered.

Shaking his head, he said, "Don't be."

She gathered her things from the table. "Promise you'll be safe."

"You first," he said.

She gave him a small, sad smile.

He reached behind her, opening the door for her, and she stepped out into the corridor. She'd been a fool to kiss him. All she'd done was make everything between them worse, because now…she wasn't sure she could let him go.

"**Naval** engagements are never fought on still water. The sea is as constant an enemy as any crew sailing under a black flag. Navigable channels are narrowed by reefs, shoals, and volcanic ridges, compelling ships onto set paths where ambushes can be readily set. Mist from vents or crashing surf can blind a lookout; submerged rocks can gut a keel before the enemy fires a single shot.

In such waters, the advantage belongs not to the faster ship, but to the one that knows the channels by memory and can read the sea's mood at a glance. A single misjudged turn can ground a vessel, or present its broadside to the cannons."

— *Captain Howard Jarvis II,* Silvamare Royal Navy

Chapter Twenty-one

The Black Reef rose from the sea, jagged and dark, glinting beneath the morning sun.

A distant boom rolled over the water.

Elin turned towards the eastern passage just as the first cannon fired. Through the drifting mist, the silhouettes of their companion ships disappeared into the reef's jagged mouth.

Another thunderous blast followed. Smoke snaked across the sky as the decoy ships loosed their released cannons.

Wood splintered, crackling in the air. She held her breath, hoping the sound belonged to the *Leviathan.*

Spray foamed over the rocks like spittle from a rabid beast. The *Maren* hugged the reef, sailing close to its edges to remain out of view. It turned hard around the bend, slipping between two spires of black basalt. The hull scraped the stone with a grinding shriek that vibrated through the deck.

"Watch out!" someone shouted.

A jet of steam burst from the water beside them with a violent hiss. A sailor lost his footing as the ship lurched, sliding across the slick planks and tumbling over the rail into the boiling water below.

His scream vanished beneath the waves.

More explosions rang out, echoing in Elin's ears.

A cannon smashed into the *Leviathan's* foremast. It snapped like a tree, taking out a section of the main deck's rail as it fell into the sea.

Through the mist, the ship wavered like an apparition, but her decks were alive with movement. Smoke pooled from the *Leviathan's* gunports. Then a burst of light tore through the eastern channel where the decoy ships were already sinking beneath the waves.

At the prow, she gripped the rail as the wind whipped past her, dressed in the Silvamari uniform Edward had given her. Her short sword, sheathed in leather, rested at her hip.

Beside her, Howie raised his spyglass, scanning the deck of the *Leviathan*, bristling with barricades and ready blades. Even from here, Elin could see the figure on the quarterdeck, tall and unbothered, pelt snapping in the wind. Hatra.

Her hand was raised towards the sky, as if reaching for something.

The first gust was sharp and precise, like a slap. It cut through the ship's sails, sent ropes thrashing, and caused unprepared sailors to stagger back. The *Maren* scraped against the basalt again; the hull groaned.

Silas emerged from the mast's shadow like a flame catching tinder, heat rippling around his hands.

"Where's my wind wielder?" he shouted. "It won't be long before Hatra breaks things."

"Emptying his breakfast," Howie said, face twisting into something sour. "He used most of his strength on the decoys."

Howie lowered the spyglass. "Silas, get Perry; do what's needed to get him ready. We need him to counter her gusts. Edward—stay with him."

Edward's eyes were on her as he appeared behind Silas. He gave a sharp nod, his brown eyes distant and battle-ready.

"Stay alive," he said.

"You too," she replied no louder than a whisper. He turned, following Silas to rally Perry.

Wind shrieked between the reef's spires. Silvamare's sails whipped in protest as Hatra's next gust barreled towards them.

A sharp crack split the air—rigging snapped near the stern, and a length of sail whipped wildly.

"Perry!" Silas shouted into the chaos.

But the only answer was another blast of wind that sent seawater crashing over the deck. Elin braced herself against the ship's rails as her boots skidded across the soaked planks. Howie barked orders, steadying the helm with one hand and gesturing with the other.

"We don't have time to coddle him now! Silas, get us a break in the wind!"

Silas grimaced, lifting both arms as heat shimmered around him. The air shifted, warping, as he shoved one palm forward, and the next gust from the *Leviathan* halted halfway, colliding with Silas's rising wall of flame.

"Get us between those rocks!" Howie shouted to the crew. "We'll use the spires to block her wind!"

The sailors obeyed, turning the ship hard.

Hiding wasn't going to get them any closer to the *Leviathan*. The decoy ships may have wasted Hatra's cannon fire, but they were no longer a viable distraction. They needed to draw Hatra's attention away from the *Maren* and towards a more immediate threat.

She looked down at the churning sea, its waves crashing against stone and built-up coral. The sun shone down on the mist, clouding the water's surface.

She was once again faced with a choice: to jump from the cliff or to shy away. Elin took a breath, tilting her head towards the sky, soaking in the sun's warmth. Its rays wrapped around her as she climbed onto the ship's railing. With trembling limbs, she set her sights on the *Leviathan*.

"Elin, don't—"

Someone called her name, but she didn't wait to be stopped.

She dove into the wild waters.

The sea was a stranger, hot and blue, wild and violent as she kicked hard, slicing through the surf bubbles brushing her face. Pressure filled her ears. Her selkie markings tingled, bracing for a change that wouldn't come.

Ribbons of glowing orange broke up the seafloor below, illuminating the underbellies of the ships with a hellish light. The *Leviathan* loomed ahead.

A burst of hot bubbles surged upward, forcing her to kick aside. She wasn't fast enough to avoid the stream; heat seared her arm. Biting down on the pain, she swam towards the *Leviathan's* hull. Her lungs strained as her fingers brushed the wood, pulling herself along until she found the rope of their anchor.

She surfaced near the bow, gasping for air—mist curled around her, shrouding her as she climbed the bow unseen.

She slipped over the rail, landing silently on the slick deck.

Moving fast, she drew her short sword, cutting ropes, sending the remaining sails into the rigging before smashing a lantern against the deck, sending a trail of flame licking up the center mast.

"Boarders!" a raider shouted.

Elin darted behind a stack of crates as a woman lunged for her. Elin slashed out at her, slicing her across the chest before disappearing into the rising smoke.

Out on the water, tucked between the jagged rocks, several rowboats crept forward, hidden in the mist. Perry—still trembling—crouched at the front of one with raised palms pushing the gloom forward.

"Steady," Edward whispered from one boat, crouched low with a blade across his knees.

He could barely see the *Leviathan*, but he smelt the smoke and heard the shouts—the ensuing commotion as Elin descended upon them, a goddess of vengeance.

His heart—gripped with terror when she'd leapt from the rail—now swelled with pride.

As the boats neared the hull, grapples were thrown, catching on what remained of the *Leviathan's* rails. Thus began their ascent.

With the pirates distracted, sails tangled, and scrambling across the deck, the *Maren* burst from the shadows of the spires.

Howie took the helm himself, steering between the outcroppings. Hatra's wind lashed at them again, but it was scattered, misdirected as she defended herself against his kingdom's best fighters.

The ships collided hull to hull with a splintering crunch.

More hooks zipped through the air as men clad in green and crimson leapt from one deck to another, then planks were dropped.

Silvamare roared as it descended upon the *Leviathan*.

Chapter Twenty-two

Elin burst from the fray near the mizzenmast, blood dripping from her sword. Her uniform was soaked through; the green had muddied to brown.

She scanned the deck; her gaze caught on a figure clambering over the *Leviathan's* side. Their eyes locked for a single breath before her attention was pulled away by an attacker.

The jarring impact skittered down Elin's arm as her steel met the pirate's. Smoke blanketed the deck, hiding her as she swept low, slicing her opponent across their gut. She rose again with a ragged breath, eyes searching through the sea of people.

The din of shouts and screams mingled with the impact of bodies against wood. The deck ran slick with blood that spilled into the frothing ocean. Edward's voice, a distant sound, called out Silas's name from behind her.

But it wasn't Edward she sought. Near the ruined foremast, a figure stood licking blood from his thumb.

Sensing her stare, he found her easily across the crowded ship; his smile cut through the noise—the same saccharine curve of his lips he'd worn when he'd killed her brother.

He lifted his cutlass, slow and taunting, dragging the blade across his own throat in imitation.

Ice flooded her veins. She had no fear, and only one thought drove her body forward: *kill him*. It repeated itself, a chant feeding her like a spell. She smiled back, a promise that this time she was the huntress and he the sole object of her desire. Ivan's smile didn't falter, but some of the color left his face as she tore across the deck.

Below deck, Silas and Edward moved as silently as the night.

The screams above had dulled to echoes of clanging metal and howling wind through torn sails. Inside, it was quiet. Wet wood creaked as they progressed down the smoke-laden hall. It curled low across the floor like the breath of a sleeping drake.

Hatra retreated to the ship's interior after they'd boarded, and they followed.

Edward kicked in the door to the captain's quarters.

Hatra sat at the far end of the room like a queen on a throne, one leg crossed over the other, her elbow draped lazily on a lacquered desk. The other rested on the chair's arm. From her fingers dangled something silver, a fur cloak—no, a selkie pelt.

Behind her, others hung on the walls like trophies, pinned with knives. Some were torn, others intact, as if waiting to be reclaimed.

A barrel fire crackled beside her, casting a hellish glow.

On her head, like a grotesque crown, was the head of a pelt—its fur matted and singed—its glassy black eyes stared forward, lifeless.

She smiled at the sight of them.

Silas stepped forward, blade leveled.

"You stole our ship," he said. "You murdered my men."

"Murdered?" Hatra echoed. "You say it like you don't do the same. Sacrificing your people every year so that you might survive. We're all the same, Your Highness."

"We are not."

She gave him a pitiful smile. "Yes, your men are dead. Yes, they died the way most men do at sea, bleeding and screaming."

Silas's grip tightened on his sword. "They were good men."

"You will die," Edward growled.

"Yes, but not today. Things have become far too interesting to die today."

She twirled the pelt in her fingers as if it weren't a piece of someone's soul.

"I saw the silver hair," she said, voice low and silky, "and figured a selkie came to seek revenge."

"I couldn't say which one is hers," she added with a twist of her lips. "They start to blur together after a while."

Behind her, four men stepped forward, awaiting their orders.

"They spare them as if they are more important than the rest of us. But on the sea, there are no exemptions, not from the gods and not from me. But I'll tell you what," Hatra said as she rose from the chair, moving with cold elegance.

"I'll let you fight me for it."

With a flick of her wrist, she dropped the pelt into the fire.

"No!" Edward shouted, lunging forward.

Hatra smiled, snapping her fingers.

A sudden blast of wind slammed into him, sending him crashing into a wall with a sickening thud. Wood splintered behind his back.

"Edward!" Silas shouted.

Edward was already pushing to his feet, blood at his temple, blade solid in his grasp.

Fire bloomed from Silas's palms, surging across the room in a blazing arc aimed straight for Hatra. Raising her arm with an open palm, she redirected it with a twist of air. The flame veered sharply off course, striking one of the pelts pinned to the wall.

Fur curled and blackened as the fire spread, catching the wallboards and creeping towards the ceiling.

"Silas!" Edward shouted, clashing with a pirate. "You'll burn the damn ship!"

Hatra laughed once, sharp and humorless.

"This ship is useless to me now," she said. "I'll just take yours when we're done here."

She stepped through the firelight, drawing her blades. Flames danced in the eyes of her selkie-crown perched atop her brow.

Elin climbed the steps to the foremast two at a time, the boards slick with blood and seawater. She adjusted her grip on the sword.

Ivan stood at the top, twirling his cutlass in slow, lazy circles.

"Elin, isn't it?" he drawled, grinning like a fox. "Finally."

She did not deign a response as she reached the top. The Butcher moved first, striking fast, the flat side of his blade glancing off hers near her shoulder. She swung back, her sword biting a shallow line across his ribs.

His eyes narrowed on her.

"You should be grateful I took your pelt," he said. "You can't deny the gods made a mistake when they made you."

"You're wrong."

"In some ways. My mother always said I was twisted in the head, but I am not wrong about you."

Their movements were a synchronized dance, each anticipating the other's next step.

"Your brother begged," Ivan crooned. "Not for his life, but for yours. He tried to bargain with me. I agreed to spare you, though I should have shared my terms of concession."

She slashed again, this time nicking his chest near the same spot. He hissed, smile twitching.

"You didn't have to kill him," she spat.

Ivan danced back with an elegant spin, dodging her next strike. His blade dropped low. She twisted out of reach.

"Ah," he said, cocking his head. "But I did."

Her jaw clenched, fury surged like a tide through her chest.

"You're a plague."

Ivan beamed. "No, no. The sea god," he drawled, "is a plague."

He struck hard. Elin blocked, but the force knocked her sideways. She slipped. Hitting the deck, she rolled, sword scraping the boards before scrambling back up, putting distance between them.

"You were never meant to exist—two natures, no loyalties," Ivan said, eyes bright with fever. "The gods don't make things like that." His grin widened. "But I'll fix what they failed to."

Ivan circled slowly, taking his time with her. Two natures. No loyalties. In a way, he wasn't wrong. That was the worst part.

"That fear in your eyes…" He licked blood from his lips. "I look forward to seeing what they do when my blade's at your throat."

He lunged for her once more; she dodged, crying out as his blade grazed the side of her leg.

Bodies lay strewn across the floor, their blood mingling with the soot and smoke curling through the air. The wall of selkie pelts burned, fire devouring fur and flesh alike, the scent thick and cloying.

Hatra moved through the carnage with brutal grace, blades flashing like lightning in the dark. She sheathed one blade. Her fingers twisted and then clenched into a fist. The air in the room shifted. Edward grabbed at his throat, choking in the absence of air.

"Edward!" Silas shouted.

Hatra launched at Silas, trying to gain an advantage with the distraction. "Do you know how long one can live without air?" she asked.

Silas deflected her blow, sending a plume of fire into her clenched hand.

Hatra hissed, releasing her hold and reaching back for her second blade, blisters healing in seconds.

Edward fell to one knee, filling his lungs with air.

One blade in each hand, Hatra's strikes were fluid, clinical—cut, pivot, cut again. The stolen pelt bound to her body glimmered beneath her coat, wounds sealing as quickly as they opened.

But she was waning; her breathing hitched, and her balance faltered.

"You stole a pelt in Frostwake," Edward said as he met another pirate's blade with his own. "Where is it?"

Hatra's laugh was choked out by smoke. "I've stolen many skins in Frostwake," she murmured with disinterest.

Still, her eyes betrayed her. For the briefest moment, they lingered on the chair she'd been sitting in moments before—where a single selkie pelt hung draped over the backrest like a discarded cloak, untouched.

Silas saw it too.

Edward drove his sword through the last pirate.

Silas drove Hatra back a step.

"Get the pelt to Elin," Edward said, joining the fight against Hatra.

Edward's blade locked with Hatra's, sparks flying.

"I'm not leaving you," Silas said.

"Please," he said.

Firelight caught in Silas's eyes—he nodded and turned towards the chair for Elin's pelt.

Hatra snarled and, with a flick of her wrist, sent a twist of wind, flinging a blade like a spear.

"Silas!" Edward shouted. He moved on instinct, shoving Silas aside just as the blade shrieked past, missing them by inches.

But Hatra's assault didn't stop as a second blade swung low with merciless precision. Steel met flesh with a sickening crack that echoed through the room.

Edward screamed as he hit the floor, crimson spilling across the boards. Blood pooled from where his lower leg had been severed from the rest of him.

Hatra turned back towards the chair, fire casting flickering shadows across her face. Her hand reached out for the pelt, ready to feed it to the flame.

"No," Silas roared.

The air combusted around him, fire surged, and he hurled himself at her—heat meeting wind in a violent clash. She met him blade to blade, a grin still curling her bloodied mouth as they collided again in the heart of the burning ship.

Elin charged, driving her boot into Ivan's ribs with all the force her body could summon, but he was faster. She searched him for a hidden pelt, but found nothing.

He caught her mid-kick, fingers tightening around her ankle like a vice, and slammed her to the deck. Her skull struck the boards with a crack that rang in her teeth. The world warped around the edges, ringing out in all directions.

By the time her vision steadied, he was already atop her—straddling her chest, his weight pressing her down. Her limbs were pinned beneath his knees, her breath trapped in her lungs. Cold steel settled across the curve of her throat, light as a feather.

Ivan grinned down at her, gleeful, alive in the chaos.

"So familiar," he murmured, blade tracing the hollow of her collarbone. "You look just like you did before. So full of dread. Already knowing the outcome."

She stared up at him, paralyzed, her heart hammering against the blade.

Anik.

His name was like a sharp pain piercing her heart. She saw his face, a near match for her own, alive and laughing, blue eyes shimmering in sunlight.

I'm sorry. I failed you. She thought only to herself.

She was going to die here, with regrets and unsaid truths. Why hadn't she spoken them when she knew life was fickle and love sacred? Anik's death, the loss of her pelt, had made her a coward, scared—like she was now.

Ivan's smile grew too wide for his narrow face—he could open his mouth and devour her whole.

"You feel it, don't you?" he whispered. "That wrongness inside you. The sea pulling one way. The land another. Let me end it for you."

The blade skimmed lower, down the line of her sternum, dragging over cloth.

No.

Not like this.

A feeling surged in her chest, something more potent than her fear.

She was a daughter of Frostwake—a creature of land and sea. In her blood, she carried the strength of glaciers and the brutality of an arctic winter. She had kissed sorrow on the mouth and crawled from the brink of her own despair.

She struggled under Ivan, trying to buck him off.

He laughed.

This would not be her end—not at *his* hands—not when she had so much left to live for.

Not when she had a promise to keep.

Ivan leaned close, breath sour against her cheek.

"Let me watch you die, little selkie b—"

He didn't finish. Elin's freed hand plunged into his chest.

The words caught in his throat, strangled by shock. His blade fell from his grip, landing on the blood-slicked deck.

Those mocking, ice-bright eyes—widened in disbelief.

His fear caught like an ember.

She sat up slowly, forcing him back into a seated position, her hand still buried in him. His heart tried to pulse within her grasp. With her other hand, she reached behind his neck. From a distance, they might've looked like two people locked in an embrace.

Elin leaned in close and whispered, "Eat your heart out, Ivan."

She tore her clenched fist free in a single, vicious pull—and shoved his still-beating heart between his lips.

It was fast enough that she knew he tasted it, understood what had happened before his eyes dimmed.

She let his body fall.

For a long breath, she didn't move. Just sat in the smoke and blood and ruin, with a heaving chest and shaking hands. The sounds of battle rang out around her as she pressed a kiss to her fingers, raising them towards the sky.

I did it, Anik.

For you.

For me.

I love you.

"**When** she left him for the sea, his heart shattered; for he did not see that to a selkie, little else ever matters. My heart aches for them. What a cruel existence, to ever yearn for what you cannot keep. And a harsher truth still, to be born for abandoning, bound in blind devotion to something that cannot love you in return."

— *Musings from a Fisherman*, from *A Collection,* gifted to the Royal Library of Silvamare

Chapter Twenty-three

Elin strapped on her weapons with trembling hands slick with Ivan's blood. She wiped them on her clothes, eyes scanning the deck. The battle was still raging. Shouts echoed across the planks, steel ringing through the smoky haze.

Someone had put out the fire she'd ignited, but still, smoke billowed across the *Leviathan's* wooden planks.

Silvamare's navy clashed with the last of the pirate crew. Some fought one-on-one, while others rushed to aid Howie as he held off three at once.

"Edward!" she shouted, then louder, "Edward? Silas?"

She couldn't make them out in the mass of bodies; she scanned the faces staring blankly at the world in pools of sticky blood. Panic eased in her chest when she didn't spot who she was searching for.

Her boots slipped on the deck as she made way for the steps, smoke burning her throat—her eyes. The heat coiled around her, like the great snakes of the Sable Isles, suffocating her.

"Edward!" she called again, descending the steps. Her voice broke on his name.

A scream, distant but familiar, came from inside the ship. She spun towards the sound, boots pounding the scorched boards, and slammed her shoulder into the nearest door, following the screams into the ship's dark, smoke-choked belly.

Smoke thickened as she neared the captain's quarters, choking her. She pulled her damp shirt over her face.

Squinting, she approached a door; an orange light glowed from its seams.

She reached for the handle, hissing as searing heat bit into her palm. She shoved the door open with her shoulder.

The moment the door creaked open, she stepped into a seething blaze of fire and blood. Smoke coiled thick in the air; flames licked up the walls; in some spots, the wood was eaten away, revealing the sea beyond.

Silas was locked in battle, slick with sweat, his blade flashing as it clashed with Hatra's. And in the pirate queen's hand was her—Elin staggered forward, breath escaping her. It was her pelt glinting in the firelight.

Cold swept through her as she spotted Edward slumped against the far wall. His blood was dark and slick around him.

He wasn't moving.

His leg—

Elin's stomach lurched, and she couldn't tell if the ship was listing or if her own balance was failing her.

Hatra's wild laugh caught her attention. The pirate queen smiled, eyes shining with delighted malice as she tossed the pelt into the fire.

Elin screamed as the flames caught fast, curling up the edges with greedy fingers.

The world unraveled around her, flattening and folding in on itself. Time bent inward, no longer linear but running through events, each overlapping until she was no longer on the ship.

She was on the shore again, the ice shelf beneath her bare feet, the wind cold on her face, pushing her back towards the sea. She watched herself pull the pelt from her back, tossing it across the ice. Forced to watch as Ivan slit Anik's throat. Watch as her brother lay dying in her arms.

Now, she stood in a room of flame and smoke, face to face with the same choice.

Would she trade her pelt for Edward's life? This time, would it make a difference?

There was so much blood. But what was there to weigh?

She had spent her whole life caught between the sea and land—torn by the pull of tides and ties. But when it truly mattered, when the moment came to choose...

Was that what Tven meant all those months ago, that some burdens were not hers to bear? Her pelt had always been a burden, a curse.

She never chose the sea. Time and time again, she chose love, the people she loved so deeply that they became a part of her.

She loved Edward; she hadn't realized how deeply that love had grown, rooting itself into her heart, her being.

She should've told him. Should've looked him in the eye and said the words before...now it might be too late.

Time snapped taut once more, minutes collapsing into seconds, and she ran to him.

"Oh—oh gods," Elin gasped, tearing at her clothes, hands slick with blood as she tied the fabric tightly above the ruin of his leg. "Edward. Edward, if you can hear me—"

Her voice cracked as his head lolled, eyes fluttering but unfocused.

"That's it," she said. "Stay with me, Edward. I'm here."

Chapter Twenty-four

Edward

He felt as if he'd fallen deep into the sea; a cold lightness carried him down towards its sandy bottom, the light dimming as he descended deeper and deeper.

He had always wondered what it would feel like. As a boy, before he understood what death actually was, he'd imagined it like sleep—familiar, painless, a door closing softly. He understood now that it was more like a tide going out. The water pulling back from the shore whether you wanted it to or not.

He wasn't ready.

He barely registered what was happening around him; that was until Elin was there, her voice distant, speaking words he couldn't quite latch onto. Her hands burned against his skin, as hot as the flame reflected in her glassy brown eyes. Her silver hair haloed her bloodied face, one he'd watched turn hard and was only just beginning to soften.

"She really is a goddess," he thought, shaped by love and forged by vengeance. The strongest soul he'd ever known.

He had known it on the ice. Since he had watched her rise up after cradling her brother's body. How she managed to keep getting up every time she fell. He had made a promise then—to a woman who didn't know his name, who had looked at him with empty eyes, and who had nothing left to give anyone. He thought at first that his promise was about duty. He realized a while ago that it was never really about duty.

He had been falling since she marched up to *Maren* with determination in her eyes. No, even before then. On the ice, when he watched her give up a piece of herself to save someone she loved.

He thought about the night in his quarters. The walk down the corridor, his coat on her shoulders, the heat of her body when she'd let him hold her. How long he had carried what he felt for her, keeping it manageable, keeping it at the distance she'd ask for. A part of him was grateful for it, the rapid growth of his affections had confused him.

Behind it chased the rampant fear that he had someone else to lose. It felt as though an hourglass had begun to countdown, and he didn't want to waste time. Not this time.

He hoped she'd find happiness, even if he wasn't there to see it.

He was sorry to have failed her and not to have lived up to his promise to get her pelt back. He was sorry he would not see what she became. She would become extraordinary; he was certain of it. He was sorry for his parents and his sisters. Sorry for Silas and Howie.

Sorry that Elin would face yet another loss.

"Elin..." he tried to say, but it was only a breath.

"Edward," she choked out, tightening the makeshift tourniquet with trembling hands. "Listen to me—" she sniffled. "You're going to be okay."

She drew a breath that shook her delicate frame. He wanted to reach out to her, to hold her one last time. But he could no longer move his body.

"Please—don't—don't leave me," she whispered.

The world's edges were creeping in closer, sound dulling, and not even the searing burn of her hands on his cold flesh could save him now.

He knew the moment she sensed it—that he was fading. Her brown eyes lit up with panic as she shook him.

"Edward, wait. I love you. I love you—I—please. I can't lose you, too."

He heard it. He wanted her to know that he heard it, that it reached him here at the bottom of this dark sea, that it was the last warm thing he felt.

"Wait," he thought. *"Not yet."*

But the darkness did not listen.

Chapter Twenty-five

Silas

Elin's pelt curled in the flames, reduced to glowing embers and ash.

Across the room, Silas faced Hatra, sword drawn, lungs burning with smoke. They had to get out of here soon, or they would die.

"Funny how the Tide forgets you," Hatra growled. "It never forgets us."

"You know," she purred, circling him with a lazy twirl of her blade, "I'm not the villain here, Your Highness. At least I'm no worse than the kings and queens feeding their people to a monster of the sea," she added. "Or the nobility hiding untouched in their castles."

Silas said nothing.

"Oh, come now," she cooed, pouting. "Don't you have a witty insult to throw my way?"

He kept his stance steady, footsteps light, sword held low. Knowing he couldn't keep up this fight much longer, he calculated a new plan. He'd give her what she wanted; he'd play her games.

"And what would you do in their place? Deny a god?"

"There are no gods, boy. Only men and monsters."

"Well," he said, "I think it's well established you're a liar. You're no queen, no lady, and yet you parade around as one."

Hatra scoffed. "I can be a lady for you, princely boy."

His nostrils flared as he guided her back, step by careful step, until her heel knocked against the desk behind her. Silas didn't waste a second. The moment her body fell back, his blade sliced through the delicate flesh of her neck.

Hatra's head hit the floor, then her body slumped off the front of the desk, a smear of red left in its wake.

Silas staggered back, bile rising in his throat, but he swallowed it down.

Turning, he found Elin crumpled beside Edward, hands pressed against his wound, blood spilling through her fingers.

Silas rushed to their side, coughing as the smoke thickened around them. The air was scorching, and he fought for every breath.

Edward's chest rose in an uneven rhythm; his skin had turned the grey of death.

"Shit," Silas snapped, falling to his knees.

He slapped Edward's face. Once. Twice. "Wake up, damn it!"

Edward didn't stir.

Elin looked past them, eyes landing on the blaze where Hatra's body was beginning to burn.

She flinched. Perched like a mockery of a crown on Hatra's scorched head was what remained of another selkie's pelt.

But enough of it remained that it might help them—help Edward.

"Silas," she said, voice trembling. "The pelt on her head—get it. It can help him."

He blinked at her, horror giving way to understanding.

Without hesitation, he darted through the smoke and tore the burning pelt from Hatra's corpse.

Elin didn't hesitate as she took it from him. She placed the pelt on Edward's head, pressing it down as if it might anchor him to this world. Then she prayed to the gods that they weren't too late.

Together, Elin and Silas carried Edward out of the burning ship and onto the deck, smoke curling in their wake.

All around them, the battle had ended. Hatra's men were either dead or disarmed, kneeling in surrender.

Silvamare's sage and crimson flag still flew proudly on their ship's mast. Their losses seemed minimal, but every uniformed body that remained too still amongst the ruins was one too many.

Sailors rushed towards them when they cleared the door, calling for Samson. Strong arms reached for Edward, but Silas brushed them off, laying him on the deck floor.

Edward's chest had stopped moving.

Silas dropped to his knees beside him. "No. No, no, no."

He pressed both hands to Edward's chest and pumped. She couldn't do anything but stand there frozen, unable to believe what was happening in front of her.

Samson, the *Maren's* surgeon, came to Silas's side, taking over the compressions.

Howie stepped beside her, with a furrowed brow and glassy eyes.

"What are they doing?" she asked in a voice that didn't sound like her own.

"He's trying to get his heart going again."

Elin brought her hands to her mouth as she watched Silas and Samson work. Howie pulled her close, wrapping a supportive arm around her shoulder, as if he might need to catch her. Or perhaps it was he who needed the touch.

There was nothing either of them could do as they stood there watching.

Silas leaned in, pressing his bloodied fingers to Edward's neck, then let out a sharp cry as he buried his head into Edward's chest. Samson sat back on his knees, wiping sweat from his forehead.

Elin could not tell if the cry was of relief or grief. The heavy wave of emotion seeping from Silas was hard to distinguish. Until she saw Edward's chest rise and fall once, then again.

"He did it?" she whispered.

"He did it," Howie confirmed, his voice tight.

She ran to Edward. Dropping to her knees, she took his hand in both of hers.

"I'm here," she said. "I'm here."

Edward's fingers weakly squeezed hers. She rested her forehead on his chest, feeling its gentle rise and fall, the ebb and flow of his breathing, the only sound she needed to feel whole.

In the dim light of Edward's quarters, only his breathing and the ship's groan kept her company. For hours, she sat in the chair Silas had dragged from the desk, unmoving, worn thin.

She couldn't look away.

She breathed him in, crisp pine, sharp and clean as Terron's Forest. The rise and fall of his chest wasn't enough to keep the shadows seeping in from the corners where candlelight failed. A phantom chorus of clashing steel echoed in her ears. She tightened her grip on Edward's hand, trying to ignore the sticky heat of it—until the memory of the Butcher's heart pulsing in her palm rose too vividly to endure.

The chair scraped across the planks as she rose, the sound intrusive in the quiet. Her muscles protested, stiff from battle and hours of stillness. She exhaled shakily as she looked down at Edward's sleeping form.

She'd almost been too late.

Behind her, hinges squealed as Edward's door opened. Silas stood in the doorway, exhaustion bruising his face.

"How is he?" His gaze slipped past her to the bed.

"The same."

Floorboards creaked under his feet as he stepped inside; the door groaned shut behind him. Though his expression remained bereft of emotion, a storm raged beneath.

"It was neither of our faults," she whispered.

His jaw clenched. "I know."

That was a lie. Edward had lost his leg protecting Silas. He would carry that burden of guilt for years to come.

Still, she didn't press. Silas had his way of dealing with grief, and it wasn't her place to tell him how he should process it. The gods knew she had enough of her own.

"You've been here all night," he said. "Go get some air, and I'll watch over him."

Elin opened her mouth to protest, but a wave of cold silenced her. Grief fractured his stoic exterior. He needed this time with Edward, and she had no right to deny it.

"You'll let me know if he wakes?"

"You have my word."

Casting one more glance to where Edward slept, she reminded herself it was just that—sleep.

"Is there anything I can do for the crew?" she asked. Since leaving the *Leviathan* to burn in the Black Reef, the Silvamari had been repairing the *Maren* and preparing their fallen for the funeral at dawn.

"Their belongings need sorting," Silas said, lowering himself into the chair beside Edward. "Howie will tell you what to do."

As she entered the corridor, the door behind her creaked shut. She leaned against it, the cold wood pressing against her spine, and tilted her head back. Silver strands spilled from her shoulders as she drew in a steadying breath. As soon as she made her way to the upper deck, she'd be barraged by the emotions of the crew, whose grief was as strong as any loss.

She took a moment to sort through her own emotions so they wouldn't be muddied with the others. Then she peeled herself away from the door before her resolve could falter. Silvamare had been there for her when she needed them most; now it was her time to shoulder their burdens.

On deck, the night sky was pin-pricked with stars, and the moon glowed through the damp, heavy air. Sweat beaded across Elin's forehead as she slowed, spotting crewmen bent over the fallen, wrapping their comrades in linen while others labored over the damaged ship, patching splintered railings and torn canvas. Lantern light caught on bruised faces, torn sleeves, and bandaged wounds. The quiet murmur of voices carried no laughter or joyful camaraderie.

Guilt churned in her chest. She'd spent hours cloistered in Edward's quarters while the rest of Silvamare carried their burdens on deck. She should have been here helping.

Howie stood near the mainmast, his head bound in a bloodied strip of cloth. He glanced up at her approach; loss etched plain across his weathered features. He drew Elin aside, out of earshot of the others.

"How are you...after Ivan?" His voice was steady, but there was an underlying frailty. It made him sound older.

Elin's throat tightened. "I don't regret what I did. There's peace in knowing Ivan and Hatra can't hurt anyone else." She exhaled, shaking her head. "But it doesn't fill me as I thought it would, especially not with its cost."

Howie's expression softened. "Sacrifice is the price the crew is always willing to pay. We were seeking vengeance of our own, remember? It doesn't make the loss any easier, though. We lost good men."

Elin followed his gaze to the linen-shrouded shapes lining the deck. Her heart swelled painfully.

She forced the words out. "Do you think Edward will wake?"

Howie did not reply right away; the soft crash of waves against the ship's hull filled the silence instead. With each moment that passed without a reply, Elin's nails dug deeper into her palms.

So much time passed that when Howie finally spoke, she flinched. "He wouldn't be alive if not for you and Silas. Recovery will be slow. He—he may not be the same as he was."

Elin's thoughts drifted to Edward's family; from what he'd shared, she was certain they would not abandon him. "He has people who love him. They'll see him through."

Frowning at her, he noted the damage to her sleeve, then the ruin of her pants. "Has Samson seen to your injuries?"

She looked down at her leg, where Ivan's blade had sliced her. It hadn't fully healed, but there was nothing Samson could do at this point to help her.

"I'll be fine," she assured him. "There are others who need him more than I do."

Howie gave a small nod, eyes lingering on her with contemplation. At last, he asked quietly, "What now, Elin?"

Elin pondered the question, studying the deck's plank grooves. Before the battle, she knew what she wanted, and it hadn't changed. But now, it felt strange to stand here and claim it.

"I don't know," she admitted. "Frostwake is behind me, at least for now, and Silvamare…I don't even know if they'll accept me."

Howie's brow furrowed. "Silvamare is a welcoming place. If you want, you could stay with the Navy. After a year of service, you'd earn citizenship." He paused, eyes searching hers. "You wouldn't be a burden. You'll be paid for your part in defeating Hatra's crew, and if you remain with me, you'll keep earning your way. As for a roof, my house is too large for one man. Edward and Silas stay there from time to time. You'd be no less welcome."

Her lip quivered. "I—I don't know what to say."

A faint smile curved his mouth. "You're family now."

She swallowed against the growing lump in her throat. "I'll think on it."

Wiping tears from her face, she said, "Now tell me what I can do to help."

The sleeping quarters were hushed, stripped of their usual chatter and snoring. Hammocks swayed with the roll of the sea, but many lay empty now, their ropes hanging slack above the meager belongings of the fallen.

The silence was laced only with the rustle of fabric and the muted scrape of boots on wood. No one had slept since the battle, and fatigue nettled at the bones of everybody on the ship.

Elin worked wordlessly alongside the others, folding shirts and tucking away trinkets that might mean everything to someone waiting at home. One sailor pressed a shirt to her face, seeking to catch the final scent of their fallen friend before setting it aside. Each item was placed into a chest to be returned to the families of the fallen.

Her throat constricted as she reached for a pair of weathered boots.

They were Milo's.

The memory of their first meeting fluttered through her mind, as fleeting as the sun in winter. His smug indignation as she pleaded to be let on; he'd been rude, but he was also doing his job. People are more complex than good or bad, rude or kind. She remembered him circling her in their duel, needling her and poking at deep wounds, teaching her the lesson Silas wanted her to learn. Yet for all his sharp words, Milo had never been cruel. Loyal to his prince, to his kingdom, to his brothers and sisters—he had been a good man.

She placed his boots in his trunk.

A sob, muffled by a clamped hand, came from across the sleeping quarters. Something delicate clattered to the ground, shattering as it met the planks. A hissed curse was followed by the clomping of boots as another sailor walked away from the broken mess.

Elin bowed her head, willing herself to keep moving, trying to shut out the stifling grimness of the room. She escaped into her own thoughts.

The sea's call was no louder than a whisper, sometimes heard on a breeze. A part of her had died over the last several months. It happened slowly, beginning the moment Ivan took the blade to Anik's throat and ending as the remnants of her pelt turned to ash.

She'd died and been reborn a woman who no longer had one foot planted on the shores and the other in the sea. Where the weight of her pelt had once been a comfort to wrap herself inside, it had equally been a burden. One she no longer shouldered, and the lightness of it was freeing. It was the shedding of an old skin that never quite fit.

The world was wide and uncharted.

Her grief remained raw and unyielding, but she was carrying it. Like the silver braid at her wrist, it would never leave her, but it no longer chained her.

The faintest pinks stretched across the navy sky, the first threads of dawn unspooling across the horizon. The ship rocked, its timbers crying out as if it too mourned that it was time to say goodbye.

Before returning to the deck, Elin had slipped once more into Edward's quarters. Still, he slept, his chest rising and falling with ease. Yet the longer he remained in that state between life and death, the more dread coiled in her chest. Sleep could be healing, but it could also be the slow closing of a door that would never open again.

She could not bear to follow that thought further. She could not—would not—stomach a funeral for him, even if that meant she had to pry his very soul from the clutches of the gods themselves.

Back on the upper deck, the crew gathered, lining up along the railing. Golden rays reached down from the sky like sun-kissed fingers shimmering in the cool morning air. The light caught on weary faces. Howie stood on the steps, voice carrying across the deck.

"To Terron and Cosmir," he said. "We thank you for the blessing of knowing these men and of serving beside them. Now we ask you to carry them in your embrace until we meet them again."

The sailors lowered their heads, a reverent hush falling over them. When Howie raised his hand, the crew snapped their salutes in unison. The sound was sharp in the still air, a final ode of respect.

Silas and several of the crew moved forward. Together, they lifted each shrouded body with care before rolling them over the side of the ship.

The sea received them with quiet splashes, ripples widening and breaking apart before fading back into the vastness.

Elin's throat ached as she watched the shapes sink, linen and flesh swallowed by the deep. The sea took them all—enemy and kin, blood and stranger alike. After all, the god of the sea was a greedy, gluttonous thing.

Morning gave way to afternoon. The bright blue sky was peppered with large, fluffy clouds, and a warmth settled over the deck, softening the hard edges of the crew's grief. A handful of sailors leaned against the rail or sprawled on coils of rope, murmuring in low voices about nothing of consequence—weather, cards, which port tavern poured the strongest drink. Others had fallen asleep, their mouths slack, not ready to return to the hammocks.

Howie dozed upright against a barrel, a blanket draped haphazardly over his lap by some unseen kindness. With his chin resting on his chest, he looked more peaceful than Elin had ever seen him.

Her own eyes burned with fatigue, but sleep remained elusive. Her body begged for its dark embrace, but her mind refused to loosen its grip. Instead, she sat cross-legged near the mainmast with a pair of sailors, playing a game of cards in the mast's shade. The cards blurred at the edges, her hands full of losing numbers.

Somewhere farther on the deck, a voice lifted in song. At first it was soft, almost a hum, but soon the melody carried on the soft breeze—an old Silvamari ballad. The words painted the tale of a cursed prince whose love went unrequited. In his sorrow, he killed the woman, then drowned himself in her blood. Yet death did not claim him. Instead, he was cursed to live forever in shadow, reliving the act until madness twisted him into something darker, less than human.

A shiver crawled up her spine. She glanced at Perry, who appeared equally disturbed, across from her. "That ought to be sung around a fire," she murmured.

The other sailor gave a weak smile, fanning his own cards. "My mother used to sing it to me as a boy. Said if I wandered out after dark, the cursed prince would chase me home."

Elin huffed a laugh through her nose. "Not much worse than the stories from Frostwake, I suppose. We were told stories of watery hands pulling children from the ice shelves if they strayed too far."

"Better to learn fear from stories," he said, laying down a winning hand, "than the hard way."

Elin smiled despite herself, showing him her pitiful cards. He chuckled.

Footsteps thundered across the deck. Silas came running, his grey eyes alight and wild. Elin's heart dropped to her stomach at his frantic approach.

Before she could form the fear on her lips, he blurted, in a near-laugh, "He's awake."

The cards slipped from Elin's hands; the world narrowed to that single truth.

"He's awake!" she cried, the words cracking with relief.

Silas grinned, nodding. She ran straight into him, arms thrown around his shoulders, tears pricking at her eyes. He held her tight for a heartbeat before pulling back, eyes gleaming.

"Go," he said. "He was asking for you."

Elin squeezed his arms, joy burning through her exhaustion, and then she was running, her feet pounding across the deck and down into the ship.

To her surprise, the door to Edward's quarters made little noise as she opened it. The afternoon sun slanted through the porthole, painting Edward in gold. His short-cropped hair caught the light, a dark halo against the pillow propped against the headboard, but his eyes were fixed on the flat space beneath the sheets where the lower half of his leg should have been.

When she stepped inside, he startled, looking away from the stump and whispered, "Hi."

Her heart tugged. "Hi."

For a moment, the silence stretched between them, heavy as the sea. Then his lips pressed together, and in a voice rough with disuse, said, "I'm sorry."

She moved closer, confusion knitting her brow. "For what?"

He didn't look at her. The corners of his mouth tugged down. "I couldn't get your pelt back. I tried. But—" His voice frayed, and he kept his eyes on the sheet bunched in his hands.

"Edward," she interrupted. "That doesn't matter. What matters is that you're alive." She sat in the chair beside him. "That you came back to us—to me."

Edward swallowed hard. His grip loosened from the sheet and sought her hand instead; his rough palm scraped against her skin as his thumb brushed her knuckles.

"I heard you," he whispered. "When I was dying. I tri—I tried to get back to you." His broad shoulders shuddered with the effort to hold steady.

"Can you still love me now?"

It took her a moment to realize he was referring to his leg, or rather, the absence of it. Her heart sank at the thought that he believed her love could be so fickle. She could only sit there, the silence thick between them, at a loss for words before climbing onto the bed and gathering him into her arms.

"I meant every word," she said. "Your injury doesn't change how I feel. It never could. I'm just...so grateful you're alive—that you're here, with me."

His forehead rested against her collarbone, his hair tickling her skin. She held him there until the tension bled out of him and the trembling slowed.

When he lifted his face, tears tracked down his cheeks. His eyes, watery in the light, searched hers. She cupped his cheek, her thumb brushing along the strong line of his jaw.

There was no more hiding, no more denying what she felt so plainly, and she would not waste another second with him.

"I love you, Edward Graves," she said. "I've been falling in love with you since the day you put that coat on my shoulders. I always feared I'd be the ruin of someone who loves me, but I don't fear that anymore. I'm here. I'm not leaving."

A ragged laugh escaped him, wet and breathless. "Good," he whispered, and leaned in to kiss her. "Because you could never be my ruin, Elin." His lips returned to hers, soft and desperate.

She kissed him back, her fingers splayed in his hair, her other hand pressed against the warm breadth of his chest.

When exhaustion overtook him again, his head sagged back onto the pillow. Still, his hand caught hers before she could move away, his soft eyes half-lidded with weariness.

"Stay," he murmured.

So she did—even if she didn't yet understand what it would cost her.

She curled against him in the narrow bed, fitting herself against his body. His scent wrapped around her, settling her mind enough for sleep. As the world grew fuzzy and her body melted into the warmth of Edward, the jagged pieces inside her shifted, reforging themselves into something new.

PART III
The Ephemerality of Ever After

SILVAMARE — FEBRUARY-JUNE

"**The** Isle of Silvamare is known for its strait, which cuts through the island as if Terron himself pulled the land apart to let the ocean through. Its mountainous peaks touch the clouds, and in its valleys, yellow-crowned trees bleed red sap into the soil, feeding the little blue flowers which blossom in the summer and are a key ingredient in procuring the sleeping drafts universally distributed for the Black Tide. Positioned between Frostwake and Drakcultus, Silvamare is of moderate weather, and its people are of modest temperament. In many ways, the kingdom of Silvamare is the warm heart linking the remaining isles of Aquerios with its overarching positive relationships with the Old Kingdom of Sidon, the Confederation of Frostwake, and the kingdom of Drakcultus."

— *Geological Features of Aquerios*, a common text

Chapter Twenty-six

From the blue waters of the Wavecrest, Silvamare rose—blunt-tipped mountains and sheer cliffs stacked against the horizon. Having only known Frostwake's frozen expanse, Elin struggled to reconcile this island with Edward's simplest description.

Green.

It was inadequate. She had never seen so many shades of it—greens that climbed the mountainsides and pooled in the valleys, greens deeper than Terron's Forest, softer than the brief warmth of arctic wildflowers. Even in midwinter, Silvamare held color. Afternoon light flashed off the highest peaks, bright enough that she had to lift a hand and shield her eyes.

It had only been a handful of months since she'd taken fate into her own hands. It might as well have been years. That woman was already fading away as the *Maren* drew closer.

Her worries remained, though they were quieter now. Would she be accepted? Could she love and be loved here? Would it be safe?

She had already chosen her course and had no intention of turning back.

Any lingering doubts dissipated as a warm arm slid around her waist. Edward's breath brushed her neck.

"Welcome home," he said.

Elin turned. Her smile came as naturally as breathing.

The ship lurched. Edward lost his balance, bracing one arm on the rail and steadying himself with the makeshift crutch he'd whittled from scrap wood. He was close enough that she found herself pinned between him and the rail. The smirk he gave her warmed her cheeks.

The selkie crown she'd taken from Hatra's burning corpse sped Edward's recovery over the last few weeks. His injury healed, and his strength was growing as he learned new ways to navigate around the ship. But recovery was not the same as ease. In rough seas, he had to remain in place. Some days were harder than others as he learned the new rules of his body. They both knew his time with the Navy was over.

Edward's head tipped, and Elin realized she'd drifted in thought—lost to the island, the future.

"Sorry," she said, turning back towards the shore.

They were nearing the strait. Two bell towers framed its entrance, and their distant chiming rose over the gulls. "It's strange," she admitted, "to think this is my home now."

"Have you changed your mind?"

"No," she said. "No. I just... I never imagined home could be anywhere but Frostwake. Anik and I talked about leaving, but I never thought—" She trailed off as the ship approached the bells: the gate to the kingdom's heart.

The towers—grey stone stacked into pillars—rose, narrowing towards points that seemed to threaten the sky. At their tops, an arch cradled Silvamare's famed silver bells. Above it, a second, smaller arch held mirrors and channels—built so that at night, flame could be set within and reflected outward to guide ships through the dark. A metal chain stretched between the towers, raised and lowered by pulleys. It dropped for the *Maren* as the bells rang out—loud enough that Elin fought not to cover her ears.

She expected something that would mark the moment her old life ended and a new one began, but there was no appreciable change as the ship sailed past the towers. Edward stayed beside her, comfortable with her silence as she took it in. That was the thing she loved most about him—he never tried to fill the spaces she needed to breathe.

Silvamare was the most beautiful place Elin had ever seen—more beautiful than the lights that sometimes danced over Frostwake's sky, more beautiful than valleys of untouched snow. She twisted the bracelet of braided silver hair around her wrist, feeling the places where the strands had frayed.

A piece of Anik was tied to a piece of her, and she had carried him through grief, through vengeance, through the miracle of love. Now she carried him with her here.

The kingdom unfurled along the strait as they sailed inward. Edward watched her, pride and joy radiating from him like sunshine, as if he could not help it.

"Welcome to the kingdom of Silvamare," Silas said, coming up behind them.

Elin turned. His grey eyes were bright, but something tense sat beneath his expression—a nervousness she hadn't seen in him before. It skittered across her skin.

"It's beautiful," she said.

Silas smiled at the passing crew, rubbing the back of his neck.

Elin tilted her head, studying him—wondering if it was her place to ask. After all, he was her prince now.

Edward leaned towards her and whispered, "He's nervous to see his mother."

"His mother?" Elin glanced back at Silas. "Why?"

Silas answered without looking at her, as if she were the one he'd upset. "Hunting Hatra was not the *Maren's* original mission. My mother and brother believed we were deployed only for diplomacy in Frostwake. My father—indirectly—gave me permission to extend our deployment."

"Indirectly?" Elin frowned. "I don't understand."

"It was his compromise. I was asking questions I shouldn't, and he gave me leave to act as Crown at Sea—if I dropped it."

"So, because you were Crown at Sea, you could make the call that not only extended the deployment but changed its nature."

"Precisely."

"And your mother knew nothing of it?"

"Not a thing."

"You're right to be nervous, then."

Silas smiled and then nodded, conceding the point.

"And this compromise he made," Elin pressed. "What were you asking?"

Silas drew a slow breath through his teeth. His playful, though nervous, aura shifted to something bitter and warm—frustration. "I cannot say."

The answer stirred a familiar ache in Elin's chest. She could almost hear Anik's dramatic gasp, feel the cool press of his cheek beneath her fingers as she pinched it.

"Silks and politics," she murmured, smiling despite herself.

Silas glanced at her. "What was that?"

"Nothing." She shook the memory loose. "Just grateful I fell in love with a lieutenant instead of a prince."

Silas laughed. "I'm glad for you both." He clapped Edward on the shoulder. "If you'll excuse me, I should go prepare myself for my mother's look of profound disappointment."

He disappeared into the bustle of the crew as the *Maren* began its final approach.

Perry gentled the wind, and the ship glided through the strait into a wide, sheltered basin, the island splitting like two crescent moons turned towards one another. On the eastern shore, the palace rose from the mountainside, carved into stone. The city itself was alive—homes and shops clustered close together, built of wood and grey stone, their windows crowded with boxes of pine and bright red berries.

The air changed as they neared the dock. Fish and brine and smoke from cook fires mingled with unfamiliar scents that made Elin's pulse quicken. Each breath was an invitation—each smell something new to learn.

Crowds gathered along the dock, their voices blending into a low, restless murmur. Howie had sent word ahead of their arrival, and families waited now—some eager, some tense, all hungry for news.

Elin smiled at the anticipation crackling through the air—until she remembered the chests.

They were carried with reverence, bearing the belongings of those who would not be coming home.

She steadied herself, bracing for the tide of grief she knew was coming. Edward's hand closed around her arm, grounding her without a word.

Commands were shouted on the deck, followed by the clunk of the anchor.

Edward's unease brushed against her senses.

"You're worried," she said.

"No."

Raising a brow, she asked, "You do realize I can feel it, don't you?"

He blinked down at her. "Can you not...turn it off?"

"I would if I could," she said. "What is it? You think they'll see you differently now?"

He leaned against the rail, gaze locked on the dock. "I just don't want them to worry. Once they see..." He exhaled. "They'll never stop fussing. I won't escape it."

She frowned, remembering what it felt like to be overwhelmed by concern—to want silence more than comfort. She nodded instead of replying.

He smiled and leaned closer. "Perhaps you'll be enough of a distraction to spare me."

Careful of his balance, she slid an arm around him. "Gladly," she said. "It sounds like they love you a great deal."

"They do."

The *Maren* grazed the dock, timber striking timber as cheers erupted from the crew and the dock. Guards held the crowd back as the gangplank was lowered.

Howie stepped forward.

"We return victorious against Hatra and her crew," he called. "But our victory didn't come without a cost. Some gave everything to secure Aquerios's shores. Your grief is not yours alone."

Members of the crew lifted the chests from the deck and descended the gangplank. Heat burned behind Elin's eyes as Howie named the fallen crew. As each name was called, a fresh wave of grief washed over her.

She tried to shield herself from the swell of emotion. Edward's thumb traced slow circles over her knuckles, anchoring her.

Silas disembarked next, immediately surrounded by guards. Elin watched as he met with each family, not missing the way guilt clung to him as he consoled them.

She returned her attention to Edward. "Do you see them?"

"No, but I'm sure they're here."

She recalled Edward's stories about his sisters—there were three. The eldest, Elide, was, according to Silas, as tall as Edward. She struggled to imagine it. Then there were the twins, Margot and Willow. They'd been a surprise, as it was believed Edward's mother was past her childbearing years.

Edward squeezed her arm and nodded towards the back of the crowd. "There."

She tracked where he was looking and saw a group of people moving through the crowd.

"Ready?" she asked.

He bent close, a wicked glint in his eye. "It's not often I return with a beautiful woman on my arm."

"I would hope not."

Edward reached for his crutch and faltered. Elin moved instinctively, but he stopped her.

"I've got it." The words came out sharper than intended. Steadying himself, he drew a slow breath, then let it out.

"Actually..." he said, "I could use your help."

She slipped an arm around his back, supporting him as they descended the gangplank together.

They had barely touched the dock when three heads of wild curls barreled towards them—then skidded to a halt, eyes dropping to the cane, the uneven set of Edward's stance.

"I'm all right," he said, pulling them into his arms.

Elin was caught between them, smiling as the twins stared at her with open awe.

"A selkie," one whispered.

A woman and a man pushed through the crowd. They were undoubtedly Edward's parents. Worry and anger radiated from his mother as she neared them. Edward's father bore only surprise and relief.

"You said this was a diplomatic mission," his mother snapped. "What diplomacy costs a leg?"

"A violent one," Edward replied, smiling wide enough to show the dimple in his cheek.

She cupped his face, shaking her head. "My sweet boy."

Then her gaze turned to Elin, and the anger vanished.

"And who," she asked, "have you brought home?"

"As the eldest child of a royal household is reared for the crown, the spare children are reared for other roles. Some are prepared for marriage alliances, leadership positions in their navies, or serving as members of the royal council. In instances where there is only one spare, however, caution is typically taken to rear them to the safest of positions, as in this world, life is precious and easily lost, even to its heirs."

— *The Doctrine of Bloodlines,* housed in the Old Kingdom Library of Sidon

Chapter Twenty-seven

Silas

The iron gates opened before him, groaning under their own weight. Palace guards welcomed him with warm smiles and respectful bows. Behind him, more guards trailed—the rest of his escort. Silas did not expect his family to be waiting for him at the docks. The king and queen's presence would only overshadow the celebration of the sailors' return after so many grueling months at sea. They deserved their moment not only to celebrate the return of their loved ones, but to grieve for those who did not return—for the ones he'd sent into danger.

The courtyard opened before him, cold beneath a pale winter sky. The sun hung low, bright and cold, casting a sharp light that glinted off the ice caught in the joints of stone and the bare twists of ivy clinging to the palace walls. Royal banners hung stiffly, their sage green darkened from the damp. At its center, two crimson mountain peaks were emblazoned, separated by the island's strait. Unfiltered light poured into the open space, striking tall windows and pale stone, making the palace as cold as the mountain face it was carved from.

He used to hate Silvamari winters, but after his time in Frostwake, he doubted he'd ever complain of them again.

As Silas's polished boots met stone, he couldn't help but feel uneasy. Six months. They'd been gone long enough to miss the winter solstice and the ushering in of a new year. It was a long time to live at sea. Twice since leaving the docks, Silas had felt as though the ground were swelling beneath him.

The walk left him too much time to think about where he'd left things with his family.

He'd caught them in a lie, and they expected him not to ask why.

Sunlight fractured through a shard of ice, casting a rainbow of light across Silas's boot. The sight pulled him back to his last conversation with his father.

Dappled light shifted across the palace walls and carpet as they passed portraits of past monarchs.

"Why won't you tell me?" he'd asked.

"We can't." His father's voice cracked. "The more people who know… the more dangerous the information becomes."

Silas frowned. "Does Linden know?"

His father hesitated. "All heirs must, for when they take the crown."

He'd suspected Linden did, but another realization had dawned on him. Sereia might know too.

"All heirs, or only Silvamari? How far does this secret go, Father?"

"Far."

Silas frowned. The secret that cost his parents their peace was one she carried too.

"Silas," his father breathed. "It's important that you let this go."

"How can you ask that of me? I don't even know what I'm letting go of."

Arden laughed bitterly, releasing him. "Be glad of it. Some knowledge is a curse."

"Your Highness." A servant bowed, welcoming Silas as he stepped into the palace. Inside the palace, he was met with warmth and, for the first time in months, tension bled from his shoulders.

"Their Majesties await you in the royal study. This way." The servant gestured for him to follow, though Silas didn't need a guide to traverse his own home. Did they think he'd slip away to his chambers without first meeting with them?

"Thank you." Silas followed the young man through the palace, avoiding the painted stares of his ancestors. He didn't want to know if it was pride or disappointment he'd find there. A set of guards opened the study's doors, allowing him to enter.

Light streamed through the tall windows overlooking the cold waters of the strait. Sunbeams captured the quiet dance of dust motes as they came together and fell apart. It was all Silas could take in before a blur of skirts and blonde hair embraced him in a crushing hug. For a moment, Silas felt more like his brother—unsure how to respond. It had been months since he'd last received a hug like this. He wrapped his arms around his mother, resting his chin on her shoulder.

"Hello, Mother."

She pulled away, brown eyes searching him for injuries. When she found none, her eyes met his. There was warmth and relief, but he didn't fail to notice that the shadows had deepened since he'd been away. His heart clenched, knowing he was at least partially responsible.

"You are well? You were not injured?" she asked, returning to examining him. "How are your ribs?" she reached out to touch where he'd been hurt during a pirate conflict offshore just months before sailing off to Frostwake.

Silas grabbed her wrist and brought her hand to his chest. "I'm back. I'm safe."

Her soft gaze hardened. Silas decided he should have let her fuss over him longer, because here was the welcome he'd been preparing for. She withdrew her hand from his chest.

"I told you not to pursue Hatra." Her voice went flat. "You are not a deckhand who can be easily replaced. You are one of only two princes in Silvamare."

"Mother—"

"Do not 'mother' me, Silas." Her fingers caught his sleeve, tugging hard. "If you die at sea, the stability of our island is at risk."

Silas looked to his older brother; a look of sympathy painted his face. Then, Linden gave him a look that said, *"Do not bring me into this."*

Silas couldn't resist. "Linden, do you have plans to die anytime soon?"

His brother cleared his throat, tugging at his collar. "I don't believe that is her point."

Silas sought his father's support next, who remained in his chair at his desk. King Arden shook his head, refusing to interfere.

"I am sorry to have worried you. Now, would you like to hear about my travels before tomorrow's meeting?"

"You will meet with me for tea every morning for the next week. Only then will I consider your apology."

Closing his eyes, he inhaled deeply because he knew what tea entailed—already his ears bled with the endless chatter of his mother's friends. "I accept my penance."

She beamed at him, hooking his arm in hers. "Good, perhaps my ladies and I can instill some sense into you." Then she led them to the small couch in the sitting area before his father's desk. Linden lounged in a chair across from them.

"So," Linden said, interlacing his fingers as he leaned forward. "Tell us about the adventures of Prince Silas Blackwater."

Silas took a breath and told them of everything that had transpired since he had last left the shores of the Kingdom of Silvamare.

Chapter Twenty-eight

As Silas recounted the events of the last several months, he watched his family's expressions alternate between pride and horror, especially as he recounted the battle at the Black Reef.

"Honestly, son, I didn't expect you to be the one to bring her down. I am incredibly proud of you," Arden said.

"All the credit goes to the crew of the *Maren*."

His father nodded in approval.

"And how is Edward?" his mother asked.

"He will be okay. He's handling his injury better than I would have."

"The *Maren* will need a new lieutenant. We'll plan a ceremony for Edward's retirement, bestowing him with royal honors."

Silas grimaced, not because Edward didn't deserve it, but because it was not something he would want. "Isn't it quick to jump to retiring him? Shouldn't we give him a chance to recover and learn to adapt?"

Linden frowned. "Silas, we shouldn't give him false hope that he'll return. Edward can't be an efficient sailor with his injury."

Silas wanted to argue Edward's capability further, but the point was moot. To change the subject, he asked, "What did I miss while I was away?"

His parents and brother shared a grim look, and Silas knew they too had grave news.

Every spring, priests from Drakcultus come to oversee the rites of the Black Tide. When the Tide passes, the most devout return with them on pilgrimage to the temples of Drakcultus. For generations, the pilgrims had always come home.

But the ones who left after last year's Tide never returned.

"I don't understand," said Silas. "What reason does he have to do so? What are we doing about this?"

"Talon claims we sent them to serve as spies and--" His father pressed his thumbs to his eyes. During Silas's absence, the grey at his father's temples had spread until scarcely any black remained.

"And?" Silas asked.

"As assassins." Linden finished. "According to Talon, a Silvamari pilgrim attempted to assassinate Princess Sereia."

It wasn't the political ramifications that left Silas feeling cold one moment and hot the next. *Attempted*, he told himself. Attempted means they failed. He'd been worried something would happen to him before he could tell her his truth, but he hadn't considered that something might happen to her. He should have. It wasn't the first attempt on her life. Since her prophecy spread, many have wished to see her dead—better that than an uncertain future.

"Is she okay?" Silas asked, praying to gods who had never cared before that she was.

"She's an Araceli," his mother said. "Even without elemental abilities, she can hold her own."

"So she killed her attacker?" It was her greatest fear that she might someday take another's life. He needed to write to her—to see her.

"No," Linden said, suppressing a shiver. "It was one of her guards. His remains were returned to us as a pile of ashes."

Greer then, Silas decided. "So he's keeping our pilgrims in hopes that we what?"

"We are keeping his wind-wielders as prisoners of our own until he releases them."

Silas gripped his armrest to keep himself from standing. "We're what?"

"It's our only leverage," his father explained.

"Those men fight and bleed beside us. Perry--"

"Stop thinking with your heart, Silas." His father rose from his desk, his temper flaring. "Despite what you might think, we have the kingdom's best interests at heart. Politics goes beyond personal relationships."

"Politics is only about relationships." Silas countered. "Sereia is not Talon. We can ask for her assistance."

Arden laughed. "Sereia is a lovely girl, but you and I both know she is a threat to Talon. He keeps her out of the kingdom's affairs. I am not even sure if they speak to each other."

"I can at least try. She can try. We need Drakcultus's wind-wielders to feel safe with us. What if we need them again? How can we expect their help when their trust has been broken? This will permanently harm the relationship between our kingdoms."

"Talon should have considered that before imprisoning our people. There's no evidence that Sereia's attacker was even one of ours."

"Silas could marry her," Linden proposed.

"No," his mother said.

Silas shifted beside her. Until now, she'd remained quiet. "Drakcultus is an ally out of necessity. Talon can't be trusted, and however fond of Sereia you—any of us—might be, we can't trust her either."

It was then that Silas realized an uncomfortable truth. Despite his mother's claim, he trusted Sereia more than any of them. He had thought little about the secret his family sheltered while he was away, but now that he had returned home, it buzzed in his ear like an insect. He could swat it away, but it would always return until he squashed it. How might he trust his family if they would not trust him?

He'd promised not to press the subject, but now he found it was all he wanted to do. He needed to find a way to slip out, to excuse himself.

His mother was speaking, but he had not heard her. She placed a gentle hand on his arm.

"Hmm?" he asked, returning his focus to the people in the room.

"I said you are pale," she said. "Are you well?"

"Only tired, mother," he sighed. "I hope you don't mind, but I think

I'll go rest."

"Not at all," she patted his cheek.

"We can have dinner sent to your chambers tonight," his father offered.

"Thank you," he said, bowing to them before exiting the room.

Memories prickled at Silas like the itch of sweat on a humid summer day; they left him sticky and warm. He thought of the night before the last Tide, of a conversation they'd shared when his father had one too many.

"There's no sense in borrowing tomorrow's troubles when a monster already laps at our shores."

"A monster?" he asked.

"God. Monster. What does it matter? A deal's a deal," his father had said.

He hadn't been sure that there was a secret then. It was his parents' reaction to his questioning that gave them away—the tension in his mother's voice as she intervened in the conversation, his father's averted eyes. The more Silas pressed them both, the clearer it became until his father confirmed it before his departure to Frostwake.

Silas could tell they wanted to share it, but also sought to protect him. Protect him from what? How was the truth any worse than the reality they faced each year as the sea god demanded their souls?

A more recent memory surfaced, and Silas could almost feel the stifling heat of the room, smell the burning flesh and fur, hear the clash of metal.

"I'm not the villain here, Your Highness," Hatra had claimed. "At least I'm no worse than the kings and queens feeding their people to a monster of the sea."

Had Hatra known the truth of the secret Aquerios's leadership kept? If she did, how? Had she learned some hidden truth about the sea god and refused to take part?

Would he go mad from not knowing? He didn't know. He knew only that in a few short months he'd see Sereia again, and he prayed—no, hoped she'd tell him. Why bother praying when no one was listening?

The walk to his chambers seemed to take ages, and he breathed a sigh of relief as he opened the doors and took in the familiar space. It was just as he had left it.

He walked straight to his desk, where he found 6 letters stacked, each from Sereia. He smiled, pleased that she had granted his wish as he picked up the stack and carried it to his bed, where he dropped onto the mattress.

He opened the most recent letter and read.

Silas,

I don't quite know what I meant to write. My hand simply found the pen, and before I could think, your name was inked across the page as though it had been waiting for me. I miss hearing from you. I hope you are safe, wherever the gods have sent you, and that your mission is bringing you purpose, if not peace.

Your last letter frightened me. I cannot imagine a world where I am not waiting for your next words, whether they come folded in parchment or spoken beside me on some sunlit shore during a spring day.

I was attacked recently. The man was unskilled and weak with fire. I disarmed him easily, yet I could not kill him. Anyone else would have done so; it would have been expected, but I could not. It was a foolish decision; perhaps it will be the death of me someday. He called me a monster, as many believe I am, though what have I truly done to deserve such a title? My only crime is the words spoken upon another's lips.

Greer took it upon herself to show him whose flame burns hotter—she won, of course.

My father has imprisoned the Silvamari pilgrims. I tried to tell him that the crime of one shouldn't condemn the whole. He will not speak to me on the matter, nor listen. I'm sorry. I pray it's resolved before spring, and that you'll return before then, too. If only I could travel, even once. Perhaps I'd find you.

Or perhaps I would vanish into the world as someone unremarkable, unfeared. Maybe I'd find another lonely soul, and we'd disappear together.

Foolish imaginings, I know.

I have no such freedom. Only these letters, and the bit of happiness they grant me.

Write soon.

Yours,

Sereia Gaiano

It seems she'd already tried to help without anyone asking it of her. Should he have expected any less?

He reminded himself of the promise he'd made himself before leaving Frostwake. He'd decided to make his feelings known to Sereia. Something he still meant to do, but the situation between their kingdoms was now strained, and then there was the matter of the secret everyone seemed to keep buried under immovable stone.

Would she share it with him if he asked? Was their relationship worth burdening in his quest for a hidden truth?

If the roles were reversed, he was certain he would tell her what she wished to know. He set down the letter and spent the rest of his night reading the ones that remained, eager for their meeting, now only weeks away.

"**An** isolated emergence of plague has afflicted the easternmost region of Drakcultus. Implementing the procedures recommended by the Governess of Health in the Old Kingdom of Sidon, Drakcultus effectively contained the disease, preventing an outbreak. Such action is especially important, as any major loss of population will jeopardize the outcome of the annual Tide."

—*Outbreak of Disease Log*, Old Kingdom of Sidon, Department of Health

Chapter Twenty-nine

Elin

Silvamare revealed itself to Elin slowly, unfolding in quiet moments—the smell of salt and pine carried on the wind, the steady rhythm of waves against a rocky shore, the way light caught on the bare spines of climbing ivy, then dripped from the budding leaves as spring crept in.

She took up a small room in Howie's home along the strait, where fishing boats passed close enough that she could hear the creak of their hulls and the indistinct murmur of voices carried over the water. Her mornings still started off with the familiar cry of gulls, a constant she believed she'd find anywhere in Aquerios. Some days, Howie took her fishing, and she'd complain that it was easier as a seal.

During those times, she often thought of her father and the letter she'd yet to write. One night, as she tossed and turned with thoughts of her father and what he might think of her disappearance, she finally knew what she wanted to say.

Papa,

This letter is long overdue, and I am sorry. Sorry for leaving without a word. Sorry for leaving you and Mama to deal with the loss of Anik on your own.

I could not bear to stay after Anik died. I knew there was nothing that wouldn't remind me of him. I did not know how to live with it, not until I found something to fight for.

The Butcher of the Black Reef is dead by my hand. I thought vengeance would fix what was broken, but of course it could not. Though I remain full of grief, I'm learning to live with it, and I am satisfied in knowing Ivan will hurt no one else.

I think I will remain with the Silvamari Navy. There is still work to be done. Too many people in this world take and take until nothing remains. But that is not the only reason I want to stay.

I have done something foolish, Papa. I have fallen in love.

I swore I never would after watching what Mama's absence did to you. I was afraid love only gave the sea another way to wound us.

But the sea cannot call me away any longer.

And maybe loving someone means accepting that one day they may break your heart or be taken from you. Maybe it means knowing that and loving them anyway. I don't know if I will ever stop being afraid of that. But I cannot spend my life running away from love simply because it may end in grief.

I have come to learn that surviving is not the same thing as living. I hope you come to the same understanding.

Love Mama while she is near. Love her while she is gone. But love yourself enough to keep living, too.

I love you.

Your little seal,

Elin

Evenings were most often spent at Edward's family table. The meals stretched long into the night, punctuated by laughter, stories spoken over one another, and plates refilled before Elin could declare she was full. She listened more than she spoke and watched how Edward leaned back in his chair when he laughed, and the way his family cared for him. Here, he seemed lighter, more himself, as if all his layers had been stripped away.

At first, Edward relied on his crutches. On harder days, he used a chair, and while he never said it, she knew those days were hard beyond the physical.

One afternoon, he removed his prosthetic and tossed it aside with more force than necessary. "Something that used to be nothing is now—" He scrubbed a hand over his face. "It takes everything out of me."

He didn't look at her. Just stared at the prosthetic on the floor.

Elin stepped closer, careful of the space he needed, and rested her hand lightly against his arm. "I know," she said quietly. "And I hate that for you."

His hand hovered for a moment before reaching for hers, lacing his fingers with hers.

Elin learned the signs—when his shoulders stiffened, when his smile tightened—and when to offer help or step back. Over time, different prosthetics appeared, some abandoned after a few days, others adjusted and refined as Edward and his father, Thomas, tested what would give him the most freedom.

When Edward felt strong enough, he showed her Silvamare as if introducing her to an old friend. They walked coastal paths where the sea broke against the rocks, wandered through market squares fragrant with produce and smoked meats, and traced the edges of the forest where the trees grew dense and dark. Their outings were unhurried, built on conversation and shared silences. Somewhere in those wandering days Elin realized she had begun to see the island not as a place she lived, but somewhere she was beginning to belong.

Days slipped into one another, marked by naval patrols, meals, and outings. Elin found herself settling into the rhythm of her new life with little effort. Comfort and peace had taken root in her. It unsettled her how easily it came.

It was easy in those early weeks to believe that this peace might last.

The *Maren* cut along the shoreline, its hull parting the water with a low, rhythmic hiss. The coast rose and fell beside them—stone cliffs giving way to narrow beaches before climbing again into forested hills. Wind snapped at the sails as Howie steered with ease, his attention fixed forward.

Elin stood near the rail with Silas. He'd been quiet since they left the harbor, though that wasn't unusual for the prince.

His gaze kept drifting towards the water, lingering there as though partaking in a silent conversation.

Elin leaned her forearms against the rail, watching the dark shapes move beneath the surface. "You've been staring at the sea like it owes you an answer," she said at last.

Silas blinked, as if pulled back from his thoughts. "It does," he said. Then, after a moment, "What does Frostwake believe about the sea god?"

She turned to look at him. "That depends on who you ask."

Silas angled towards her, curiosity sharpening his expression. "Explain."

"Most people think the sea belongs solely to the god," Elin said. "That it's his domain and his hunger, therefore it's his mercy we must ask for." She shrugged. "But selkie lore is...different."

The ship rolled beneath them as she chewed on her lip. "In our stories," she continued, "the sea isn't only *his*. It's also the Mother's. A living force that births us, carries us, and takes us back when it must." Her fingers tightened briefly on the rail. "It's hard to explain. I don't know that I believe it myself."

"A god and a mother," Silas murmured. "That seems...at odds."

"Terron isn't the only creator of life. Cosmir made the amphipteres, the sea god," she tilted her head, "the leviathans. Are the two really so at odds?"

Silas's gaze drifted back to the water.

"In Frostwake," she went on, "we understand the sea is full of spirits. The Sluagh, for instance—water spirits. Perhaps those beliefs are left over from before—before the Tide, before the death of the drakes, the merfolk..." She inhaled slowly, wondering how long until the selkies joined that list.

"It's hard to reconcile the sea god as the creator of anything," Silas replied.

The wind filled the brief silence that followed, snapping the sail and carrying the cry of a distant seabird.

Elin smiled sadly at him as they stood side by side, watching the coastline slide past, the sea stretching endlessly beyond it. News of pirate activity all but ceased after they'd cut down Hatra, but there were still crews out there.

"You don't stay down," Silas said after a time. "It's inspiring."

Elin let out a soft breath that might have been a laugh. "Well, when you fall, you're only left with two choices."

Silas studied her, understanding settling into his expression. "It's no wonder you and Edward suit one another."

"He misses you," Elin said without hesitation. "He's doing well. Some days are harder than others, but he's adapting." She paused. "He gets frustrated when he needs help, but he's learning when to accept it."

Silas nodded, gaze distant again.

After a moment, Elin asked. "How does it work here? When the Tide comes."

Silas exhaled slowly. "On the day, names are drawn across the island. Those chosen are assigned guards. Their sacrifice is celebrated," he winced at the word. "There's a feast." His mouth tightened. "Afterwards, they're brought to a preparation hall. Given a draft, much like the one the rest of the island takes to block out the Tide's call."

"And then?" Elin asked.

"Their bodies are laid along the outer shorelines," Silas said. "They sleep through it, just as they do anywhere else."

Elin closed her eyes, the roll of the ship beneath her suddenly too present.

"It's different in Frostwake. They still get the draft, but you don't know it's you before you're taken. The chief draws the names in private, then orders the warriors to gather the sacrifices. Their unconscious bodies are left tied to stakes on the shore while the rest of us move inland and pray that it was enough."

When she opened them again, she was staring down at the water, watching it ebb endlessly.

"You know then," Silas asked. "That Frostwake is on the brink of collapse."

"Of course I know. The sea god does not give second chances. The year Frostwake cannot meet *his* demands...will be the year of its end. I read in the paper that Frostwake survived this year with Silvamare's assistance. Where did the souls come from?" she asked.

Silas rubbed the scruff on his neck. "We emptied our prisons. We'll have to call on more innocents this year to make up for it. It will buy Frostwake time, but we cannot sustain it forever."

Elin's heart weighed heavily in her chest, wishing she could slip beneath the waves and forget her troubles. "I have not heard from my father," she admitted. "I do not know if he was spared from this year's Tide."

"I can try to find out for you," Silas offered. "Though it might take a while."

"Thank you," she said, tapping her fingers along the *Maren's* repaired rail. Silvamare's Tide was only months away. The promise of summer had once filled her with joy. In Frostwake, it was a promise of warmth and life. Wetlands buried under months of snow blossomed with flowers and whispering grasses. Animals came out of the forests, with their babies in tow. But now, summer loomed over her like a noose, threatening people she'd grown to love.

As the ship continued its patrol, the sea stretching wide and unknowable beside them, Elin found herself wondering—without knowing why the thought cut so much deeper than before—who would be spared and who would be damned.

"In all my time, I have found but a single cure for an affliction of the soul, one which can kill as well as it may heal, and that is love."

— *Musings of a Fisherman,* Second Edition, incomplete

Chapter Thirty

Elin had been told to dress for a hike.

She stood just outside Edward's family cottage, tightening the laces of her boots for the third time, her nerves alive beneath her skin. A hike. With Edward. She tried not to let the word spiral into concerns she didn't want to voice.

Edward noticed anyway.

"It isn't strenuous," he assured her as he adjusted the pack slung over his shoulder. His newest prosthetic was fitted snugly beneath his trousers, an improvement from the last, offering him greater movement and endurance. Still, she worried. "I promise. I just want to show you something. It's my favorite place on the island, and this is the best time of year to see it."

Elin told herself not to think too hard about what being alone with him might mean. She searched his face, then nodded. "All right."

He smiled, relief softening his expression. "Good."

Heidi pressed a basket into Elin's hands before they could leave. "You'll need this," she said, eyes alight. "Eat well."

"Thank you," Elin said, a little surprised.

Behind her, Heidi's daughters dissolved into giggles and darted away down the hall as soon as Elin looked at them.

Elin paused, glancing between them and Edward. "Why are they acting like that?"

Edward frowned, then shrugged. "I've long since accepted that the inner workings of the female mind are a mystery I was not meant to solve."

She laughed despite herself, rolling her eyes as she stepped past him.

The trail wound upward through pine and ivy, the ground soft beneath their boots. The air was cool and clean; the sky stretched pale blue overhead. Edward remained steady as they walked, and Elin relaxed as the path unfolded before them.

They talked as they climbed—about nothing and everything. About the absurd, about Howie's stubborn refusal to retire, and which of Heidi's dishes Elin liked best and why Edward would forever defend the one she found unbearable.

When Edward slowed, she noticed at once.

"Do you need to stop?" she asked.

"Just a moment," he said, already lowering himself onto a sun-warmed stone. "This thing's clever, but it still likes to remind me who's in charge."

She knelt beside him as he adjusted the straps, fumbling with a clasp. Elin reached out to help, and their hands brushed. It had been a while since they were last alone. They'd stolen quiet moments here and there, but they never lasted. There was always one interruption or another.

"You're doing better," she said softly.

He looked up at her, his expression softening. "I am. Though it's hard to admit my limits," he said. "And how much I hate having them."

Elin squeezed his hand gently. He reached for her, pulling her in for a kiss. It was gentle and familiar, but it made something in her chest tighten, a fear that she was claiming something she couldn't keep. When they parted, Elin rested her forehead against his, breathing him in.

"Ready?" he asked.

She nodded.

The trail opened; the trees thinned until the land became a wide, open valley.

Elin stopped short.

Grasses rippled in the breeze, silver-green beneath the light, and thousands of wildflowers dotted the field beyond—white and pale blue, delicate and determined, stretching as far as she could see. A narrow path cut through the valley, winding towards distant peaks dusted with frost. The sky above was impossibly clear.

"It's... stunning," she breathed.

She turned back to him—and stilled, her breath hitching. The world narrowed on him, kneeling in the grass with a small silver band between his fingers.

"Elin," he said, voice steady despite the emotion in his eyes. "We've both learned the hard way that time is a gift. I don't want to waste any more of it without you by my side. Will you marry me?"

For a heartbeat, she could only stare at him, the valley blurring at the edges of her vision. She couldn't have this. Old fears rose unbidden. She was born for leaving, a creature destined to be called away. No, that was not who she was, not anymore. She could have this. She would stay.

Dropping to her knees before him, she said, "Yes." The word tumbled from her again and again. "Yes."

His smile brightened as he slid the ring onto her finger, the silver cool against her skin.

"How soon can we—" she began breathlessly.

"As soon as possible," he said, not letting her finish.

She laughed, the sound breaking into a joyful cry as she leaned into him, arms wrapping around his neck. The valley stretched around them, endless and alive, and for a moment it felt as if the world had paused to bear witness.

Elin cupped the nape of his neck, pulling his mouth to hers. This time, when they kissed, she readily leapt from the cliff, falling into the breathless, weightless moment before the plunge.

The world could fall into chaos around them, and they wouldn't know because here and now, the world was only made of them.

They sank into the grass together, laughter dissolving into breathless quiet. Edward's hands were warm and steady—anchoring, even here— and Elin let herself drift into it, into the strange, terrifying peace of being held without needing to brace for the impact.

Wind rushed through the grasses, low and constant, as she met the plunge.

When she came apart, it felt like surfacing after a long submersion—lungs burning, heart racing, the world rushing back too fast, too bright.

"I love you," she said, the words spilling out of her.

Edward pressed his forehead to hers, breath trembling above her. "I love you."

They lay tangled in the grass as the sky deepened and stars pricked awake overhead. Edward brushed twigs from her hair as she traced idle patterns over his chest, grounding herself in the truth of him.

She'd lose her pelt a thousand times if it always led her here.

Because there was no place on land or sea that felt more like home than Edward Graves.

And for the first time in a long while, Elin knew—without doubt—that she was happy. Even if some part of her was still waiting for it to be taken away.

Chapter Thirty-one

The next day, when they returned from their hike, Elin and Edward were met by an unabashed gaggle of girls, eager to confirm what they already suspected—that they were gaining a sister. Laughing, they announced they would marry as soon as possible. From there, plans moved quickly. Too quickly, some part of Elin thought.

The days that followed blurred together in a flurry of movement. Elin helped gather flowers, which stained her hands green and left them sticky with sap. Heidi helped her with her gown, measuring and making adjustments. Edward's sisters argued over ribbons and seating, while neighbors appeared with offerings of bread, wine, garlands, and congratulations.

She found herself momentarily frozen, a silent observer as flowers found vases, voices mingled, and laughter chimed around her, as though she were witnessing a life that hadn't yet become hers.

Before she knew it, she was standing before a mirror, scarcely recognizing herself.

Her hair had grown out, silver waves falling to the middle of her back. The front pieces were drawn away from her face in a series of neat braids. The gown had once belonged to Heidi and had been altered to fit her frame. Layers of gauze fell around her, lace sleeves ending at her wrists, a modest train that whispered against the floor when she shifted her weight.

She twisted the bracelet of braided silver hair around her wrist, her excitement tangled with something fragile. Fear crept in, cold and familiar. What if something was already gathering, waiting to reclaim her pain—waiting to remind her that nothing this good was ever allowed to last?

What was the price she would be asked to pay?

She lifted her hand to her cheek, half-expecting it to pass through her, as though this moment were nothing more than a dream. Instead, her fingers met warm, solid flesh. A quiet sigh of relief escaped her.

She turned towards the window. Sunlight streamed in, catching on her selkie markings. The silver flecks at her temples shimmered, alive beneath the light.

Her thoughts drifted to her parents. She had written to them shortly after her arrival, telling them where she had gone and what she had done. What they thought of it, she did not know. Perhaps the letter had not yet reached Frostwake. Perhaps their reply was still on its way. She tried not to linger on the third possibility—that they had chosen not to answer at all.

The creak of the bedroom door pulled her from her thoughts. Heidi stepped inside and smiled at the sight of her.

"You look beautiful," she said.

Then she noticed Elin's expression.

Heidi crossed the room at once, concern softening her voice. "What is it?" she asked. "Is this too soon? Too fast?"

"No—no, it's not that," Elin said. "It's the opposite, actually."

"I don't think I understand."

Elin reached for her bracelet, twisting the band around her wrist. "I've always had this feeling," she said, choosing her words with care, "that I'm running out of time. Like I was born holding my breath. It's like I've been swimming against an invisible current, trying to outrun something." She let out a quiet laugh. "Fate, maybe."

Heidi studied her for a moment. "You have been through a great deal, Elin. Anyone would be nervous before their wedding. I was." She smiled faintly. "And I've seen you and Edward together. I've never known a better match. For a long time, I wasn't sure there was anyone else for Edward. Not after—"

"After Cassidy," Elin finished.

Heidi nodded. "I choose to believe the gods have their reasons," she said. "That there is purpose, even when we cannot see it. There is enough darkness in this world to blot out the sun. Let us not allow it to take hold when light manages to break through."

Elin hadn't realized she was crying until Heidi brushed a tear from her cheek.

"Thank you," Elin whispered.

"There's no need," Heidi said.

A knock sounded at the door, and Silas stepped inside. His smile was bright, unmistakably relieved. He was leaving the next morning for the spring congregation in Silvamare and feared he'd miss the wedding.

"Heidi, can I have just one moment alone with Elin?" Silas asked.

Elin's skin cooled. Heidi looked between her and Silas. "I'll see you outside," Heidi said.

Elin gave her a tight smile as Heidi turned and left the room.

"I'm sorry about the timing, but I have news about your father," Silas said, stepping further into the room. She waited for him to continue.

"He is fine; so is your mother. The villages had to restructure after this year's Tide. It is why you haven't heard from them yet. I made sure they know where you are and that you're safe."

Relief flooded her. "Thank you," she said, hugging Silas. "Thank you for doing that for me."

"I would do anything for you," he said. "And for Edward."

She gave him a watery smile.

"Are you ready?" he asked.

"Yes," she said, meaning it. She had never wanted anything more.

Slipping her arm through Silas's, they stepped out of the cottage.

Beneath the wisteria—now heavy with flowers—Edward's sisters and father waited, already seated. At the base of the tree stood Edward, with Howie beside him. Edward stood tall, shoulders squared, his expression open and radiant.

His warmth hit her before she reached him. Joy poured from him so freely that Elin felt her remaining worries loosen their grip. For this moment, she was willing to believe this was only the first of many happy days to come.

She hadn't been prepared for this. Emotions came from every direction at once. Margot and Willow's joy was bright like summer light, a wonder that hadn't yet learned to protect itself. Howie's was gruff and tender, the warmth of a man who loved deeply.

She was walking through the most concentrated warmth she had ever encountered from a group of people, and it was almost too much—overwhelming in the way standing too close to a fire was overwhelming, the way you wanted to step back even as you're tempted to lean in.

As they neared Edward, Silas delivered her into his waiting presence, then stepped away to join the family.

Elin met Edward's warm gaze and placed her hands in his. He looked down at her, expression open and eyes bright. His hands trembled around hers.

Howie's eyes crinkled as he smiled, welcoming their small audience.

Elin tightened her grip on Edward's hands and held fast to the warmth between them, determined to remember this moment—every breath—no matter what the future demanded.

Edward licked his lips, then took a shaky breath. His eyes crinkled when he smiled at her, and her heart leapt. With him, she wanted to believe they could stand strong against the world—wanted to believe nothing could keep them apart.

When Howie proclaimed their marriage, Edward rushed to pull her close and kissed her as she laughed. All this time, she'd feared where fate would bring her, but fate had brought her to him. And with him, she was safe.

That night, she lay awake long after the candle had gone out. The cottage was quiet. Outside, branches moved against the window in the light breeze off the strait. Beside her, Edward's breathing had slowed into the rhythm of sleep.

She stared at the ceiling, thinking about the version of herself who had stood in Edward's room on the *Maren*, telling him it would be a mistake to love her. Who had believed that she was built for leaving. Who pushed him away and ran because she was too scared to risk love.

So much time she wasted fighting the inevitable. In the dark, she turned towards Edward. He lay on his side, the expanse of his back facing her. She moved closer, trailing her palms across his skin, before kissing the curve of his neck and whispered, "I love you."

The rustling of leaves filled the quiet as she pressed another kiss to his shoulder.

Then Edward turned toward her, silently gathering her against him. His arms came around her, and he pressed a kiss to her hair. His breath warmed her ear, and he whispered, "You don't know the half of it."

He nipped at her softly, and she arched into him, her body flushing hot. "Can't sleep?" he laughed breathily.

"No," she said, brushing her lips against his. She felt his smile before he shifted above her, propping himself on his forearms. His brow furrowed as he took her in, his expression at odds with the blooming warmth she felt from him.

"What is it?" she asked, bringing a hand to her cheek.

He reached for her hand and brought it to his lips. "Nothing," he said, pressing a kiss to her knuckles. He never looked away, as if blinking might make what he was seeing disappear. "I have never seen you look as you do now."

Raising a brow, she said, "Tired? That can't be true."

Edward shook his head. Then reached down, brushing silver strands from her face. "No. Soft."

He pressed a kiss to her temple. "It's called happy," she said, as he moved to her cheek. "I am happy."

His hot breath caressed her neck before he ran his teeth against the delicate skin where her neck met her shoulder. Her breath hitched. "You," she whispered. "Make me happy."

Edward made a pleased sound. She laughed quietly into the warmth of him. Later, when his breathing finally slowed and the breeze had stopped, she lay with her head on his chest and listened to his heart. She fell asleep to its steady rhythm.

"**Like** every sailor before, my first love was the sea, followed by a creature birthed from its depths, and my heart died with the last breath of my greatest love born of a passionate dalliance. One should be so lucky to love and lose and find once more the embrace of open arms and hearts. One does not require a life of absence if they don't wish it."

— *Musings from a Fisherman,* from *A Collection,* gifted to the Royal Library of Silvamare

Chapter Thirty-two

Silas

Silas traveled to Drakcultus for the annual spring congregation as he had for years, though the honor was not technically his to bear. It should have been Linden's, but his brother had never taken to ships or open water, leaving Silas to fill the role.

The voyage became a bright spot in his year. He knew the currents of the Silver Sea as well as the inflections of Drakcultian speech. He spoke their language fluently—along with several others—and had spent enough time in foreign courts to understand when a pause meant caution and when it meant deception. His father trusted him in negotiations, allowed him to sit in on trade discussions, and sometimes even deferred to him, as this would be his responsibility when Linden took the throne.

The Silver Sea lived up to its name the week before their arrival—its waters stretched wide and bright, smooth as beaten metal beneath the sun. As a younger man, Silas had stood at the rail and watched the light fracture across its surface in distorted reflections of the sky above.

The wind favored them from the start of their journey. Perry wielded the wind with a proficiency far greater than when they'd first met. They made excellent time.

When the pale cliffs of Drakcultus broke the horizon—days before expected—he felt the familiar tension in his chest.

Soon, he'd be reunited with Sereia.

In Drakcultus, they were received in the King's study overlooking the sea. It provided a glimpse of the palace garden; there, people walked the stone paths, disappearing and reappearing behind the blooming flora.

They exchanged pleasantries before getting to the real purpose of their meeting. Together, they discussed current and proposed trade agreements and projected yields before their conversation moved to a topic both kings had avoided.

"I apologize; I was forced to detain the pilgrims. Surely you understand I had my daughter's safety and the stability of my reign to consider," Talon said. "Those are matters that require caution."

Arden inclined his head. "Of course. You have my assurance that Silvamare will implement stricter screening before this summer's pilgrimage. And I thank you for returning my people in good faith." News reached them the day of Edward and Elin's wedding that the pilgrim's ship was just days away. Silas thought the timing was pertinent to the success of this year's meeting.

Once more, the conversation shifted.

Talon turned his attention to Silas. "I must congratulate you on neutralizing the Hatra threat," he said, voice heavy with appraisal. "Your kingdom must be very proud."
Silas bowed. "The credit goes to our Navy, Your Majesty, and to the wind-wielders who assisted us. Perry, in particular, proved indispensable in the capture."

Talon smiled, surprise almost breaking through his otherwise neutral expression.

"As a gesture of continued goodwill," Talon said, "Perry may remain with your fleet. Consider him a permanent attachment." His gaze narrowed on Arden. "Have you uncovered how Hatra captured the *Leviathan?*"

"We have not," Arden replied. "She left no Silvamari prisoners, and the crew we managed to capture refuse to speak."

"There are ways to persuade men," Talon said.

"There is a matter left undiscussed from our last exchange," Arden said, glancing toward Silas. "Now is a better time than any to address it, lest it be brushed aside once more."

"You are free to explore the palace," Talon told Silas, gesturing towards the door in dismissal.

He inclined his head. "Your Majesty, might I inquire about the whereabouts of Princess Sereia?"

Talon's brow lifted, incredulous.

"Forgive me," Silas bowed before taking his leave beneath the weight of the king's gaze.

He knew only fragments of the palace. A corridor to the council chamber. A gallery that overlooked the harbor. The outer gardens. Beyond that, Drakcultus's palace remained a maze of carved stone and narrow passageways unfamiliar to him.

He was not permitted to wander alone.

Two Silvamari guards followed at a respectful distance. Two Drakcultian soldiers shadowed them just as closely. It was a false courtesy; the Drakcultian guards were supervising.

He attempted confidence anyway, choosing turns as though he remembered them. Sunlight filtered through high, narrow windows as he passed murals depicting the gods: Cosmir crowned in light, Terron carved into mountains, the Tide's retreat.

After walking several corridors and one descending stair, he realized—with irritation—that he had made an unintentional loop.

Once more outside the heavy doors of Talon's private study, voices carried through the stone, tight and aggravated.

He should have continued walking. Instead, he slowed down.

"...they deserve to know," his father said.

A sharper voice answered. "I told you before—"

Silas caught only fragments after that. Words too muffled by distance and thick doors. *Tide. Sacrifice. Danger.* Then—

"You would doom us all."

The statement cut through the air, causing him to still.

One of the Drakcultian guards shifted. "Prince," he said, a subtle but unmistakable prompt.

Silas resumed walking. By the time they reached the next turn, he had lost any appetite for exploration within stone walls. To his right were doors open to the outside.

"I will take to the gardens," he said, more to the air than to his escorts.

The guards followed as he walked the winding path through manicured terraces and flowering shrubs until the palace gave way to warmth and open sky. The sea stretched wide and blue beyond the last steps. He descended towards the shore where the sand ran gold and soft beneath the sun.

The air was fresh here—salted and breezy, perfumed from the garden nearby.

He exhaled slowly, tension loosening in his chest.

Whatever argument boiled behind those doors, he'd not been meant to hear it.

Standing on the shore, the tide curled in gentle, harmless ribbons around his boots. Drakcultus rose behind him in pale stone and gleaming spires, and yet the words from the corridor would not release him.

Tide. God.

They deserve to know. You would doom us all.

He replayed them in fragments, trying to stitch together the meaning, growing more certain they were discussing the secret. He longed to know what his father's intentions were.

Had he challenged the withholding of its knowledge?

Talon almost sounded frightened. What made the secret so dangerous that it warranted such a warning?

Silas rubbed his face, fatigue settling in behind his eyes. A sound carried over the surf, bright and unrestrained.

A laugh.

Silas turned towards the sound. Three figures made their way down the garden path towards the beach, the sun flashing off fair skin and dark hair. He recognized them immediately.

Sereia walked in the center. She and Greer were shoving one another, shoulders colliding in playful offense. Callum followed a few paces behind, watchful as ever, his posture relaxed, but his eyes scanned their surroundings carefully.

Greer gave Sereia another playful shove—harder this time. Sereia staggered, nearly losing her footing in the sand.

Silas expected her to stop. Instead, Sereia launched herself forward, hitting Greer in the middle. The two of them went down in a tangle of limbs and laughter, sand flying in golden arcs.

It ended with Sereia pinned in the sand, Greer grinning above her in triumph.

Sereia only laughed. Then she looked up towards the shore, eyes widening as she found him. The smile that broke across her face was unguarded and incandescent—it stole his breath.

Greer released her, and Sereia wasted no time. She crossed the sand in quick strides and threw her arms around Silas's neck.

He stilled in surprise—hands hovering as though uncertain where they belonged. Then instinct overtook hesitation, and he held her close.

When she pulled back, her cheeks were flushed a vivid pink. Silas had never seen her like this—unguarded, almost giddy. Her shoulders lacked their usual rigidity. Her movements appeared light, unmoored, as though she were close to floating.

"Sorry," she said, pressing her fingers to her mouth to contain a laugh that escaped anyway. "I—I wasn't expecting you today."

She attempted composure.

He watched the effort with quiet bewilderment as she straightened her spine and lifted her chin, arranging her features into something more befitting a princess of Drakcultus. It was a valiant attempt.

It failed.

Sand clung to the loosened strands of her black hair, which had fallen free of its braid. She wore black trousers and a loose white shirt, sleeves rolled carelessly at the forearm—dressed for practicality, not ceremony. Her pale skin, almost luminous beneath the sun, gleamed with heat and exertion.

But it was her eyes that unsettled him. Her pupils were wide despite the glare, and there was a looseness to her movements Silas had never seen before. The corner of her mouth kept twitching upward, as though her smile was threatening to slip free again.

"Sereia," he said, studying her face. "Are you well?"

"I am splendid," Sereia declared, chin lifting with theatrical dignity. "Most especially since my company has improved so handsomely."

Silas regarded her with open bemusement.

Greer and Callum reached them. Callum alone wore armor, dark steel catching the sun. He inclined his head, composed as ever. Greer, by contrast, looked unrepentant.

Sereia and Greer exchanged a glance—quick and conspiratorial.

Callum sighed. "Prince Silas," he said, "what a pleasant surprise. You may have observed that my cousin is...somewhat liberated from her usual decorum."

Greer's mouth twitched.

Callum continued dryly, "Greer's concern for Sereia's recent solemnity compelled her to acquire a quantity of ceremonial herbs from Adoratia. Purely for scholarly testing, of course."

Silas stared at them. Understanding dawned on him.

Slowly, his gaze shifted to Greer.

Her smile was both radiant and feral. She was beautiful in a fierce way, sharp and wild. Silas resisted the instinct to give ground when she leaned closer.

"I can confirm," she murmured conspiratorially, "that it is an exceptional harvest."

Behind her, Sereia lifted the back of her hand to her mouth, unsuccessfully suppressing a grin. "I do apologize," she said, attempting gravity and achieving none. "I am not entirely myself. And I did not expect you for several more days."

"The winds favored us," Silas replied. "And you need not apologize for finding a moment of unguarded pleasure. I, for one, am quite glad to have found you this way."

Her smile deepened. "Then Terron himself must have arranged it," Sereia declared, slipping her arm boldly through his. "We were about to walk along the shoreline. You will join us."

It was not a question.

"I would be honored," he said.

They walked the length of the shoreline until the sun tilted westward and the gold of the sand softened into amber. Somewhere along the way, the brightness in Sereia's eyes gentled. The last traces of the herbs faded, leaving her movements steadier, her smile more deliberate.

Greer, meanwhile, had returned to herself entirely, regarding Silas once more as if assessing livestock—cool, appraising, faintly amused. He pretended not to notice. After a moment, her attention shifted to Callum instead, who bore it with stoic endurance. Even in conversation, Callum's gaze never stilled. His head turned incrementally, tracking the horizon, the palace walls, and the guards stationed along the grounds. Vigilance was second nature to him.

Silas spoke of his travels, sparing them the more brutal details.

"I am glad you are well," Sereia said when he finished. "And that you are here." She hesitated, then admitted, "I had been worried. When your letter arrived last week, confirming your return... I do not think I have ever felt relief like that."

"You were often at the front of my mind," he confessed. "The aim was always to make it back here."

She tilted her head and said, "You do wonders for my esteem. I am honored that my companionship is desirable enough to prevent you from dying at sea."

"I speak only what is true."

They lapsed into a quiet that did not require filling. The waves moved in patient rhythms at their feet. Greer and Callum drifted ahead, giving them the illusion of privacy without relinquishing their watch.

And then he remembered.

"Your dreams," he said, recalling the nightmares that plagued her sleep.

She faltered. It was subtle—a pause too long, a breath caught and corrected—but he noticed. A faint flush touched her cheeks. Ordinarily, he might have been pleased to have caused it. This time, he was uncertain how he had.

"Your nightmares," he clarified gently. "Do they still trouble you?"

"Oh." She blinked, as though returning from somewhere distant. There was relief in her voice. She looked towards the water, the breeze lifting the dark strands of her hair.

"I still dream," she admitted, glancing at him. "But the nightmares have gone."

The days that followed settled into an almost numbing rhythm.

Mornings belonged to stone chambers and carefully measured speech. Silas stood beside his father as trade was debated and pilgrimage safeguards were revised.

There were a handful of disagreements—small at first, then less so. Talon's patience thinned when the Tide was mentioned. Arden's responses grew firmer when matters of ritual were pressed. Their councils watched each exchange like sailors studying a change in the wind.

Once, late in the week, Silas passed the study and heard voices again—low, urgent. He did not linger this time. He caught only fragments. Faith. Obligation. The cost. The meaning escaped him, but the importance did not.

Afternoons, however, remained sunlit.

He walked through the gardens with Sereia, or the shoreline where the sand held the day's warmth. Sometimes Greer shadowed them with thinly veiled suspicion, untrusting of anyone in her cousin's presence. Sometimes Callum did, silent and vigilant. Silas tried to memorize it all— the cadence of her laughter, the way she argued doctrine with playful ferocity, the softness that appeared only when she forgot to guard it.

He told himself that there would be time.

Time to speak plainly. Time to confess what had long lived between inked lines and unsent letters.

But as the week wore on, the dissonance grew harder to ignore. The kings were arguing about something far greater than trade, and as spring progressed, the Tide loomed ever nearer.

Silas had waited long enough. If there were a secret dividing their kingdoms—if it concerned the Sea God, the Tide, or whatever choice could doom them all—

Then he would not remain ignorant of it.

If Sereia knew the truth of the Tide, he would hear it from her.

Chapter Thirty-three

Elin

The morning fog hung low over the garden. Dirt caked beneath Elin's nails as she dug out the carrots for tonight's dinner. Strands of hair slipped from her braid, clinging to her temples.

Elin looked up at the miserable sky; its towering grey clouds and the soft pressure in her bones promised an evening storm. "I don't know, Elide," she said, peering through the swaying grass in the garden. "We may be rained out tonight."

Elide squinted up at the sky, frowning. "Oh, I hope not. There will be someone in attendance whom I'd really love to dance with."

Tonight's dance would be Elide and Elin's first, and Edward had the honor of escorting them both. Elide spent the last several days teaching Elin the numerous dances performed at the city's dance hall.

"I have not heard you talk of this before? Who is it?" Elin asked, smiling at her.

"It's George," said Margot in a singsong voice. Elin looked behind her to where Margot and Willow were gathering spinach.

"Oh, I've seen him. The baker's son? Why would he ask *you* to dance, Elide?" Willow asked, wiping a hand across her apron. It left brown streaks across the pale linen.

"Willow, you're just jealous because a boy like George would never talk to you," Elide snapped.

Willow stiffened. "Am not. Boys are gross anyway. I just want to dance."

"You can dance anywhere," Elin said.

"You know, you're right," Willow said, reaching for Margot. Margot stumbled as Willow pulled her up. Then the two were spinning in circles, a swirl of skirts and giggles.

"They are such a nuisance," Elide muttered, though she was smiling.

"I think siblings are meant to teach you patience. There were times my brother and I would leave things in each other's bedrolls and—"

Elin stopped speaking. A skittering sensation crept across her skin. She rubbed her arms, trying to subdue the chill.

"Are you okay?" Elide asked, appearing at Elin's side, brow furrowed with concern.

"Yes, I just..." Elin looked towards the city; the clouds were breaking up, allowing the sun's rays to pour down like liquid light over the crowded buildings. "I felt something...odd—anyway, Anik and I irked each other all the time as kids. It's the job of siblings."

"I just wish they didn't do it so well," Elide sighed.

Elin pulled another carrot, trying to ignore the way the dirt clung to her sticky skin. She looked to where the twins were now chasing one another at the foot of the garden. They paused, waving down the path at something unseen.

The sensation sharpened.

Elin rose from where she crouched, narrowing her eyes at the figures approaching. One walked while the other rode horseback, an empty wagon pulled behind them. Edward and Thomas were returning from their most recent supply delivery. Since Edward's retirement from the Navy, he'd been working with his father to build various items for the Navy's ships.

Elin and Elide approached the men as they stopped at the base of the wisteria tree. Edward held tight to the saddle as he dismounted, stumbled, then reached out for the trunk of the tree to steady himself.

Edward's hot irritation licked against her. She pushed the sensation away, approaching him with a smile. His irritability was quickly replaced with a softer warmth as she wrapped her arms around him. "Welcome back," she said, pulling away.

He kept his hand at the base of her back, pulling her back in for a brief kiss. Her smile fell as she met his eyes. "What is wrong?" she asked.

"I'll tell you—"

"What are you ladies doing?" Thomas asked. The question sounded more out of habit than interest.

"Well, Elin and I are pulling carrots, and the twins are...well, being the twins," Elide said, frowning at Margot and Willow.

"That's nice," Thomas said, his gaze not wavering from the city in the distance.

Elide's eyes narrowed on her father. "What is it?"

Elin looked to Edward, then to his father. Neither spoke for a moment. The sensation turned into a sting. She suppressed a wince.

Edward pulled her close. "The Silvamari pilgrims returned," he said.

She tried to pull away to get a better look at his face. Edward hesitated before releasing her.

"Isn't that a good thing?" she asked, studying him.

Thomas looked away from the city. "It would be, but it's brought with it plague."

Elide gasped softly.

"Plague?" Elin asked. She'd heard the term before, but it wasn't something they had in Frostwake.

"Prince Linden might have been exposed. He was just rushed to the palace." Edward said, looking towards the stone spires.

"That's horrible. What—what will happen?" she asked.

Elide came to her side. "There's been small outbreaks before. They pass quickly." Elide assured her. "It won't stop us from enjoying the dance."

Thomas's jaw set. "It might be best if we stay away from the city for a while, Elide."

"What? No. No one was let off the ship, right? What's the harm?"

Thomas rubbed a hand over his face. "The ship came from Drakcultus," he said. "We don't know that it wasn't on other ships. These things...can spread quickly."

Elin grabbed Elide's arm, giving it a gentle squeeze. "We'll go to the next one. I promise."

Elide closed her eyes and nodded once.

As the day progressed, the sky grew darker; clouds smothered out the sun's light. Thunder rumbled outside, and the patter of rainfall drifted from the open window of the Graves' dining room.

The smell of roasted vegetables and honeyed bread wafted across the table. Edward handed her a plate of bread, offering her a piece before passing it on.

The bread was still warm inside when she bit into it. Its sweet, buttery taste melted against her tongue, and she stifled a groan. She understood why Edward had missed it while at sea. Silvamare's bakers had ruined any other bread for her.

Elide spent much of dinner in silence, only picking at her plate. Since learning she could not attend the dance, she'd remained somber.

"You're quiet tonight, Elide," Heidi said.

"I am just tired."

"No, she's upset about the dance. She wanted to dance with George," Willow quipped.

"You really ought to mind your business, Willow," Elide snapped.

Silence fell over the table, broken only by the scrape of utensils. Elide chewed on her lip, slumping in her seat. Margot and Willow were splitting their third biscuit, and Heidi and Thomas were in the middle of a silent exchange. Under the table, Elin reached for Edward's hand, threading her fingers through his. He squeezed her hand in reassurance.

Thomas's chair scraped against the floor as he slid back. "Elide, I know it's not the same, but we can dance anywhere."

"To what music?" Willow asked.

"We can make our own," Thomas said.

Edward huffed a laugh beside Elin as Thomas began to sing. He rose from his chair, approaching Elide with a tone-deaf tune that made her smile.

He pulled Elide from her chair, twirling her in front of him.

Edward leaned in, his breath hot against Elin's neck. "Might I dance with my wife?" he asked.

"It took you long enough to ask," she teased. Elin took his

outstretched hand.

Edward pulled her close, joining Thomas's singing. Soon, all the Graves were out of their seats, dancing offbeat and singing out of tune, and somehow it was the most beautiful thing Elin had ever seen.

Edward held her tighter, as if he were afraid of her drifting too far from him. She held him back, listening to the sound of his heartbeat as they swayed.

A clatter came from the other end of the table. Margot had tripped on a chair leg. She laughed, catching herself before delivering a performative curtsy.

Elin smiled as the thunder rumbled outside, but her gaze lingered on a chip she'd missed on her porcelain cup.

Notice Concerning the Return of the Silvamari Pilgrims

Prince Linden Blackwater was present at the docks for the public return of the Silvamari pilgrims, who had been held for questioning in connection with the attempted assassination of the Drakcultian heir, Princess Sereia Gaiano. As the ship approached the harbor, it became clear to those present that something was amiss. The vessel showed signs of disorder, and no passengers came forward to greet the port.

Guards were ordered to surround the ship. Before the perimeter could be secured, a child was thrown from the deck into the water, landing near Prince Linden. The prince immediately entered the water and retrieved the child, bringing them safely to shore. A guard then took the child from his care.

A woman aboard the ship cried out that if the passengers were not permitted to disembark, the children should at least be allowed to leave, so they might have a chance to live. When the Port Master asked what danger they faced, she declared that plague was present on the ship.

Upon the declaration, the vessel was placed under immediate quarantine. No passengers were allowed to disembark. Prince Linden Blackwater was escorted to a private wing of the castle and ordered into isolation until the period for the appearance of symptoms had passed.

This notice was printed and distributed with urgency for the awareness of the public.

Chapter Thirty-four

This morning, Silas was not summoned to the day's meetings. He did not question it. Instead, he sought Sereia.

He found her along the garden path that curved behind the eastern wing of the palace. The air was warm and heavy with jasmine. Greer followed a few steps behind them, close enough to intervene, far enough to pretend she was not listening.

They walked in companionable quiet until the path opened into a small alcove overlooking a reflecting pool. White petals drifted lazily across the water.

They sat.

"There is something I have been meaning to ask you," Silas said at last.

Her expression shifted, the blue of her eyes complemented by the pink rising in her cheeks.

"Oh?" she asked, the word light but lined with suspicion.

Silas hesitated before glancing towards Greer.

"Would your cousin grant us a measure of privacy?"

Greer lifted a brow in slow, deliberate refusal.

Sereia suppressed a smile. "Greer," she breathed. "I'll be okay."

Assessing him as a threat, Greer's gaze sharpened on him. "This is unwise," she said.

"And yet," Sereia replied, "I remain capable of judgment."

Greer exhaled through her nose and stepped down the path, remaining within sight but out of earshot.

Silas watched her go before turning back to Sereia.

"There is something being kept from me," he said. "From both our houses. I've heard enough to know it concerns the sea god. The Tide. The heirs are entrusted with truths others are not."

He held her gaze. "I know you are hiding something."

The color drained from her face. It was subtle, but unmistakable. The brightness left her eyes, replaced by distance. For a fleeting moment, she did not seem to see him at all. Her attention turned inward, as though some unseen calculation had begun behind her gaze.

"Sereia," he pressed.

Her composure returned with practiced precision. Her expression smoothed.

She looked at him—calm, if not a bit puzzled. "I am not certain what you mean."

Silas felt the shift as clearly as if a door had been closed between them.

He recognized that look. He had seen it in council chambers and in negotiations—moments when information was being intentionally withheld.

She was not naïve about politics. It was easy in casual conversation to forget that she was the daughter of Talon. There was no forgetting it now. Disappointment settled in his chest.

He had thought she would trust him. Perhaps he had been foolish enough to believe that whatever existed between them extended beyond diplomacy.

"Sereia," he whispered, fighting to keep frustration from sharpening his tone. "Must we pretend? Are we not friends?"

"We are," she said. "Of course, we are. But I do not know what you are alluding to."

He studied her for a long moment. "The royal houses are hiding something. Something is not right about the sea god. About the Black Tide. And all of you are keeping it buried. No one will tell me."

"Of course something is not right with the Black Tide," she replied evenly. "It takes our people each year. But that does not mean there is a hidden truth behind it."

"There is," he insisted. "My father and brother have admitted as much. They say it is better that I do not know."

Her gaze flickered.

"Then perhaps they are right," she said. "We are not entitled to every truth. Those in power carry burdens that must sometimes remain unseen. Secrets are not always cruel. Sometimes they're for our own protection."

"Do you truly believe that?"

"Yes." She did not elaborate.

"Then you are content to keep yours from me?"

"I never claimed to harbor any."

"But you are," he pressed quietly. "I know you are."

"If I knew anything of the Tide or the sea god that could spare our people," she said, her composure thinning, "do you think I would sit idle? Do you think I would allow innocent people to be marched to the shore each year if there was something—anything—I could do?" Silas reached for her hand. She pulled away. "Or do you not know me at all?" she finished.

Silas exhaled, frustrated with himself, with her, with the unseen thing between them.

"I thought I did. But how can anyone truly know a person who is withholding truth?"

She laughed once, incredulous. "Have you never withheld anything? Never lied? Never concealed? Did Cosmir descend from the heavens and appoint you guardian of righteousness?"

Her voice rose despite herself. "I have written you letters I have written to no one else. I have entrusted you with fears I have never spoken aloud. And you repay that with accusation?"

The hurt in her voice was unmistakable. Silas swallowed. The argument was slipping beyond his control.

"We both know your prophecy," he said. "Have you considered that whatever is being hidden may be what leads you to fulfill it? That in keeping secrets, you might—"

He stopped himself, but it was too late. She became very still.

"Might what?" she asked calmly. "Kill my family? Tear down the world's kingdoms?"

There was no tremor in her voice, only a cold distance. "I did not realize you were so frightened of me as well."

"I am not frightened of you," he said, though uncertainty crept into the edges of his voice. "But Hatra knew something. She was Drakcultian. How could a rogue captain grasp fragments of this mystery while you claim ignorance?"

At that, she closed her eyes. The sunlight caught along the planes of her face, casting a soft shimmer. She tilted her head upward as though listening for something beyond him. After a moment, she released a slow breath and opened her eyes again.

"As you know," she said carefully, "all records of the sea god were destroyed at his command when the Black Tide began. The priests teach we offended him; now this is our penance."

She met his gaze. "Whatever secrets exist belong to the divine. And if there were something to be done, don't you think someone would have done it by now?"

"How am I meant to know?" he asked. "No one will tell me."

"Then you are not meant to know." She rose from the bench, giving Greer a nod. "I am tired," she said. "Thank you for your company. I imagine I will see you later tonight."

"Sereia—"

She was already walking back towards the palace, Greer falling into step beside her.

Silas remained seated a moment longer, staring at the rippling water. He had come seeking the truth. Instead, he had driven a wedge where there had once been understanding and ease.

And he did not know whether he had been wrong to press, but he knew he'd been wrong in hurting her.

Chapter Thirty-five

Silas found his father in their chambers overlooking the harbor. The curtains were open. Ships drifted in the distance, their sails slack in the afternoon heat.

His father stood rigid at the window, tension carved into his expression. "These meetings are unraveling," he said. "Talon is being more difficult than usual. His proposals are...unreasonable."

"I had the same observation," Silas admitted.

"It feels as though he wants this relationship to fracture."

Silas hesitated. "Do you think it's because of the attack on Sereia?"

"No," Arden said without pause. "While we are speaking in confidence, I never believed it was one of our own who attacked her."

"Why?"

Arden was quiet for a moment. "In light of recent conversations, I just don't know what to believe."

His father rubbed his temples. "Silas, I fear I've made a mistake."

"What sort of mistake?"

"It is easy to say the wrong thing in the heat of the moment."

"Will you elaborate?"

"No. Do not concern yourself. I am certain I can amend it."

Silas gave a small, humorless breath. "I may have done the same."

Arden looked at him more closely. "What happened?"

"I offended Sereia."

That drew a short laugh from his father. "Then it seems we both spent the day offending a Gaiano. We should watch our backs."

Silas almost smiled. "And our fronts."

Arden's expression softened before becoming serious once more. "I will mend matters with Talon. You should do the same with Sereia. Aquerios cannot survive a conflict between our kingdoms."

Silas nodded. "What was he pushing for?"

Arden did not hesitate in replying. "A proposal. Sereia to Linden."

Silas went still.

"I declined," Arden continued. "Talon did not take it well. He is threatening trade restrictions, amongst other measures."

"Did you explain why it was not a wise match?" Silas asked.

"I did. He does not care how other islands might perceive such an alliance. He believes none would challenge him without placing themselves at risk."

"Talon has always ruled with only himself in mind," Silas said.

Arden gave a slight nod. "Even so, this must be repaired."

Silas looked out towards the water.

There could be no confession on his part, no reckless admissions, no matter how earnest. Whatever he felt for Sereia needed to remain only his to carry.

There was no version of their lives in which they could simply choose each other and walk away from all they were embroiled in. They weren't free in that way.

Perhaps that was the lesson he had failed to grasp.

His father and Linden had kept their knowledge from him, not out of spite, but because there was nothing he could do with it. He had pressed for answers they could not give. He had done the same to Sereia. And all it accomplished was hurt.

If the truth were meant to surface, it would do so in its own time.

Until then, silence was sometimes a mercy.

"I will apologize tonight," Silas said.

Arden rested a hand on his shoulder. "Good."

On his way down to the beach, Silas paused beside a flowering bush that had crept beyond the garden's edge. He plucked a single bloom without thinking.

He found Sereia near the shoreline. Greer stood close, watchful as ever. Callum was beside them, dressed in formal attire befitting his station. As the son of Prince Elric, he carried himself with the same controlled vigilance Silas had come to expect.

He approached. "May I have a word?"

Greer's glare was immediate and unrestrained. Without a doubt, Sereia had told Greer what unfolded between them. He averted his gaze, unwilling to let her shame him.

"Please," he said to Sereia.

She studied him for a moment, then gave a small nod. Without speaking, she stepped away, leading him several paces down the sand. Greer did not follow, but her eyes did.

Silas lifted the flower.

"May I?" he asked, gesturing towards her ear.

She nodded again.

He tucked it behind her ear, fingers brushing her cheek as he pulled back. She closed her eyes at the touch.

When she opened them again, there was something new in her expression—a challenge.

"I'm sorry," he said.

"For which part?" she asked.

"All of it." He swallowed. "It was selfish of me to put you in that position. To demand answers you cannot give. I should have known better. I know things are not simple for you—"

"Gods, Silas," she cut in, offended. "I do not want your pity. Do you think me so fragile that I cannot withstand disagreement?"

"That is not what I meant." He took a breath, steadying himself. "I did not wish to hurt you. I regret that I did. Your friendship matters to me. I have no desire to lose it."

"I was not hurt by the questions," she said quietly. "It was that you used something beyond my control against me."

She held his gaze. "Honestly, you were one of the few people I thought I was safe with in that regard. But now...I don't know, it's going to take some time to forgive."

He inclined his head, disappointed, but he hadn't expected immediate absolution.

"If we are to remain friends," she continued, "you cannot do that again."

"I will not," he said.

Silence passed between them, observant as it waited for which of them would break it.

"I must begin the long work of earning back your trust." He extended his arm. "Allow me to start by asking you to dance."

Her eyes lifted, and despite herself, she smiled. "You are insufferable," she murmured, though there was little heart in it as she slipped her hand into the crook of his arm.

They joined the outer ring of dancers circling one of the larger bonfires. Flames rose high, sparks drifting into the night like brief, dying stars. It was a ritual as old as their acquaintance.

They had danced like this every year since their first meeting.

It had always been easy between them. They moved as though they already knew where the other would step, when the other would turn. Two bodies sharing one rhythm.

"I will miss you when you leave," she said, breathless from the dance.

"I think I will miss you the moment I step onto the ship," he replied.

She rolled her eyes. "You will not."

"You cannot presume to know how I feel."

"Can't I?"

Their smiles met in the firelight, both in this moment unguarded.

On the final turn, he caught her off balance and lifted her at the waist. She gasped, startled, hands bracing his shoulders as he spun her. When he set her down, she swatted at him in mock reprimand, though she was laughing.

When the music faded and the dancers thinned, they slipped away from the fire.

They found a stretch of sand where the tide reached just shy of their feet. The waves rolled in silver beneath the moon, light breaking and reforming across the surface.

They sat side by side, and for a time neither spoke. It was their way.

After a while, Sereia rested her head against his shoulder and exhaled.

"When you leave," she said, almost idly, "will you steal me away?"

His heart stuttered.

He turned, only to find her already looking up at him. Their faces were close enough that even in the dim light of the moon, he could make out the various blues in her eyes.

His mouth went dry. He wet his lips, buying himself a moment.

"That was the plan all along," he said. "I am in no hurry to return to Frostwake, but Sidon would be an excellent place to hide you."

"Sidon?" she repeated, amused. "Why not Silvamare?"

"That is the first place your father would search."

She huffed a quiet laugh. "Even in a game of pretend, I am not certain he would trouble himself."

He frowned.

"Promise me you will keep yourself safe," he said.

She shifted away from him at that—just enough to widen the space between them. The loss of warmth was immediate. He resisted the instinct to pull her back and instead pressed his hands into the sand.

"I am as safe as I am ever allowed to be," she said. "I cannot promise more than that."

He nodded, though he hated the answer.

She was burdened by so much—expectation, suspicion, prophecy...history. It turned so many against her, yet she bore it without complaint.

He reached for her then, unable to stop himself, and drew her into his arms. She did not resist. For a moment, he held her as though he could stand between her and every threat circling beyond the firelight.

He'd nearly abandoned his resolve. She should know—not to bind her or to burden her—but so she would understand that she was not alone. And that someone saw her as she was, not as a prophecy, or an heir, or a bargaining piece.

"Sereia, I want to tell you something."

Meeting his eyes once more, she waited for his response.

"I—"

"Silas." His father's voice cut through the night.

Arden approached with two Silvamari guards, his expression stripped of all ceremony.

"We must leave. Immediately."

He stood at once. "What is it?"

"A Drakcultian vessel has returned from Silvamare." Arden's voice wavered. "There is an outbreak of plague."

The world tilted.

"And your brother—"

Sereia's hand squeezed his arm.

"Linden is afflicted," Arden finished. "It does not appear—" He stopped himself, unable to finish.

The sea was too loud; it roared in his ears. Heat licked beneath his skin, but all he felt was the cold.

"Your Majesty...Silas...I am so sorry," Sereia said, her gaze moving between them. "What can I do? How may I help?"

"Pray, Princess," Arden said. "I fear that is all anyone may do."

He turned to Silas. "You have a moment."

Sereia was already speaking. "I will secure our fastest wind wielder. You will not lose time."

Silas could barely hear her over the rush still filling his ears. Emotion pressed in from all sides—fear, dread, guilt for not already being home.

Then she was in front of him, hands rising to cradle his face. Her blue eyes searched his, wide with concern.

His gaze fell to her mouth. If he leaned down, just a fraction, would everything else disappear? Would the world narrow to this small, survivable thing?

"Silas," she whispered, pulling him back to her eyes. "It will be alright."

He did not know how she could say it so certainly. Perhaps she'd been so used to telling herself the same lie. He nodded anyway.

She rose onto her toes.

For a breath, he thought she meant to close the distance fully. That she had felt what he had too. But her lips brushed his cheek instead—gentle and soft.

"I will pray for you," she whispered. "Go. Be with your family."

"I wish I could bring you," he said before he could stop himself.

"Don't say that."

He gave her a faint, sad smile and started towards where his father waited.

"Silas."

He turned.

Standing alone on the shore, her red gown caught the wind, silvered by moonlight. "Promise me you will be safe."

He swallowed.

"I will," he said, though the words felt thin.

Chapter Thirty-six

It began as all dreams do—in darkness, then the slow spill of light through waking eyes.

Hazy blue shapes and threads of silver sharpened into an island split in two.

Silas had described his home to her once. She knew it now at a glance—though she had only ever seen it in paintings, in the fragile architecture of her own imagining.

Windows were boarded. Signs hung on cottage doors in warning.

Graves had been dug in long, hurried trenches, the earth still raw where it had been disturbed. Bodies lay where there had been no time to bury them.

Stay clear, the signs warned. *Plague.*

A gnawing hunger crept along the shore, lapping at rocky beaches, recoiling when it found nothing.

She'd never known anger to be cold, but she felt its chill in her veins, turning blood to ice. The ocean churned.

In the distance, the sound of silver bells clanged, frantic and uneven. Pine needles rustled and branches creaked as the sea retreated, denied its due.

The sea receded far out on the horizon, unveiling leagues of seabed and taking sound with it.

Bleary figures stepped away from their homes, weapons in hand. Not enough souls remained to save them from the god's greed, but still they were brave enough to meet it.

The wind howled a high, keening cry.

They'd only a moment to catch their breath before the sea returned, a wall of fury unleashed. It swept away people and homes, trees and boulders, and smashed against mountain faces. Filled the mouths of the innocent until Silvamare and its people were consumed.

Hundreds of lifeless eyes found hers. Their bodies bobbed on the ocean's surface, mouths agape in silent screams.

This was the Black Tide. Grief ran as deep as the hunger that drove the sea god—bottomless. Bodies sank into the inky depths, and she felt it—as if the hunger were her own, gnawing and endless.

Reality burned sharp as a new horror took root.

Silvamare was going to fall.

Silas would die.

And she was—

No, she was not helpless.

Was this a warning from the gods, or only her fear painting horrors in her sleep? It was too vivid to be anything other than an omen. These dreams had found her before, and they'd yet to prove her a fool.

Silvamare's Tide was still months away. There was time. If only she could wake and tell her father.

"Sereia," a voice called from the inky depths. She thought she recognized it. Her eyes strained, trying to see to whom the voice belonged.

It happened fast. Pain lanced through flesh. Something cold and scaled gripped her, pulling her down into the deep. Water filled her mouth as she tried to scream.

And then she was in her room, upright in her bed with damp cheeks. Throwing off her sweat-soaked covers, Sereia stumbled out of bed. As her mind fought to clear itself, a familiar, comforting voice slipped in through the fog.

"Sereia," Lucius began, *"there is nothing you can do."*

"I can try," she said aloud.

She flung open the door to her chamber and braced herself against the cool draft. Goosebumps scattered across her skin. Callum, her cousin and tonight's personal guard, startled at the sight of her.

"Sereia, what—"

He took her in, damp hair sticking to her face, blue eyes wide with bewilderment. "Sereia, what's happened?"

She ignored him, pushing past, moving as fast as her feet could carry her.

Callum cursed, following her.

He was calling for her to stop, but she couldn't hear him. The world was a distant thing, irrelevant compared to her mission.

"What will you tell the King?" Lucius asked. *"That you had a bad dream? He won't listen to you sane. Why would he listen to you now?"*

He was right; she knew it. Still, why would the gods deliver this dream to her if she wasn't meant to do something? She asked Lucius just that.

"Who says the gods gave you that dream?"

Two guards stood outside her father's private chamber. They stared at her with perplexed expressions, which she ignored.

"Is he in there? I need to speak with him."

Her voice sounded strange—detached, as if she might still be dreaming.

"I am not a child running off to sleep at the foot of my parents' bed after a nightmare, Lucius."

"That's exactly how it's going to appear to him."

She shoved Lucius from her mind, feeling his presence brush against her mental barrier, not forcefully, though he could break through if he wanted to.

The guards exchanged a look and then informed her that the King had gone to the council chamber.

"Are you well?" one asked.

"Thank you," she said, already shifting away. A hand reached out to grab her, and she startled back, bumping into something solid. She turned to see it was Callum.

"I've got her," he told her father's guards. They nodded, and Callum pulled her down the hallway away from her father's chamber. Once they were out of sight, he spun her around, bracing his hands on her shoulders.

"You're scaring me, Sereia. What has happened?"

She tried to pull away again, set on getting to the council chamber, but while she was faster, Callum was stronger. "I need to see my father. Now."

"I gathered that, but why?" His green eyes searched her face; they shone with worry and confusion.

"Because something terrible is going to happen, and I think he's the only one who can prevent it."

Callum released her and ran a hand through his blond hair. His face was shadowed with fatigue after many long nights guarding her door. Guilt crept in, but it could override her need to see her father. They had so little time.

"Stop what, Sereia?"

"The fall of Silvamare."

The words fell from her lips, heavy as rocks, and she was once again sprinting down the hallway. Callum didn't call after her this time, only followed.

Light poured out from beneath the unguarded council chamber doors. She paused for a moment before opening them.

Lords and advisors filled the long table, too many for an informal audience, too few for a full council. Cloaks lay draped over chair backs. Most looked as if they'd been pulled from their beds.

No Araceli were present, not even her mother.

A prickle of unease crept up her spine; meetings of consequence never excluded them.

Her father stood at the head of the table. King Talon looked up as she entered, his expression hardening at once to annoyance.

An old ache stirred in her chest. She was his only child, his sole heir—and yet, there had always been the sense that if he had been granted another path, another child, she would not be standing here at all.

"Father," she said, stepping forward before Lucius's doubts became her own. "I need to speak with you."

Talon gestured to the room, in a motion that said, go on.

The chamber was silent, and a dozen pairs of eyes were on her.

She told them about the dream. Of the boarded-up windows and warning signs. Of the Tide rolling in and drowning their neighbor to the east. She spoke, urgency lending a brittle edge to her voice.

When she finished, the silence was heavy.

Talon regarded her for a long moment. Then his mouth curved into a wintry smile. "Are you a child, Sereia," he asked, "or are you unsteady in the mind?"

Her stomach dropped.

"Interrupting governance," he continued, gesturing to the table, "to speak of monsters beneath your bed?"

Heat crept up her neck. "Forgive me for interrupting," she said, voice stronger than she felt. "I was not informed that there was a meeting. I was concerned."

A chair shifted.

Prince Elric leaned forward, fingers laced together. "It is a difficult season," he said, tone mild and conciliatory. "The approach of the Tide weighs heavily on us all. You may have overheard talk of unrest—perhaps even plague. With that and the strain of anticipation, the mind can conjure terrible things."

She opened her mouth—to ask why she had not been told of this meeting, why the Araceli were absent, why this meeting had been called in secrecy—

"That will be enough," Talon said sharply.

The finality in his tone snapped her jaw shut.

"You are dismissed," he continued, looking past her shoulder. "Callum, see that she returns to her chambers."

"Yes, Your Majesty," he said.

Shame pooled low in her stomach, creeping up her throat. She bowed, aware of too many eyes on her, and turned away before any of them could speak.

A hand caught her arm just beyond the door. Callum guided her from the chamber before she could say anymore. The doors closed behind them with a final, echoing thud.

They walked in silence for several paces.

"I'll do it myself," she said at last, pulling her arm free. "I'll send a letter."

Callum hesitated. "Are you certain it wasn't just a dream, Sereia?"

She stopped and turned on him. "You think I would put myself through that if it was only a dream? Do you remember when I told you our grandfather was going to die that night?"

Her cousin frowned. "He was old. He'd been ill."

"And he died in his sleep. Just as I said."

"That isn't foresight," he said. "Anyone could have predicted it."

She searched his face. "Do you think I'm being foolish?"

The pause was answer enough.

"I would never think you a fool," he said at last. "If you wish to write…I'll see that the letter reaches a ship bound for Silvamare."

Relief flooded through her, loosening the tension that had built up since waking. "Thank you."

She wrote the letter, willing her hands to be steady and her vision clear. A fool she felt indeed, but it was a small sacrifice to make if it might save the lives of thousands.

When she sealed the letter, she prayed to Terron, to Cosmir, even to the sea god himself, not just that it would arrive on time, but that it would prove her father wrong.

That she was not, as he believed, a childish fool.

And then she prayed once more for a man with dark hair and soft eyes, that he might live to see another Tide.

Chapter Thirty-seven

The chiming of bells marked the hour as Elin navigated the rain-swept streets of the city square. She stayed vigilant, though her mind struggled to accept how quickly Silvamare had changed. Once radiant and bursting with activity, the city now held its breath. Most people on the streets were there out of necessity, forced to take the risk. It didn't take long for the plague to take hold, then burn like a wildfire. Before Queen Reina stopped releasing the health reports, they'd learned the plague had already reached the mountain villages.

The ship with the returned pilgrims arrived only a week after Silas's departure. Days later, vinegar barrels were placed outside each shop, and the palace shuttered its doors. A week later, the bodies piled up in unprecedented numbers.

Walking down the cobbled streets, Elin kept her distance from passersby—holding her breath when they drew too near, moving her bag out of the way lest someone accidentally touch it.

Death and grief coated her like sap. She wanted nothing more than to return to Edward's family home in the countryside, where the air was clean and untouched by grief. *For now.* She shoved aside the intrusive thought as she reached behind her head, checking that her mask was still secured.

The door to the bakery was held open by a sizable stone. Beside the open door was a washtub. Elin scrubbed her hands with vinegar before approaching the counter.

The city baker was a plump woman with ruddy cheeks and thin lips, giving the impression that they were permanently pressed together. The result was that she always appeared in one of two ways: lost in thought or raging mad. Only her eyes softened her—round and bright, the color of sunlight breaking through leaves.

"Three loaves, please."

She nodded, turning to pack Elin's order. Elin rocked on her heels, looking around the shop.

"I heard they are running you lot ragged with patrols," the baker said.

"It is only a precaution," Elin replied. She'd returned only yesterday from a patrol. Reina ordered them with greater frequency, though each ship only carried a handful of crew members. Howie reported that there were growing concerns of raids now that Silvamare was in a weakened state. With fewer crew members, everyone had to take on numerous tasks to keep the ships running. By the time the week was up, the only thing she could do upon coming home was sleep.

"Oh yes, just as quarantine is only a precaution."

Elin smiled thinly. The woman's sarcasm was sharp on her tongue.

A tingling feeling brushed the back of her neck. She turned, expecting someone behind her, but there was no one.

"Here you are," the baker said. She handed Elin the wrapped loaves. After stuffing them into her bag, Elin dropped a handful of coins onto the counter.

"Terron be with you."

"And you," replied the baker.

Elin slipped out the door and back onto the street.

A cart pulled by horses squeaked down the center of the street. The wheels hit a divot in the road, jostling it, and an arm covered in oozing black welts fell, dangling from the back. She turned away from the dead cart, picking up her pace.

The plague would not take her as easily as it would the rest of the Graves family. It was why she offered to go into the city instead. She could endure the horrors around her if it meant keeping the family she considered her own safe.

From the doors of homes hung various signs—some were warnings: *Plague. Stay away.* Others: *medicine, hot meals to go…body pickup.*

The palace was no longer releasing the death counts, likely to avoid making the public more frightened than they already were. The Tide was only two months away.

Elin stepped off the walkway and onto the street, avoiding a gathering of praying people. They crowded around a statue of Terron; the priests arranged an altar at its foot for offerings. Their voices were frenzied, piled one on top of the other, fighting to be heard over the others. Many had turned to the God of life, leaving money at the temples, praying with the priests, listening to speeches providing them with hope that the gods still loved them, that this would pass. Though not everyone appealed to the divine. The plague turned others resentful towards their passive overlords. For every group of worshipers Elin passed, there was another who raged at the gods, blaming them for their lot.

Who was to blame and who she was to seek salvation from, Elin did not know. She couldn't help but feel indifferent, not towards their circumstances but towards the gods. Aside from the sea god, she didn't believe they played any role in Aquerios, not anymore. They had their fun, painted their canvas, and moved on.

Again, the hairs on her neck stood up. Since leaving the bakery, she had made several turns, suspecting someone was following her.

Once again outside the baker's door, she cast a sidelong look inside, but it was her periphery that she focused on. A tall figure, obscured by the shadows of their hood, was trailing behind. Elin's heart thumped painfully in her chest. She needed to confirm what she suspected lest she lead them home. Two doors down from the bakery was an alley open on both ends. It would offer her an escape should she need it, but also provide her with a space away from others to confront the person.

Approaching the corner, she made a sharp turn, pressing herself against the mossy stone, blending into the shadows. Her hand slipped into her pocket, fingers closing around the dagger Edward had given her. Sweat beaded off her brow, and her breath was humid beneath her mask;

she pushed past the dizzying feeling threatening to overtake her.

The hooded figure stepped into the alley.

In two strides, she had them pinned to the opposite wall, blade at their throat.

"Why are you following me?"

They remained silent.

Elin peered under the shadow of the hood, brows furrowed in confusion. Something about them was familiar enough to make her hesitate, but she kept her dagger against their throat. "Remove your hood."

An old, wrinkled hand reached for the hood's hem, pulling it back to reveal a leathery brown face and cloudy eyes.

"Wh—what are you doing here?"

"You've changed," Tven said, in a voice that belonged far from here.

At a loss for words, she stared blankly at them. Their last meeting came flooding back to her, and she fought the urge to recoil from the shaman.

"I'm sorry, Elin," Tven said. "I could not speak what I knew."

An icy cold swept over her, sending her body humming. Her hand shook against the dagger's hilt.

"You knew," her voice cracked. She'd suspected it, but they confirmed it. "You knew Anik would die."

"I did."

She stepped closer, leveling her voice. "And you said nothing."

"You think fate can be changed because you love someone?"

"We could have tried!" Her breath hitched. "He is dead. I thought it was my fault."

"It was how it needed to unfold," they said, grief dimming their cloudy gaze. "He is with the Mother now."

She sneered at Tven. "There is no Mother. Only the sea god—and he takes." Her blade nicked their neck; a bead of blood slid down their throat. She looked away.

Tven's hand rose, light but steady around her wrist.

Sweat beaded on their forehead, slipping from the corner of their tattooed eye like a teardrop.

"The Tide will never be sated. It will take more than it has in centuries."

Her limbs were heavy, as if she'd been scooped out and filled with stones. "From Silvamare?"

They nodded.

"You come here—now—when my people are dying, to speak in riddles?"

Tven's gaze shifted—not to her, but towards the palace spires beyond the alley.

"When the prince sails, you must sail with him."

She followed their gaze. "What does Silas have to do with this?"

"When the water recedes," they said, "he will still be standing."

"I don't understand."

"You will."

"There's more, I know it."

"There's an order to things—a way events must unfold if we wish to have a future beyond the Black Tide."

"You need to leave Silvamare," she said. "It's not safe."

They gave her only a solemn nod.

"I did not come alone."

Her hand tightened reflexively around the dagger's hilt. "What do you mean?"

"There is someone who wishes to see you."

Her pulse skipped. "Who?"

"They remain aboard our vessel. We cannot stay long."

"Why didn't you bring them with you?"

"You said it yourself." Their gaze flicked to the street beyond the alley. "It is not safe."

Only a handful of names flashed through her mind. None dared rise to her lips.

"Meet us at the north pier," Tven said. "After moonrise. It is your only chance before we depart."

"And if I don't come?"

They held her gaze. "Then you will regret it."

She looked towards the sea, as if she might glimpse it through the stone. A cool breeze swept down the alley, tossing her hair behind her.

She turned back towards Tven. They were gone.

Nausea fought to snake its way up her throat. She bit back the acid, casting a glance towards the palace spires. When her heart returned to a steady beat, she slipped out of the alley.

On her way back to the cottage, she kept her head on a swivel, watching for the hooded figure. As she did, she caught glimpses of the docks between the buildings lining the strait.

She halted her steps, spotting a large group of guards congregated at the base of a vessel. Her heart clenched in recognition. Silas and the King had returned, and soon they would learn of Prince Linden's fate.

Pain and grief pressed in, needling her sweat-streaked skin. She needed to get home, to get away from the city.

If she could get back to Edward, she could breathe again.

She broke into a run; her mask made breathing difficult, but she fought through it.

Thoughts of her brother rose up, her grief and fear overflowing as she imagined Silas learning what had befallen Linden. She stumbled over loose stones. Fell once, scraping her palms when the path turned to dirt. Once out of the city, she ripped off her mask, drawing deep breaths. But she didn't stop running. If she did, everything would catch up to her: her losses, her fears, Tven's warnings and omissions, the misery of the plague, and the unbearable understanding that Silvamare was in terrible danger.

She didn't slow down when she reached the shadow of the wisteria, or when the cold air itched her skin. Her scraped palms stung as she dipped her hands in the bowl of vinegar set outside the door. Ignoring the pain, she scrubbed aggressively at her skin as if she might wash it all away. How dare Tven come here? How dare they corner her and tell her it's her destiny to lose over and over? Have the gods no mercy?

The Mother. Elin's lip curled in anger. She put far too much power into opening the front door, causing her to nearly tumble as she crossed the threshold. Discarding her grimy attire into the wash bin, she then slid into a clean dress, evidently placed there for her on the bench by one of the girls. Her mind racing, she moved unseeing through the cottage until she found Edward.

He was sitting at the kitchen table, cutting fresh vegetables. Upon seeing her, he set the knife down and rose from his chair.

"Elin?"

She yearned to share the truth with him, but the words refused to escape her lips. She could only respond with a slight shake of her head. He walked towards her, his handsome face etched with a deep furrow of worry.

Her arms encircled him in a desperate hug. Strong hands reached up, their touch a gentle caress as he threaded his fingers through her hair. He made soft, comforting sounds and then asked in a soothing tone, "Elin, what happened?"

Her throat tightened, a raw, aching pain spreading through her chest as a strangled sound escaped her lips. He said nothing and held her until the worst of her tears had passed. Until she could speak the words her heart wished to deny.

Chapter Thirty-eight

A sharp breath escaped Edward's clenched teeth as he sat on the bed's edge, fingers digging into his thigh.

Elin quickly crossed the room.

"You don't have to come," she said, watching his hand grip the place where his leg had once been. "I can meet Tven alone."

He exhaled slowly, as if forcing the pain back. "I am not comfortable with that."

"If the pain is too bad tonight," she pressed, kneeling before him and resting her palms on his knees, "then listen to it and stay. I will be fine."

"When you returned from the village," he replied, meeting her eyes, "you looked as though something inside you had cracked. I can endure some discomfort if it means I do not sit here imagining Tven dragging my *wife* into another dark place."

"Edward."

"Elin," he said dryly, shifting to reach for the prosthetic where it leaned against the wall. She moved, giving him space as he fitted the socket with practiced movements and secured the straps. "Still, I would rather limp beside you than sit here imagining the worst."

She steadied him as he rose, though he pretended not to need it. "Then take your cane."

He grunted, the sound a low rumble in his chest, as he reached for the cane leaning by the door.

Instead of walking, they mounted the old family horse, a decision that saved Edward a considerable walk over the difficult, uneven terrain. The animal shook its head, a faint tremor running through its muscles, as Edward swung himself onto the horse. Elin followed, steadying herself behind him.

The pier glowed under the flickering torchlight, the flames hissing and crackling as the wind swept in from the strait. Above them, the crescent moon hung pale and sharp, resembling a fishing hook cast into the dark sky. Each clatter of the horse's hooves on the cobblestones seemed to break the mournful stillness, the sound rippling across the water.

At the north pier, a small vessel rocked in the sloshing water, lanterns swaying gently along its hooks. Footsteps sounded on the gangplank.

Elin slid off the horse, then turned to help Edward. He waved her off with a frown, determined to dismount without assistance, but when his boots hit the ground, he swayed, pain flickering across his features before he mastered it. He inclined his head, giving her a small smile.

Tven approached, their woolen cloak stirring in the wind. "I am glad you came." Their gaze settled on Edward. "And who have you brought with you?"

"This is Edward," Elin replied, lacing her fingers through his. "He is my husband."

"Husband?" a woman's voice echoed from the ship.

A figure descended the gangplank, her face obscured beneath the shadow of a selkie hood. Her belly curved round and full beneath her dress.

Elin's heart stuttered.

The woman lifted her hand and pushed back the hood. Short silver hair caught the torchlight, and large coal-black eyes met her own.

Elin's hands flew to her mouth as a sob broke free. "Arnaq?"

Arnaq smiled. "Hello, Elin."

Elin closed the distance between them in a rush, wrapping her arms around her friend as though the sea might rip her away. When she pulled back, she searched Arnaq's face, disbelieving. "I cannot believe you are here," she said, breath trembling. "Why are you not migrating with the others?"

"Something strange is happening in the sea. It didn't feel safe and I…I wanted to find you."

Tears fell freely as her gaze dropped to the curve of Arnaq's belly. "Oh, Arnaq… this is wonderful. Who is—" Before she could finish the question, the answer had already formed in her thoughts. "Anik?"

Arnaq nodded, tears sliding down her cheeks.

Edward stepped close behind Elin, resting a hand on her back as she bit down on a sob.

"May I?" Elin asked, shaky hands hovering uncertainly.

Arnaq guided them down, pressing Elin's palms against her abdomen. She felt a firm kick against her hand, startling her.

Life, insistent and unashamed, in a world that seemed determined to decay.

"Do my parents know?" Elin whispered.

"They do," Arnaq replied. "Your father has built a yarnaga beside theirs for when I come to visit. They are very excited."

Elin laughed softly through tears. "Is Ila with you?"

"She's with the herd. I did not wish to risk the journey with them, not now."

Another kick pushed into Elin's palm, drawing a watery smile from her.

"I've tried for years," Arnaq murmured. "I had almost lost hope."

She held her hand there, cherishing the touch, reluctant to break it. For one fleeting moment, she imagined such a life in her own womb—and the thought terrified her as much as it ached.

"Hello, little one," she whispered. "You are due any day now, aren't you?"

"I hope so," Arnaq replied.

"Anik would have been delighted," Elin said, her throat tightening.

"He would have," Arnaq agreed, a quiet laugh escaping her. "Can you imagine him attempting to change a diaper?"

Elin huffed a feeble laugh. "I have, actually."

The amusement evaporated as swiftly as it had appeared. Elin's brows knitted together. "Arnaq, you cannot remain here."

"I know," she said. "I was uncertain where to find you after you left, and I needed you to know that a part of Anik still lives. Silvamare may be your home now, but Frostwake has not forgotten you. Do not disappear from us."

"I won't," Elin promised.

Arnaq turned her gaze to Edward. "I remember you. Thank you for what you have done for us, and for her."

He shook his head. "Elin has done just as much, if not more."

Arnaq squeezed Elin's hands. "You've never shied away from the hard path. I know Tven has spoken to you. Whatever you do, just make certain this child knows their aunt."

Elin nodded, biting down on her lip.

"Our time is up," Tven announced, appearing beside them.

Elin startled, having nearly forgotten their presence.

Arnaq drew her into one last embrace before turning back towards the ship. Elin watched as Tven and Arnaq boarded, lantern light casting long shadows across the dock. Her heart ached painfully.

Edward drew her close, steady as an anchor. "It feels dark now," he said, "but I can see a light beyond it. We will reach it."

"You truly believe that?"

"I must."

"We will have to fight for it," she said. "Tven did not bring hopeful news."

"It wasn't a death sentence either."

She managed a small, tired smile. "Ever the optimist."

He pressed a kiss to her temple as the vessel eased away from the pier.

"Come," he mumbled. "Let us go home."

They mounted the horse and turned from the water. Behind them, the ship cut through the strait, its lanterns shrinking against the vast black. Elin twisted in the saddle, watching until the mast thinned to a fragile line beneath the hooked moon and then vanished.

Upon their return to the cottage, they were surprised to see the number of lit-up windows for the hour. As their horse meandered further up the path, Elin straightened and lifted her head to look at Edward. His brows were scrunched as he took it in.

"I thought they'd gone to bed before we left," Elin said.

Edward urged the old horse to move faster, kicking up dirt as it went. "They did."

They shared a look as they descended from the saddle.

"You go ahead," Elin said. "I'll put him away."

Edward's jaw ticked as he looked between her and the house. "I'll be fine," she assured him. "Go check on them. I'll be right there."

He planted a quick kiss on her temple before turning toward the cottage.

Quickly, Elin removed the horse's saddle and reins before running her hand over the creature's jaw. It filled her with warmth, and she smiled weakly.

Closing the stable gate behind her, she ran to the cottage door, scrubbing her hands with vinegar before hurrying inside.

Edward stood in the entryway, holding Heidi in his arms. Tears traced her cheeks. Her fear and panic wormed their way under Elin's skin, raising the hairs along her neck.

"What has happened?" Elin demanded.

Heidi's face crumbled. "It's Margot," she cried. "She woke with a fever, and I can't get it down."

Blood drained from Elin's face. "Have you called on a physician?"

Edward's father exited the girls' room next, his skin sallow. Thomas shook his head. "There are none. Perhaps we can appeal to Silas for the aid of the royal physician, but there's no one willing to treat the sick. Not now. And if it's the..." Thomas trailed off, unable to finish the sentence.

"I will check," Elin said, already walking toward the girls' room. Edward moved to follow her, and she whirled around. "No," she said. "Stay here, just in case."

He began to protest, but Elin put her hand up. "Please," she said. "I know she's your sister, but please just let me make sure it's not plague first."

"I'll wait just outside the door," he said. Elin wanted to protest further, but knew it was pointless.

The girls' room was lit by candles burning on a small table between two beds; it lit the room in an orange hue and caught on the girls' curls. In the smaller bed, Elide held Willow close, running her fingers over her hair. Her eyes never left Margot's slight frame lying limp on the larger bed.

Elin had been prepared for a pungent, sour taste on her tongue when she stepped inside the room. Instead, she was met with the tangy-sweet taste of an ordinary fever. Her shoulders slumped as she sat on the bedside Margot, careful not to disturb her. "Thank the gods," she said, running a hand over Margot's forehead.

Elin turned towards the bedroom door, finding three pairs of worried eyes on her. "It is not the plague."

Their relief flooded the room, though it did nothing to cure the underlying anxiety that Margot was ill and they'd have to wait to see if she'd get any better.

"**Our** navy has captured and imprisoned three pirate crews plundering the northern coast. Three of the four ships were intercepted while attempting to attack migrating selkies."

—*Sidonese Naval Reports*, from the Old Kingdom of Sidon

Chapter Thirty-nine

Silas

He'd always known his home as vibrant and alive, the people warm and welcoming. Like the sunrise, Silvamare once promised new beginnings, carrying with it a wealth of hopes, dreams, and infinite possibilities. He rode his horse through the uneven cobblestone streets; the grandeur of his kingdom now felt foreign and unrecognizable.

Guards maintained a wide berth, keeping the people far away from him and his father. Pine-fresh air was now tainted with smoke from burning bodies. Sounds of despair came from different directions: grieving cries, angry shouts.

The few Silvamari he could see through the wall of guards revealed masked faces and listless eyes. As they approached the palace, the green ivy choked the stonework; the royal banners hung worn from exposure. Even the gleam of their guards' armor had gone dull. There was no denying that Silvamare was facing its dusk, and when it fell, they'd be met only with their end.

He didn't immediately understand that his brother had died.

Upon their arrival at the palace, he and his father were led to one of the smaller sitting rooms near the entrance. His mother stood by a window;

only a sliver of her profile was illuminated by the filtered light. One hand covered her mouth, the other wrapped around her waist. She did not move upon their arrival. In that moment, his mother seemed more like a statue than a human.

Silas's gaze moved expectantly across the room, searching for the face he'd been most desperate to see. His eyes darted over the couches and chairs, finding nothing, then scanned the shadowy corners of the room.

Disappointment left a bitter taste in his mouth.

He turned to the only other person in the room. The royal physician had served his family for decades, predating his parents' rule; the man was ancient. There were very few in Aquerios who were lucky enough to have such a long life.

"Where is my brother?" he asked, interrupting the silence.

He turned, seeing his father still in the doorway. His father stared at his mother, who remained as still as a portrait by the window.

"Prince Linden was very ill," the physician began. "We tried everything we could, but it wasn't enough."

Silas shook his head, brow furrowing. "I'm aware of his illness. Where is he?"

He fought against the crushing weight in his chest, even as it bled into his arms and then his legs. At the continued silence, he asked more questions.

"Have you called on other physicians? W—When is he expected to recover?"

"Silas," his father said from the doorway.

"No," Silas said, but the shattered sobs of his mother confirmed the truth he refused to accept.

Linden Blackwater was dead.

Beside his brother's entombment, the words rang in his ears.

It wasn't enough.

The possibility of Linden being dead was something he avoided considering on their journey back. He'd naively thought he'd visit him in his chambers, already on the mend.

Silas couldn't remember their last exchange, what words they had spoken, or if he'd hugged him. Did he tell him that he loved him?

He leaned forward, resting his head on the cold stone of his brother's resting place. He drew in slow, trembling breaths, fighting the inferno that clawed at his skin.

"Why?" The question was as light and fleeting as a breath.

His question of "Why?" came again, this time with a force that demanded an answer. He struck the stone with his fist, and a searing pain shot up his arm. With each blow against the stone, his anger surged, a tempest in his chest.

The ship had come from Drakcultus.

Talon had imprisoned his people, returning them infected. It was *he* who had inflicted this plague upon them.

This was *his* doing.

He was the one to blame.

The pounding echoed inside his skull, then burst out as a shout, and flame burst from his palms. A choked sob escaped his lips. His shoulders shook as the force of his grief poured out.

When he settled, tears welled in his eyes as he murmured, "I'm sorry, Linden."

He didn't know how long he stayed there. By the time a servant arrived with a message from his parents, his tears had long since dried, and the glass ceiling's light had faded.

The clanking of silver against porcelain was the only sound to fill the dining hall as Silas ate an early dinner with his parents. It was the first they'd shared since their return, since Linden's passing. The silence clamped down on the room with the weight of all four seas.

His father sat at the end of the table, his mother to his left, and Silas next to her. If he cared about proper etiquette, his place would now be to the right of his father, where Linden once sat. There were many reasons he sat where he did, and he tried not to think of them as he brought a piece of roasted duck to his mouth. He didn't taste it as he stared at the empty chair. Losing his brother was hard enough for his mind to accept.

His new role as heir to Silvamare, even more inconceivable.

He looked around the room, noting the lack of servants. The palace staff was reduced, both by precaution and by loss.

Needing to fill the silence, he put down his utensils. Despite their grief, there were matters to attend to. Concerns to address. "I've read the most recent reports," he said at last.

His mother flinched at the sudden intrusion.

In a gesture meant to provide comfort, he took her hand in his. Ignoring the chill of her skin, he continued. "The death toll is rising. We will not meet the quota without outside support."

His father paused, peering up at him over the rim of his wineglass. He took a long sip before placing the wine back on the table.

"It is a minor concern," Arden replied. "Your mother has secured aid."

Silas reached over the table, scooping an additional helping of vegetables onto his plate. He wasn't hungry, but needed something to do.

"From whom?"

"Sidon."

"And if their ships are delayed?" Silas pressed. "If the winds turn? If pirates intercept them?"

"It's only two months away. When did these assurances arrive?"

Arden's eyes lifted.

"If you have read the reports," his father said, "then you know Sidon has captured three pirate crews. They've requested assistance in locating a fourth. A vessel last sighted sailing east, towards us."

Silas leaned back in his chair.

"This is not the time to chase pirates."

"It is precisely the time," Arden replied. "When the Tide passes, we will be weakened."

"We are already weak," Silas hissed. "Our people are dying."

"Which is why," his mother said carefully, "it is best to have a member of the royal family away from the island."

Silence fell. His parents meant to preserve him, to spare him from the grievances of their people. They wanted him to run from the plague, the Tide, while their people were forced to endure it.

The thought curdled in his stomach.

"I refuse to leave my people at a time such as this," he said.

His mother's amber eyes met his, and he found he could not read them.

"You are the heir now," she said.

"I am Silvamari," he answered. "I will not ask of them what I will not endure myself."

Arden's jaw tightened. "You speak like a warrior, not a king."

Silas met his father's gaze. "A king who hides while his people suffer is no king at all."

His mother withdrew her hand.

"Any of us may die at any time," she said. "Linden has proven that."

The name settled between them like ash.

"We have ruled for decades," Arden said. "You've been heir for a week. This is not exile. It is preservation."

"It feels like exile," Silas replied.

"And if the island falls?" his mother asked quietly. "Would you have our bloodline end with you?"

"If the island falls," Silas said. "I will fall with it."

His father studied him for a long moment.

"You may choose your crew," Arden said at last. "Take those you trust. Remove the pirate threat. Return before the Tide."

Silas did not respond.

They placed him in an impossible position. Leave his kingdom in their time of need—on the knife's edge of ruin—to eliminate a pirate threat. Or defy his parents' wishes, remain in Silvamare, and risk the safety of his people after the Tide.

Seeing that Silas was considering his position, Arden offered something he recognized his son could not resist.

"Upon your return, I will tell you the truth about the Tide. About the sea god."

Air caught in Silas's lungs. He had begged for nearly a year to understand the Tide.

Now, when Linden lay cold in stone, the truth was dangled before him like bait.

His father knew he was hungry for this knowledge, and only when he'd just learned to quell his desire did his father deign to feed it.

"You would bargain with this? Will I not need this knowledge regardless of my decision?"

"I will withhold it until I am dying if I must," Arden said.

"We are trying to keep you alive, Silas," his mother said.

He stood. "If I go," he said slowly, "it will not be to spare myself. It will be because pirates threatening our shores while we're weak puts us at risk. It will be for the island's future."

His parents looked at him expectantly. He hated that their bribery was working, that he hadn't quelled his thirst enough to resist what they offered.

"When I return," he said. "I expect the truth."

He pictured the courtyard, where his people would assemble for the drawing, risking everything to face a lottery that could cost them their lives. Where would their heir be then?

And if he were delayed at sea, he could miss the arrival of the Tide. If something went wrong, if he was not there—

He swallowed the thought.

If his parents and his people needed him back at sea, then he would go. Though the machinations his father used to get him here would be hard to forgive and even harder to forget.

He'd given in—and already knew he'd regret it.

Chapter forty

Elin

The Graves family room was surrendered to chaos. Chairs were pushed back from the hearth, clearing a space on the worn rug where Margot and Willow—cheeks flushed with triumph—had appointed themselves the arbiters of a new game. Margot's fever had broken just the night before and already she pounced around full of life.

Willow stood with hands braced at her hips, chin lifted, drawing in a dramatic breath before flinging her arms overhead as though summoning lightning from the rafters.

"Storm!" Elide cried.

Edward leaned back on his palms. "No," he said mildly. "That's the girls when they don't get their way."

All three sisters gasped in outrage before the room dissolved into laughter.

Elin sat cross-legged near the hearth, watching the scene unfold. There was something stubbornly miraculous about it—the way joy found ways of surviving. The plague had narrowed the world to careful distances and masked faces. It had emptied streets and quieted markets. But here, within these walls, warmth remained.

A knock struck the door.

The laughter died at once. They glanced at one another, confused.

Thomas rose from the floor and crossed the room. The hinges gave their usual weary protest as the door opened, and cool air, faintly scented with blooms from the wisteria, slipped inside.

"Oh," he said, surprised. "Come in, Your Highness. Captain Howie."

Elin's spine straightened.

Silas entered first, mask secured over his mouth and nose; Howie, a solid shadow behind him. Even masked, there was no mistaking the tension in Silas's posture—everything about him was wound tight.

Edward rose, his gaze meeting hers.

Do you know what this is? she asked, arching a brow.

His slight shake of the head was answer enough.

Silas's eyes met hers immediately—a cold grey. Once, not long ago, they'd been warm.

"I apologize," he said evenly. "We didn't mean to intrude."

"It's no intrusion," Thomas replied, stepping aside to make space.

The twins, oblivious to the undercurrents, beamed up at their prince. Silas gave them a brief wink, and they collapsed into quiet giggles.

Then he looked back at her and Edward. "We need to speak with you. Privately."

Edward inclined his head towards the narrow corridor. "Kitchen."

They moved through the narrow passage; the door closed behind them with a muted thud that felt louder than it was.

"We have orders," Silas began, wasting no time. "We are to patrol the Black Reef. A crew eluded the Sidonese. They believe it's taken shelter there."

"When do we leave?" Elin asked. "I'm not due back until the start of next week."

"We sail at dawn," Howie said.

"Dawn?"

Silas held her stare. "We do not have the luxury of slow preparation. I intend to return before the Tide."

Edward reached for her, wrapping an arm around her waist. "How long will she be gone?"

Silas did not hesitate. "You're coming too."

Elin's hands reached out, bracing the kitchen table. The air in the room became too thin to breathe. "What?"

Edward's brow furrowed. "Silas—"

"You've been reinstated," Silas said, clipped.

It was Edward's turn to stare. "Reinstated."

Heat spread up Elin's neck, flushing her cheeks. "He hasn't trained in months. He has a prosthetic. You're asking him to put himself in danger as though nothing has changed."

Silas's gaze flicked to her, sharper than she'd ever seen. "Edward will be fine."

Something passed between the two men—a conversation made entirely of expression. A language they'd learned long before Elin had entered their world.

Edward gave a single nod. "I'll adjust."

Though Elin didn't miss the way his jaw tightened, as if doubt threatened to slip out.

Silas's shoulders eased, but his expression remained unchanged.

"My parents ordered me to assemble a crew I trust implicitly," he said. "There is no world in which Edward is not part of that crew."

Elin swallowed. "Why are they sending you?"

For a fraction of a second, Silas's expression cracked, and Elin felt the emotion he was keeping walled up—his anger and his grief.

She sucked in a breath. Noticing it, Silas pulled back his emotions as if he'd learned how to hold them close.

"They want me away from the island," he said at last. "They believe distance will serve us until the plague settles. Illness has infiltrated the palace once already."

Edward's voice was quieter when he spoke again. "Will we return before the Tide?"

"Yes," Howie said.

Concerned by the flicker in his confidence, she crossed her arms. "Anything could delay our return. How can you be so—"

Silas's gaze cut to hers. She straightened at the severity of it. "Your duty is to follow orders," he said. "Ours is to give them."

A chill raked up her arms despite the spike in the room's temperature. She felt his regret almost as swiftly as he did, but he did not retract his words. They were true after all.

"I did not request this mission," he added. "But I have been persuaded it serves my kingdom."

Edward studied him as though reading currents beneath still water.

"We'll prepare," Edward said at last. "We'll say our goodbyes."

Silas nodded once.

"Attaboy," Howie said, slapping his hand on Edward's shoulder before leaving the three of them alone.

Silas and Edward watched each other, their stares unmoving. There it was again—that unspoken conversation flowing between them. An apology? A warning?

"Thank you," Silas said.

Then he was gone.

Supplies arrived before sunset—medicine, preserved goods—along with formal assurances that the Graves family would be spared from this year's Tide drawing in recognition of their service.

Heidi did not hide her fear. "What is he thinking?" she demanded. "You nearly died last time."

"And if you're attacked?" Thomas pressed. "If something happens at sea—"

Edward let them speak. When they finally ran out of words, he said simply, "It's adapt or die." He didn't look at them when he said it. None of them needed to be an empath to know which outcome Edward expected.

Later, when they were alone in the narrow hall, Edward whispered, "This mission isn't about pirates."

She looked up at him, cold seeping into her skin. "What do you mean?"

"Silas doesn't trust his parents."

Her brow furrowed. "When did he say that?"

A faint, humorless smile painted Edward's face. "He didn't."

She stared at him, raising a brow.

Edward shrugged. "I've known him a long time. He wouldn't put me in this position unless he was certain it was for the best."

Elin knew to what lengths Silas would go to ensure the safety of those he loved. Edward had told her as much before. If this mission wasn't really about hunting pirates, then what was it about?

Tven's voice rose in her memory, calm and unyielding.

When the prince sails, you must sail with him.

Edward did not believe in prophecy. He had dismissed Tven as a relic of another age, an empty hope people clung to. But now, as he stared down at her, she knew from the way his eyes turned contemplative that he was reconsidering.

If they were to accept one part of the prophecy, they would have to accept it all.

Dawn arrived colorless and thin.

In the cottage garden, only the tallest of flowers broke through, flashes of orange and blue in the mist.

Heidi pulled Elin into a tight embrace. "I know you already know this, but keep an eye on him. He rarely asks for help when he needs it."

Elin smiled warmly. "Always."

Heidi turned to Edward, who had only just pried his sisters away. He held his mother close, whispering something Elin couldn't hear before kissing the top of her head.

Thomas emerged from around the cottage, slightly out of breath, carrying something wrapped in linen in his hands. "Oh, good, I didn't miss you."

Edward frowned. "What is it?"

Thomas turned the bundle over once, as if checking it, then held it out. "Go on," he said. "Take it."

Edward hesitated a moment before taking it.

He unwrapped the linen, brows furrowing.

Elin stepped closer, stopping at the sight of the new prosthetic. It was sleeker than the one he wore, reinforced with bands of metal. The joints were different, appearing to mimic the interworkings of a real foot and ankle.

Edward turned it in his hands, studying it.

"I didn't tell you about it because I wasn't sure if it would work. I thought I'd have more time…but now that you're being sent off…" He waved the thought away, pointing at the prosthetic ankle. "There's a joint here, and I added an internal cord and spring. It should move with you, giving you a more natural gait. Hopefully, with practice, you'll be able to move almost as well as before."

Edward stared down at it, lips pressed into a tight line. "I don't know what to say," he said, unable to hide the roughness in his voice.

"'Thank you' is a reasonable start, isn't it?" Willow piped.

"Yes," Edward laughed, shaking his head. "Thank you. Truly."

"You two, come back in one piece, alright?" Thomas said, pulling her in for a hug.

"We will," she said.

"Stay out of the city," Edward reminded them. "Silas promised everything you need will be sent to you while we're away."

"Don't you worry about us," Heidi said, reaching for her husband's arm. "We'll be just fine here, waiting for you."

With a final goodbye, Elin and Edward turned down the path, past the wisteria, towards the city docks.

The *Maren* waited in the strait, her hull rocking against the tide as if impatient for departure. As they stepped onto the gangway, Edward laced his fingers with hers.

She cast a final look at the city; her gaze catching on the rooftops and winding streets of Silvamare, before stepping onto the deck.

The crew was smaller than before—only trusted faces and the surgeon who had helped save Edward's life.

Near the helm stood Perry, still on loan from Drakcultus. He lifted a hand in greeting, his easy grin cutting through the heavy morning air.

The sight of him eased some of the worry in Elin's chest.

If Perry sailed with them, they would return before the Tide.

Chapter forty-one

The weeks to the Black Reef passed in disciplined monotony.

The crew kept themselves in constant motion, seeing to the needs of the ship. They slept in rotation, ate in silence, and spoke only when necessary. Every day was a held breath, one Elin feared would remain trapped until their ship returned home.

There were no sails on the horizon. No skirmishes. It should have been a comfort, but the lack of life, even at sea, gnawed at her.

Despite being by Edward's side, sleep came in fragments.

The ship creaked softly beneath her, the steady rhythm of the tide doing little to quiet the unease in her bones. She lay awake, staring into the dark. Her hand went out for Edward, only to find nothing.

With her silver hair falling over her shoulder, she propped herself up on an elbow, her eyes squinting in the dark.

A sharp crack split the night, then another. She slipped from the bed and climbed up the deck.

The night air was a wet breath against her skin. Lantern light swayed with the tide, casting frantic shadows across the planks.

Edward stood near the mainmast.

His shirt, wet with sweat, clung to his form as he moved with his blade in hand. He moved through a sequence—strike, pivot, recover—again and again; the rhythm faltering with his movements.

He didn't notice her.

She folded her arms as she watched. His footing was off as he favored one side over the other.

Moonlight caught the blade in blue sparks as he swiped at an unseen threat.

"Couldn't sleep?" she asked.

He stilled, chest rising and falling as he turned towards her. A sheen of sweat glimmered orange under the lanterns.

"You could say that."

She stepped forward, reaching for the other training blade leaning against the mast.

They took to their stances without a word.

She moved in; their first clash rang into the night. She didn't ease him into it. Her strikes were measured and forceful; she came at him just as she would any threat because that was who he would need to stand against. Not his wife. Not a friend. The person with the other blade would fight to the death.

He struggled to fend her off, moving more slowly than before. But his eyes were focused, watching her with intent.

She pressed. Feigned left.

He corrected, but not fast enough.

Her dull blade met his shoulder just as he stumbled back. The deck pitched beneath them, and he reached for the nearby handrail.

He squeezed his eyes shut. "Again," he said, opening them.

This time, he moved first, stepping into her space before she could set her footing, blade angling to occupy her guard.

She shifted to meet him. He waited until her weight committed to one direction before shifting his own. His blade slid down hers, catching at the hilt and turning the force aside. The motion upset her balance enough to expose her.

Edward stepped in and stopped his blade an inch from her ribs.

Some of the night crew wandered over during their fight, watching with curious eyes.

A scattering of applause, clapped in an uncomfortable discordance.

Edward nodded his thanks, and the crew wandered back to their assignments.

He turned away, crossing to the rail. He leaned on his forearms, his gaze fixed on the dark stretch of water ahead.

She waited a moment before joining him. His hand found hers in the dark, and he pulled her close. With her ear pressed to his chest, she listened to its unsteady rhythm.

"This doesn't feel right," he said. "We shouldn't have left."

Tracing small circles along his back, she nodded. "I know."

They stood like that for a long while, watching the horizon slowly pale with the coming day.

When the jagged spines of the Black Reef rose from the water at last, they did so beneath a too-bright and empty sky.

The sea lay deceptively calm between the teeth of stone.

No mist curled from its mouth. No heat shimmered along the jagged rocks. When she'd last seen the Black Reef, it was as alive as any monster.

Elin stepped closer to the bow, peering over the carved figurehead of a merwoman and into the sea below.

All she felt was absence beneath the water.

She closed her eyes, pushing her awareness beyond herself, but there was no brush of life. No distant pulse of movement. The creatures that dwelt here had fled.

What did they know that she didn't?

A chill slipped down her spine.

"Look there," someone muttered.

Elin reached for the hilt of her short sword as they slipped between the basalt pillars of the eastern channel. The remains of the *Leviathan* drifted within the ring of rocks—blackened ribs of timber bobbing in and out of the water.

Flashes of the battle flickered in Elin's thoughts. She blinked them away, wiping her clammy hand against her pants.

No other vessel could be seen hiding within. The only life Elin could sense within the Black Reef belonged to the *Maren*.

"If there were a crew sheltering here," Edward said quietly beside her, "they're gone now."

Elin looked at him; his skin was sallow as he stared at the blackened remains.

"Are you okay?" she asked.

"I'll be better when we're home," he said.

She nodded, glancing over the *Maren*. Silas stood at the helm, his gaze fixed beyond the wreckage, as though seeing something she could not.

"We hold position; we'll spot them if they return and then give chase," Howie commanded.

Silas's head turned slowly. "No."

Goosebumps ran up her arms.

"We've seen enough," Silas said. "There's no one here. Turn the ship around."

Howie did not move. "We have our orders."

Tension rippled outward, infectious amongst the crew.

Elin stepped closer. "What do you mean? We've completed the mission. There is no crew."

Howie's jaw tightened. "You're developing a bad habit of questioning your superiors, Elin."

Emotions warred within the captain. They pulled at him in a silent battle, one he was losing. Stepping closer, she rested her hands on Howie's shoulders. "Howie, what are you hiding?"

His pale blue eyes looked into hers. It cracked something in her to see all the pain he carried, the small flicker of faith he clung to. He was a man led by love for his kingdom, his gods, but above all else, for his crew.

"Why do you want to keep us here?"

He couldn't look at her.

"I was ordered," he said carefully, "to keep the *Maren* at sea until after the Tide."

The words floated over them before settling like a weight.

"*After* the Tide?" Elin repeated.

"There is concern," Howie continued, "regarding the viability of Silvamare."

Silas's composure broke. A wave of heat broke out across the ship, rippling from him. Elin could taste it, like coals in her throat.

"I knew it," he hissed. "I knew they were lying."

Edward approached, his face blank, his movements controlled. "Our families are there," he said. "Are you telling me I left my family in Silvamare to die?"

No, she thought. *No, not them, too.* Stepping back, she grabbed fistfuls of hair.

"It is not certain," Howie replied, though the certainty in his sorrow betrayed him.

"I am the Crown at Sea," Silas said. "You will sail this ship home. Now."

Howie closed his eyes briefly, as though steadying himself against an invisible blow.

"You are a man who still thinks like a boy," he said. "Let us do the only thing we can."

Silas's jaw flexed. "And what's that?"

"Pray for our home."

Silas almost laughed, disbelief dissolving into fury. "Pray?" he echoed.

Flame flickered faintly beneath his skin, a restless simmer along his hands, as though the fire within him strained for release.

"We are sailing home," Silas said, each word precise. "Do not test me, Captain."

Elin couldn't breathe. Tven had known this would happen. *When the prince is called away, you will not leave his side.*

This was why.

They had been intentionally removed. Exiled. Protected? Sacrificed?

If they turned back now, would they sail towards salvation or ruin? If they remained here, hidden in the Reef, could they live with themselves knowing they had abandoned those they loved?

The argument continued, voices rising and colliding—but the sound warped, stretching and thinning as though she were submerged beneath water.

A pulse began in her ears.

Her bones strained beneath an invisible weight.

"All of you, stop."

Her voice cut across the deck.

They turned, but she was not looking at them.

Her gaze was fixed on the horizon; the sky had split.

A wall of grey—so dense it was nearly black—advanced with unnatural speed, swallowing light, devouring the barren blue expanse.

Elin's stomach dropped.

She felt storms long before they showed themselves. Hours before their arrival. She could usually taste the change in the air, feel it in her bones.

She had felt nothing—until it was already too late.

"This isn't natural," she whispered.

"How long?" Silas demanded.

"I don't know," she said. "Not long."

Edward reached for her in two strides, hands bracketing her face. "You didn't feel that coming?"

She shook her head. "This—this has never happened."

The first low rumble of thunder rolled across the water.

Howie turned towards the crew. "Prepare the ship!"

Orders shattered the stillness.

Edward pulled Elin close, pressing a kiss to her hair. "We'll get through this," he murmured. "Then we'll sail home."

The sky went dark, and the sea began to rise.

"**𝕷ate–spring** and early summer bring with them a season of storms across the Wavecrest Ocean. Cold air from the north clashes with the hot, humid air in the south, forming life-threatening storms. Ships are advised to take alternative routes when possible."

— *Maritime Weather*, a common text.

Chapter forty-two

The crew worked with a desperation that bordered on frenzy. Sails were hauled. Lines secured. Men scrambled across the deck. Perry worked to weave the winds in their favor, to drive the ship away from the coming storm.

Overhead, the sun burned mercilessly as they hauled canvas, secured cargo, and lashed anything that might become a weapon when the sea rose against them.

The wall of cloud advanced without pause—an iron curtain swallowing the horizon inch by inch.

Wind barreled into them.

It whipped at their clothing and threatened to topple them over.

Waves rose in black ridges, folding over themselves, slamming against the hull with a force that thundered. The *Maren* climbed and plunged, as though the ocean meant to break her apart piece by piece.

A wave broke over the deck, slamming into Elin hard enough to steal the breath from her lungs. Her fingers slipped against the soaked wood before catching on a length of rope.

Someone shouted—cut short as another crash swallowed the sound.

The *Maren* lurched again, violent and sudden.

Light vanished.

The clouds knitted together overhead until even midday was like the bottom of the sea.

There were no stars. No horizon.

No sense of direction. Time had dissolved.

They were trapped in an endless cyclone. The ship heaved violently, pitching them from wall to wall. Crates tore loose despite their efforts. Somewhere above, something snapped with a crack like bone.

Without the sun, the horizon, or the stars, it was impossible to keep track of the days they spent below.

They slept when they could, bracing themselves against walls so they would not be thrown across the hold. They woke unsure whether hours or days had passed. The air grew thick with dampness. Each time the hull groaned, Elin flinched.

Sometimes the sound of retching could be heard over the storm's roar.

Each time the *Maren* dropped violently into a trough, someone whispered a prayer.

Between the worst of it, when the storm seemed to pause, if only long enough to build back up its strength, they took to playing cards and sharing stories. They argued over trivial things, holding on to the ordinary. Pretending things were as they'd always been.

Silas shaped flame into figures to distract them.

Winged serpents flying through clouds.

A pine rising from embers.

An earthen giant with mountains for shoulders.

He told them of ancient Silvamari who carved their histories into living trunks, found in hidden groves, planted by men bound to Terron's beasts. He spoke of how stories lived, even when cities and people fell.

The firelight hollowed his face; his eyes glowed a reflective orange.

Edward sat with his shoulder pressed to hers. He never drifted far.

If the sea split the hull and swallowed them whole, it would not take them alone.

There was no sudden end to the storm. It was a gradual exhaustion. Elin felt it weaken as the pressure eased, bit by bit.

The blows against the ship's hull grew sporadic. The groaning timbers settled into uneasy creaks.

When the silence finally arrived, it felt foreign.

It was Howie who unbarred the hatch.

Cold night air spilt in.

They climbed slowly, blinking up at the glimmering sky. No one knew how many days they had been entombed.

"Four," Edward insisted.

"Five," Silas countered.

She couldn't form a guess; she only knew it felt like a lifetime.

Howie stood at the helm with a sextant and a face carved of stone. He took his measurements in silence.

When he finally spoke, his voice was steady.

"We're roughly three weeks' sail from Silvamare."

"Three weeks."

Three weeks was too long.

Depending on how long the storm had held them captive, they would reach home just before the Tide—

—or after it had already passed.

Elin watched Silas and Edward speak in low tones near the helm. She did not know what had been said to secure Howie's agreement to sail home now, but she suspected persuasion had little to do with it.

She watched the captain when he charted their course. He held himself with a poised resignation, but he could not hide from her his grief, nor his relief.

Resting her chin on the starboard rail, Elin looked down at the murky water, watching a piece of driftwood bob along a gentle wave.

Elin had the distinct sense that Howie knew exactly how many days the storm had stolen and that when they reached Silvamare, the Tide would be long finished.

She wouldn't mention it to Edward; she'd let him hold on to his hope as she did to hers.

It was all she could do to keep from falling apart.

Chapter forty-three

Heidi

The square filled slowly, as it did every year. People came in cautious clusters, keeping distance where they could. Masks covered their mouths and noses, muting what little conversation remained. No one lingered too close.

The Graves family arrived together. Despite their reprieve from this year's Tide, they risked exposure for their friends whose names were in the drawing.

Heidi kept the twins near her side, a hand resting lightly on each of their shoulders. Thomas walked ahead, clearing a path through the crowd, with Elide following close behind.

Last year, during the drawing ceremony, it rained. The sky had torn open and poured down until they'd been soaked to the bone. But this year, the sky was an unblemished blue. The sun bore down on them, hot and unyielding.

There was no dais set at the front of the square. No driftwood bowl, nor guards forming a perimeter. No priest from Drakcultus was present to read the names.

"What's going on?" Elide whispered.

Thomas didn't answer. He was looking towards the center of the square—towards a cluster of people gathered around a series of nailed postings.

More people pushed forward to read it, craning their necks. Others stood frozen where they were, as though waiting for someone else to say what it meant.

A wrongness slid beneath Heidi's ribs and stayed there.

"Stay close," she breathed to the twins.

They moved together through the crowd. By the time they reached the front, someone had already begun to read the notice aloud.

His voice trembled. "The Crown of Silvamare regrets to inform its citizens..." He faltered, swallowing. "Due to the current conditions of plague and loss, this year's Tide quota cannot be met."

A ripple passed through the square.

People shifted, and someone laughed—a short, sharp sound that didn't belong.

Heidi pulled the twins closer so that they were in front of her.

"That's not possible," another voice said. "What of our allies? Where's our support?"

The man kept reading. Heidi held her breath so that she wouldn't miss a word.

"The sea god will not be denied. All remaining souls will be claimed."

A heavy silence descended.

"They're lying," Margot said.

"They have to be," Willow agreed, tugging on Heidi's arm. "There's another way—there has to be—"

Heidi shushed them.

"The Crown advises citizens to remain with their families. Should any attempt resistance, they do so at their own risk," the man continued.

A woman near the front cried. It started softly, a single broken sound, and then others joined it—voices rising, overlapping, unraveling into something that could no longer be contained.

"No," someone shouted. "No, that's not—no—"

A man shoved forward, tearing the notice from the wall. "This is a lie," he said, louder now. "They've made a mistake."

Another voice cut through, sharp with panic. "They wouldn't lie about this!"

"Why not—"

"Not this—never this—"

The crowd broke.

It surged towards the palace gates; people shouted, demanding answers. Others pulled away, grabbing hands, calling names, trying to gather what remained of their families.

Heidi held the twins close as bodies bumped past, the fear of the plague forgotten in the face of destruction.

"Thomas," she said.

He faced her, and the look on her face brought him to a sudden halt.

"We need to go," she said.

He nodded once.

They moved quickly, pushing through the crowd as it unraveled around them.

By the time they reached the outer streets, the city was already beginning to break.

Voices echoed through the alleys. Doors slammed. Somewhere in the distance, something shattered.

"What does it mean?" Elide asked, her voice too loud, too thin. "They said—what does that mean?"

"It means we need to leave," Heidi said.

They didn't bother packing much. There was no time for it, and some instinct told Heidi it wouldn't matter, anyway.

Thomas grabbed what he could carry—water, a small pack, a knife. Elide helped the twins pull on their boots. No one spoke of what they were leaving behind.

"Stay together," Thomas said as they stepped back outside.

The streets in the city were worse now.

Smoke curled into the sky from a cluster of buildings in the square. The Graves dodged bodies as people ran in every direction, some shouting, others silent with shock. A man stumbled past them, his face slick with sweat, his mask hanging loose around his neck. Dark blotches climbed his throat.

Heidi pulled the twins away.

"Don't look," she murmured.

They moved faster towards the docks, towards the only option that made sense.

They slowed as they neared the strait.

The water stretched out before them, wide and indifferent.

They'd been too late.

Elide stepped forward. "They cannot all be gone."

"We shouldn't have gone back for our things," Thomas said. "We should have left as soon as we heard…"

Heidi reached for him, holding him close.

Behind them, Silvamare was burning.

The sounds of the city falling reached them—shouting, breaking, the distant crack of something collapsing. The wind carried it across the water, thin and distorted.

Heidi closed her eyes.

When she opened them again, Thomas was still staring out at the horizon, as though something might appear if he waited long enough.

Nothing did.

He exhaled slowly.

"We can't stay here," he said.

Heidi nodded, tightening her grip on the girls' hands.

"Come on," she said.

With nowhere else to go, they turned back towards the cottage.

They passed others on their way back, watching the last of their hope drain at the sight of the empty docks as they too came to understand.

There was no way out.

"In the early days of the first Tides, the sea god was met with resistance. Aquerios's greatest warriors tried and failed to battle against the god, even with their divine gifts; their otherworldly patrons had abandoned them. Hardened and tested as they fought to eliminate the twisted beasts of the realm, infected by curses and rotten hearts, some plagues were too great. One by one, they died. And with them some of the earliest histories of Aquerios."

—*A History of the First Tides*, from the Library of the Old Kingdom of Sidon

Chapter forty-four

Arden

Arden had grown to believe that secrecy was a mercy.

He carried that belief for years, polishing it into something noble. It did not feel noble now.

He remembered with painful clarity the night his mother first entrusted him with the truth of the Tide. She dismissed the court, barred the doors, and spoke in a voice stripped of ceremony. There had been no dramatics, no attempts to soften the revelation. Only the facts: the bargain struck generations before, the creature beneath the water, the annual cost to keep it sated.

He listened without interruption. When she finished, the only thought that came was that he wished he had never heard it at all. It only filled him with a sense of helplessness and a permanent unease in his belly.

Linden had borne the knowledge differently. Even as a boy, he had possessed a brutal pragmatism that Arden both envied and resented. Where Arden grieved the cruelty of the arrangement, Linden assessed what must be done to survive it. He understood, even then, that ruling was often an exercise in choosing the least ruinous path.

Silas was most like him.

As a child, he had been all heat and instinct, quick to emotion and quicker still to defend those he loved. Time tempered him; responsibility had taught him restraint. Yet emotion remained his first language. It was one of many reasons he kept the full truth from Silas. Let him believe the Tide was a trial to endure, not a sentence waiting to be carried out.

He hoped now, as his kingdom made its final stand against the Tide and the monster behind it, that Silas would survive it and live to someday forgive him for the lies—all of them.

If Silas ever learned the truth—that the moment Arden was born, the seers had named him the final king of Silvamare—how could he forgive him for keeping that knowledge buried? How could any of them understand that he'd—just as his parents—thought it better if they didn't know what fate would befall them? Sometimes ignorance was the greatest gift of all.

Standing now beneath the glass-domed ceiling of the mausoleum, Arden prayed for a final gift, no longer fearful of being greedy in his asking. He sent a plea to the gods: had they any mercy in their hearts, they'd let something of Silvamare survive.

Reina stood at his side amongst the tombs of their ancestors, the carved histories rising around them in solemn ranks. Moonlight filtered through the dome above, pale and distant, painting her features in silver. He held onto her, feeling the steadiness of her heart against his chest.

Outside, the sea battered the city walls.

Inside his mind, a colder pressure gathered.

It arrived as an intrusion, a presence pressing against the boundaries of his thoughts until it forced its way through.

"What is this?"

"We have too few souls to give," Arden answered.

"Then I will take what remains."

Arden sent one final plea into the darkness. *"If there is mercy in you, grant it now."*

"I have none."

Reina's fingers tightened, and though she could not hear the exchange, she sensed the shift in him. He pulled back to look at her, and at the slight movement of his head, the last fragile thread of hope left her eyes. Tears slipped free, silent and unrestrained.

He drew her against him, pressing her close as though his body might serve as a shield against the inevitable. For years, she had been the steadier force between them, guiding him away from decisions born of pride or fear. In her presence, he found clarity when doubt threatened to consume him. Now there was no clarity to be found, only the quiet knowledge that whatever came next would find them together.

The first impact struck the mausoleum with a force that shuddered through stone. A crack splintered across the great door, thin lines of water forcing their way inward and spreading across the marble floor. The air grew heavy with salt.

Another blow followed, closer, more violent. Glass along the upper walls fractured in jagged lines, and the moonlight dimmed as a dark mass rose beyond the dome.

Reina lifted her face to his. He lowered his forehead to hers, allowing himself one last moment of stillness.

"I am grateful for the life we shared," he murmured.

She kissed him softly, as though committing him to memory. "I love you."

"Always," he answered, water pooling at his feet.

The final fracture came from above. The glass ceiling split in widening veins, the sound sharp and inevitable, until the structure could bear no more.

When it gave way, the sea descended in a single, crushing surge. The water slammed into them, stealing their breath and balance. He locked his hands into the fabric at her back and held fast while the force of it tried to wrench them apart.

He did not release her.

Not as the chamber vanished beneath churning black. Not as air fled his lungs.

He held her until there was no more strength left against the darkness, until the Tide stole their souls. Until all was lost.

And then there was nothing but the weight of the sea consuming what had once been a kingdom. It vanished beneath the Tide as though it had never been at all.

The Crown of Silvamare,

I fear I may sound foolish, perhaps even mad, but I write out of grave concern for Silvamare upon the coming Tide. I am plagued by dreams of its fall, vivid beyond any I have known. Though I am no prophetess, and most dreams are nothing more than restless wanderings—I cannot shake the sense that this one is different.

May the winds be favorable as this letter finds you, so that Drakcultus may yet be of help, should you require support beyond your allotted quota. Silvamare, and your family, are in my prayers as you endure your losses and continue to navigate the outbreak.

I also pray—fervently—that I am wrong, and that I am proven nothing more than a foolish woman, prey to the hysterics of nightmares. Perhaps you may give me grief for it at the next congregation. I ask only that you do not share news of this letter with my father, should it prove unnecessary. I would consider it a personal debt.

—*Princess Sereia Gaiano,*
Heir to the Crown of Drakcultus

Chapter forty-five

The coastline of Silvamare revealed itself in fractured slivers of silver and shadow beneath the full moon.

At first, it was easy to believe nothing had changed. The cliffs stood as dark, familiar slopes; the rocky sweep of shoreline caught the light in uneven strokes. But as the *Maren* drew nearer, a quiet wrongness settled under her skin.

Something drifted in the water. She watched as splintered beams and lengths of rope passed them by, rising and falling with the current.

"The storm must have come through here," someone muttered from behind.

She nodded, biting her lip.

As they crossed fully into Silvamare's waters, a chill burrowed deep into her bones—as though something essential had been siphoned from the land itself. Silence pressed against her ears. An old rhyme stirred in her mind—a warning about tides that lured children from shore. For a moment she feared the water spirit had returned, but the silence on deck was lucid, collective.

There were no cries of night-birds.

No insects stirred in the brush as they skirted Silvamare's shore. No lantern light shimmered along the slopes, marking the scattering of homes.

The island did not feel asleep; it felt empty.

Whatever had carved the life from Silvamare was not a water spirit; it was worse.

Her heart hammered. Pressure built in the air—heavy, electric. Along the darkened horizon, the sea was rising—lifting into a wall that did not break.

The wall came on with such ferocity that she was forced to question if they'd arrived too late—or too soon.

The ship entered the mouth of the narrow strait leading towards the heart of the island.

At its mouth stood the bell towers, looming and neglected, their great chains sagging in the water. Their beckoning flame extinguished. A sudden gust tore through the channel, wrenching an uneven toll from the bells. The sound clanged violently, vibrating through the air, echoing down the waterway like a warning call.

Clouds swallowed the moon in a single sweep, plunging the strait into abrupt darkness. The crew lifted their faces towards the sky, and in that suspended moment no one moved, as if each man feared that motion itself might confirm what they were beginning to understand.

No one spoke the words aloud, but they all knew what it meant.

Elin had long believed three fates shadowed her life. The first had arrived the night Hatra's crew stole her skin and murdered her brother. The second she had thought conquered when she chose the land and chose Edward, believing she had stepped beyond the sea's reach.

Now she understood that what she had taken for peace had only ever been a reprieve.

The water beneath the *Maren* shifted with sudden violence, a deep convulsion that sent a wave crashing across the deck. Men were thrown off their footing. Elin reached instinctively for the railing but grasped only air as the ship lurched hard.

Edward. The thought pierced through the chaos, sharp and singular.

Her boots lost purchase. The deck rose to meet her, and the impact drove the breath from her lungs. A heartbeat later her head struck the planks with a crack that scattered light across her vision. Saltwater soaked through her clothes as she rolled onto her side, dazed.

She pressed trembling fingers to the back of her skull and drew them away slick with blood.

When she forced herself upright, the sea was fully upon them; rising in dark walls that eclipsed the strait. The wind howled down the channel, and another wave crashed over the rail, dragging loose equipment towards the edge.

Somewhere through the roar of the water, she heard Edward shouting her name.

The sea was reclaiming what it had been owed.

From some fates, there is no escape.

Extended Content Warning:

The Ice in Our Veins is intended for adult readers. While it does not contain explicit sex or graphic torture, it explores heavy emotional themes, including loss, trauma, and violence. Reader discretion is advised, especially for those sensitive to depictions of grief, physical harm, or systemic injustice.

See below for a full list of trigger warnings. I've tried to be as thorough as possible.

While some of these warnings may reveal spoilers, you know yourself best—read at your own pace and skip whatever you need to.

Content Trigger Warnings

The Ice in Our Veins contains depictions or mentions of:
- Violence and Gore
- Death of a sibling (on-page; emotionally intense)
- Murder and physical assault (including fatal stabbing and combat)
- Limb amputation (on-page, a character loses a leg in a fight)
- Mental Health and Emotional Distress
- Grief and trauma (sustained focus on loss, especially of a sibling)
- Nightmares and flashbacks
- Abuse and Power Imbalance
- Systemic exploitation (e.g. selkie pelts stolen and used for power)
- Mild sexual content

Other Sensitive Themes:
- Body horror
- Infertility
- Religious/mythological elements
- Piracy

Author's Note

The Ice in Our Veins wasn't a part of my original plan.

It began with Isabel—someone who was only meant to exist as a side character of the *Black Tide Trilogy*. As her story took shape, it became clear that what she carried—her grief, her choices, and the life she lost—could not be contained within the margins of another narrative. This book exists because her story demanded more space.

In the process of telling it, Isabel became Elin.

Like Elin, I have known grief, loss, and the feeling of not quite fitting where you are. Pieces of that found their way into this story.

Frostwake's culture was inspired by nomadic indigenous groups of the Arctic, including the Inuit, Chukchi, and Siberian Yupik. Its landscape and atmosphere draw from Scandinavian environments, while elements of its mythology—such as the selkies and the Sluagh—are rooted in Celtic folklore. While this world is fictional, I approached its creation with respect and intention, drawing inspiration from real cultures without attempting to replicate them.

This is a story about the cost of love and the choice to bear it anyway.

Acknowledgements

The Ice in Our Veins was written during a time in my life when I stopped letting what felt probable dictate what was possible. For a long time, I played it safe and in doing so, I left behind pieces of myself I cared deeply about. In my final year of college, a creative writing class reminded me how much I loved storytelling, and I haven't let it go since.

When I began writing the *Black Tide Trilogy*, no one supported me more than my husband. He encouraged me to pursue self-publishing wholeheartedly and has stood beside me every step of the way. I'm not sure I would have come this far without him. Thank you for believing in me and for being my best friend. I love you.

To my sisters—thank you for reading the earliest drafts and for cheering me on from the very beginning. Your support has meant more than I can say.

And to my beta readers: thank you for your time, your insight, and your honesty. Your feedback shaped this book in ways I couldn't have done alone.

The Salt in Our Blood

Black Tide Trilogy - Book 1

subject to changes

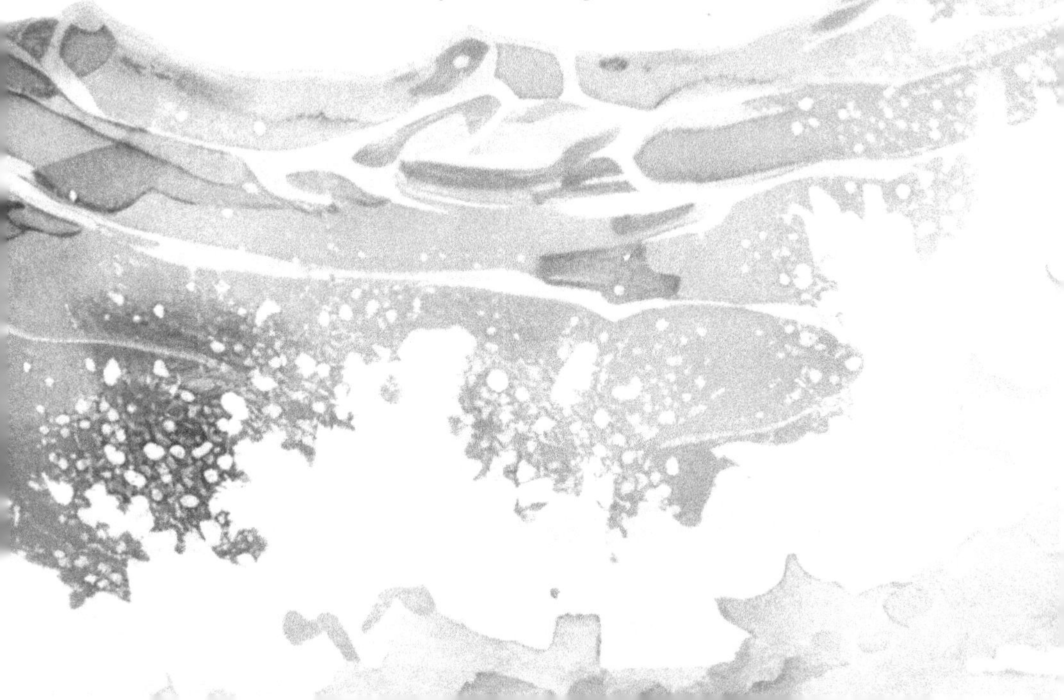

"Forged in a nightmare too twisted for even the vilest of souls to envision, the darkness crept upon him like a living thing. Hungry. Relentless. Desperate to devour the last flicker of light drowning in an ocean of blackened hate. Within this unholy cage of sorrow and rage, he waited. Not to escape, but to damn another of his own flesh and blood.

So he sang, and the sea listened.

A lullaby of ruin carried from blood to blood, carried by the tide until it reached her.

And when the salt at last found her veins, the nightmare might finally end."

Chapter One

Three Months Ago

Sereia Gaiano only defied her father once, eight months ago, and now she was made to suffer.

Before the devastating Tide arrived, she had already envisioned the kingdom of Silvamare's demise, a recurring dream of its eventual ruin. Only a thought, and she was plunged back into the vision. The Tide consuming the island, screams echoing in her ears. Lifeless eyes staring into hers as the sea god claimed their souls.

In trying to warn her father of what she'd seen, she'd only embarrassed him. He dismissed her, unwilling to consider it had been more than a dream. She'd written to Silvamare's King and Queen, anyway.

It made no difference, and she had been forced to suffer since.

She'd do it again, though, if it meant Silvamare never fell. If it meant Silas never fell with it.

"Promise me you will be safe," she'd asked him.

"I will."

It was the one promise he couldn't keep.

Standing in the moon's glow, a cool spring breeze wrapped around her as she leaned over the balcony rails. Below, waves licked up the sides of the tower, their crests breaking into moon-silvered fingers. She let her arm dangle over the rail toward the waves. *Go on*, she thought, *if you're going to take me, do it now.*

Sea spray shot up, flecking cool droplets across her cheek. Sighing, she brought her other hand to rest under her chin and looked out over the expanse of the Wavecrest.

She thought her father might let her out today--to finally leave her chambers, she was ready to return to her role as the quiet, dutiful daughter. But the king had other plans in mind for their meeting, seeking to expand her punishment by denying her permission to attend the annual summer celebrations in Adoratia. She replayed it in her head, the ripples of the sea blurring with memory until she was once again standing in his study.

"Father, I assure you I am of sound mind. I have had much time to think on my actions and promise no embarrassment will come to you from my behavior," she said.

"I am pleased to hear this. Still, the matter is settled. You may return to your chambers."

A knot tightened in her stomach, her gaze darting towards the exit, her words tumbling out in a rush, a plea for freedom.

"You cannot continue to restrict my movements or determine if I may fulfill my duties. It violates the Drakon treaty to prevent my presence—"

"You were not so disappointed when I denied you attendance at the Drakcultian Spring Celebrations."

"The Gaianos and the joint houses have never accepted me. I have no role in the celebrations." Nor did she want one.

"You've never expressed an interest in a role. If you did, I'd happily welcome it. You are a Gaiano. Though who can blame the others for being wary of you? You are a woman. One that has shown they can't be trusted."

"I am your heir. You would violate law, risk conflict with Adoratia to punish me for something I've already been punished for?"

"You will not go. That's an order."

Sereia's nostrils flared; heat flooded her cheeks. She would keep her calm. "Father, I am sorry for sending the letter. But how could I have not?"

"Would you do it again?"

She said nothing. She didn't want to lie, but she didn't want to stoke his ire.

"There are consequences to your choices, your words. How you still don't understand that is beyond me."

"If you took the time to teach me, to properly train me as heir—if you spent less time fearing me and trying to control me, I'd actually learn something from you."

The king slammed his hand onto his desk. She flinched.

"You will learn your place," he said, voice cold and empty.

The air in the room thinned. Her lungs collapsed as her father ripped away her breath, his magic like ice in her lungs. Sereia reached for her throat, stars dancing before her eyes, blotting out her vision.

"You will remain in your chambers until I determine you may leave."

There was no air to reason—to plea for his mercy. She staggered back toward the wall of shelves before slumping to the ground.

Hours passed before she woke in her chambers. The sky had shifted from the vibrant blue of noon to star-pricked night. Her throat burned, and she coughed, rolling onto her side. She blushed red up her neck, embarrassed by the realization that someone had returned her here.

Moonlight poured through the glass of her balcony door; the promise of fresh air had her lifting herself from her bed. She nearly cried as the night air kissed her skin.

Here she had festered, a storm of resentment brewing with every passing moment. When she'd first learned the news of Silas's death, it was like a cold plunge into icy water. Then it was fire, unbearable rage. She took out her anger on her father, blaming him for his inaction. Her father claimed she suffered from delusions, her mind too fragile to handle the shock of Silvamare's fall.

He'd locked her away for months, claiming it was for the betterment of her health. She knew it for what it was.

Her knuckles turned white as she gripped the rail, her breath coming in short gasps.

She was not a bird meant for a lifetime in a cage.

Pushing away from the rails, Sereia returned to her room.

Her skin was hot, and the sensation that she might burst into flames was enough to force her out of her dress. She couldn't help it; a mocking laugh bubbled up and out. Her mother would be relieved to see Sereia could conjure an actual flame rather than the drowned one they kept secret.

She tossed her dress aside without thought, sending papers fluttering from her desk. A disgruntled sigh escaped her as she scooped up the pages from the floor, their soft, worn texture and folded corners speaking of countless readings. She put them in a drawer, a place of safekeeping for the times she would later choose to torment herself with dreams that could never be.

It was becoming harder to remember herself, to harness her inner strength. Her father sought to break her spirit, one she already kept tempered to quiet the fears of others. Many in the palace thought her destined to become a traitor. From the moment her prophecy left the prophetess's lips, she'd been treated like a viper.

"I am not a prisoner," she told herself. *"I am still free to make my own decisions, and I will control my destiny."*

Now she only needed to prove it to herself.

She slipped into her dressing gown before approaching her bedroom door. She knocked three times. The door cracked open to reveal a familiar face. Greer, her cousin and personal guard, smiled at her. Though the smile did little to hide the concern in her green eyes. "Are you okay?" she asked.

Sereia nodded. "Yes. I just wanted you to know I'm going to bed."

"Okay," Greer drawled so that it sounded more like a question. "Tomas and I will continue to stand here in complete and utter silence," Greer called over her shoulder.

She frowned in his direction before returning her gaze to Sereia. She raised a brow at her.

"I said I'm okay," Sereia reassured her.

"We're going to get you out of there," Greer promised. "He can't keep you locked up forever."

Sereia said nothing, but offered her cousin a weak smile before shutting the door.

Moving silently through her room, she changed into her lightest dress. Then at her vanity, she donned a mourner's mask. The black gauzy material crossed over her nose, falling to beneath her chin as she tied it around her head. Only her eyes remained visible, their vibrant blues stark against the moon white of her skin and the blackness of her hair. She donned a cloak next, the oversized hood dulling the bright effect of her eyes beneath shadow.

Sereia returned to the balcony. She wrapped her hands around the railing. Her heart thudded in her chest, adrenaline already filling it.

"It would be a shame if you hit the rocks," a voice cautioned.

A shaky breath escaped her, and she smiled.

"Indeed. You'd have to find someone else's mind to intrude on, offering unsolicited advice," she sent back.

A dark chuckle rumbled through her skull, causing goosebumps to rise along her flesh.

"I understand the need to escape that which you cannot control, trust me, my child. I only ask that you be safe."

"I'll be sure to miss the rocks then," she said with a heave as she stepped up onto the ledge.

She pushed back flashes of dreams—recent nightmares where the ocean's water closed over her head, her hands reaching for a lifeline that wasn't there as she was dragged below.

Lucius offered no further reply, but she felt his presence linger, wary as she dove for the sea below.

The force of hitting the ocean's surface was so intense it almost took her breath away. A pins-and-needles tingle vibrated through her muscles from the impact. The chilly waters stripped the warmth from her skin, but she embraced it all because she was free. Outside the stone walls of the palace for the first time in months, Sereia feared it might only be a dream. That was until the need to take in air reminded her she was very much awake.

She was careful as she broke the surface, only rising to breathe to limit the chance she'd be caught by a patrolling guard as she skirted the palace shore, making her way toward the city.

Breaking the surface once more, Sereia spotted the small strip of beach she'd sought. She swam to the shore, rising from the current. Her damp clothes clung to her. She righted her hood and adjusted her mask. Water dripped from her hood and sand clung to the hem of her clothing as she made her way up the beach toward the city. She walked past a couple sitting on the shore, passing a cup of what was likely ale between them.

"Lovely evening for a swim," she said. It wasn't.

They smiled at her, taken by the oddity of it. "So it seems."

The cool spring breeze sent shivers through her wet skin, and she fought the clattering of her teeth.

She continued on, ignoring the stares she received as she neared the city streets. Once in the city, no one paid any mind to her. Just one of many oddities to be seen so late at night.

It was warmer on the city streets; the fires were spaced closer together.

Sereia kept her hood low as she moved through the streets of Drakcultus, slippers whispering over stone polished by centuries of tides and travel.

The streets were well-maintained, and lanterns hung at intervals, driving away the shadows of night. Stone buildings rose on either side of her, tall and ornate—proud, much like the family that built them. Still, no amount of pride could hide the truth. There were signs of strain if one knew where to look. Many homes and windows sat dark and boarded up.

Drakcultus, like the rest of the world, was shrinking.

As she continued along, slipping past bodies in the crowded street, she found herself in the square. A mural she'd only ever seen during the day stretched along the inner curve of the square: a drake with jaws clamped around the serpentine body of an amphiptere. Blood spilled in painted rivulets, flowing downward into the sea.

A ripple of noise pulled her from her thoughts—raised voices filtered through her ears, a sharp crack of something breaking.

A crowd had gathered outside a tavern, bodies pressing inward toward a widening circle of chaos. Curiosity tugged at her, and before she could talk herself out of it, she slipped into the outer edge of the bodies. Her nostrils were assaulted by the mingled odors of sweat and the sharp tang of spilled ale.

Two men stood nose to nose, spit flying as they hurled insults at one another. She nudged the man to her right, her voice carrying a curious tone as she asked what they were fighting about. He revealed that the red-haired one had apparently made a move on the other's wife. Their quarrel had spilled from the tavern into the street.

The curses they flung were creative enough to warm her cheeks beneath the mask.

She felt the rough metal of the tankard as it was thrust into her hands, a wave of ale spilling onto the cobblestone street. She hesitated only a moment before lifting the mask just enough to drink. The ale burned its way down, heat blooming in her chest, loosening muscles that had been tight for months. Without a word, she passed the tankard to the next person.

The redhead struck first.

The crowd roared approval. Coins clinked as bets were placed. Flesh met flesh with sickening thuds, turning wet as blood was spilled. Each blow was punctuated by cheers and jeers.

Greer would have delighted in this. She would have elbowed her way forward and wagered shamelessly.

Silas would have stepped between them, she thought.

Her hand instinctively went to her chest, where a hollow ache bloomed.

She'd left her tower because she was tired of feeling like a captive, but it was also to escape the quiet. The quiet forced her to sit with her burdens. She wanted to surround herself with enough noise to drown out her grief, even if just for a night. Nevertheless, she thought of him.

Soon the city guard would arrive to break up the fight. She scanned the streets, searching for a glint of steel. The crowd was growing quickly; the audience beginning to join in on the violence.

Before she could escape the growing crowd, a man was shoved backward. He stumbled into her, and she lost her footing on the stones. For a heartbeat she felt the ground tilt—then firm hands caught her.

She looked up at her rescuer in surprise.

A mourning mask covered the lower half of his face. The sight of it pricked at her conscience. She wore hers as a disguise, but mourning had once been the reason she first bore it. Traditionally, the masks were only worn after a recent loss.

Her gaze lifted above the mask. Storm-grey eyes stared back at her. They were alight with amusement.

Her chest clenched so hard it hurt to breathe. A flood of emotion threatened to pull her under. She forced herself to look away. They are only eyes, she told herself.

"Th—thank you," she managed.

He said something more, but the words were swallowed by the crowd's roar and the pounding in her ears. She leaned closer without thinking, trying to catch what he said.

He bent toward her, mouth near her ear.

"Are you hurt?"

The nearness startled her, but she did not move. His voice was low and smooth, a caress that made her heart stumble.

"No," she said, forcing composure into her tone.

"Though I would have righted myself."

"And rob me of the chance to come to your rescue?" There was a thread of dry humor.

Despite herself, the corner of her mouth curved. "I am no thief."

"And I'm no hero."

"A villain then? If so, I ought to seek better company." She didn't move.

"Is that what you seek then? Company?"

"I—," she began. "I seek to follow where the night takes me. To be someone else, if only for tonight."

"It seems we both seek to escape ourselves then," he said. "Care for a walk? I imagine the city guard will arrive anytime now."

A sense of uncertainty caused Sereia to hesitate.

"I promise to be a perfect gentleman," his eyes crinkled in a smile.

He motioned towards an unobstructed path; his hands were stained with ink. She complied, stepping away from the densely packed group.

"What is your name?"

"I am no one," she said.

His brows furrowed. "You cannot be no one."

"Fine, I'll be your lady then. A gentleman would not wander about with a random woman on his arm, now would he?"

He nodded his approval, then held out his arm for her to take. "My lady, it is then."

She took his arm; the sleeves of her cloak were still slightly damp.

"Why are you wet?"

"I went for a swim," she said, pursing her lips to keep from laughing.

"Interesting," was all he had to say as he led her away from the crowd onto the open streets of the city.

They walked aimlessly, their steps falling easily into rhythm. Somewhere between one lantern and the next, they began to invent themselves.

He was a storyteller, he decided. A wanderer who traveled from island to island, spinning tales for coin and applause.

"And you?" he asked.

"A dancer," she replied without hesitation. "I perform during your storytelling."

He hummed approvingly. "We've traveled together for years."

"The crowds adore us."

"Especially when we scandalize them."

She arched a brow beneath her hood. "Scandalize them?"

"With a kiss, now and then," he said lightly. "It keeps attendance high."

Before she could reply, the thunder of hooves split the night.

A horse tore around the corner ahead of them, the rider reckless and blind to anything in his path. The stranger reacted instantly, pulling her sharply against him and pivoting so the animal surged past with inches to spare.

Her heart leapt into her throat.

"That is twice now you have rescued me," she said once her pulse steadied.

"I cannot lose my lady to a horse," he replied. "It is not an interesting enough story for my audience."

"Indeed, I'd hate to bore a crowd with such a boring, albeit embarrassing, demise."

His arm remained around her a moment longer than necessary before he released her.

Her gaze drifted to the mourning mask covering his face.

The question arose before she could stop it.

"Who do you mourn?"

She felt his muscles tense beneath her touch.

"My parents," he said after a moment. "And my brother."

The pain in his voice was heavy. She wished she hadn't asked.

"I'm sorry," she whispered.

"Who have you lost?" he asked.

She worried her bottom lip.

"A friend—to the Tide last year," she said.

He was silent.

"That is a long time to wear a mask," he finally replied.

She withdrew from the crook of his arm. They had wandered far now, away from the well-lit streets. Mist curled in from the sea, silvering the stones and swallowing the edges of the world.

He didn't press for a reply.

"Life grows around grief," she said at last. "It softens the sharp edges."

She swallowed as she tried to think of a face she'd once committed to memory in stark relief, but now the edges were softer, little details lost with the passage of time.

"That realization is its own kind of loss, causing the ache to bleed a little more. I fear the day it stops," she added.

He stopped walking, and she followed.

In the fog and shadow, they face each other, both little more than an outline against the dim light.

"I fear that too," he whispered. "When grief becomes soft and distant, carrying nothing but the memory of pain." Then, almost too quiet to hear, "A face in the mist, scarcely a face at all."

Her chest tightened at the echo of her own thoughts.

Without thinking, she stepped closer and lifted her hand to his cheek. The fabric of the mask was cool beneath her palm. He covered her hand with his.

To any passerby, they would look exactly as they claimed to be.

A gentleman and his lady.

"I don't make a habit of midnight companionship," he admitted softly.

She smiled faintly. "Is this still pretense or is that real?"

His laugh was a breath of warm air that she felt through the fabric between them. "It's real."

The mist continued to thicken around them, silver clouds hiding the world around them. Clouds shifted in the night sky, blotting out the remaining moonlight.

"The person you lost," he began. "You loved them very much?"

She sucked in a breath. "I still do."

"Have you ever been in love?"

"Once," he admitted.

"What happened?"

"I thought I had time," he said. "It was complicated, and I needed time to figure out how to make it work, but I—I didn't have enough of it."

"I never told him either," she confessed, shivering against a cool breeze.

He pulled her into him, wrapping his arms around her, a warm shield against the cool night.

"This is still pretense?"

"For a little longer, if that's okay?"

"It is."

His fingers brushed the hem of her mask, and she stilled.

"May I?" he asked.

It was dark, too dark to make out defining features, enough to keep her identity hidden. Her heart thrummed in her chest. Her mind screamed at her to think, but her heart—her reckless, broken heart—was louder.

"Yes," she said shakily.

His fingertips brushed her cheeks as he pulled the mask down. Her breath fogged between them. The heat of his thumb under her chin sank deep as he lifted her face toward his.

She lifted her hands to his face, feeling the lining of his mask. She paused, hesitating. He rested his calloused hands on hers, guiding the mask down his chin. His stubble was rough against her palms.

She'd never allowed a stranger to touch her so intimately; it was dangerous. She knew she needed to end this. Yet, as they stood in the darkness, the heat of their shared breath between them, there was an undeniable familiarity to him. What was the harm in pretending a little longer?

"I have the strangest feeling," she admitted. Her nose brushed his.

"What is it?"

"That you're no stranger at all."

"I feel the same."
"How is that possible?"
"I don't know—"

The Black Tide Trilogy is coming fall 2026

In the world of Aquerios, the sea god demands sacrifice.

Each year, souls are taken to appease the Black Tide, and in return, the kingdoms are spared from the horrors that lurk beneath the waves. But the balance is failing. The cost is rising. And the world is beginning to collapse.

When Princess Sereia of Drakcultus begins to question the truths she was raised to believe, she uncovers something far more dangerous than rebellion: a buried history, a power misunderstood, and a fate she's tried her whole life to avoid.

As the Tide rises and the gods demand more, Sereia and those bound to her must decide whether the truth is worth the cost of their lives and the fate of their world.

Sweeping, dark, and romantic, *The Black Tide Trilogy* is an epic fantasy of grief, love, and defiance—where the sea takes everything—and still demands more.

About the Author

T. René Thornhill writes emotionally rich, character-driven fantasy centered around women who refuse to follow the endings they're given. Her work blends myth, lost kingdoms, aching romances, and complicated monsters.

She studied history, culture, and human conflict—subjects that now shape the worlds she builds. She lives in the Midwest with her husband, two daughters, and a rascal of a dog. When she's not writing, she's chasing around her children, experimenting in the kitchen, reading, or building new worlds in her head while doing the dishes.

You can connect with her on Instagram @t.renethornhill, or visit trenethornhill.com to join her newsletter for a free novelette: *The Tides in Our Blood*, exclusive content, behind-the-scenes updates, and book news.